ET]

Eternal Ecstasy

Other Titles by Setta Jay:

The Guardians of the Realms Series:

0.5) Hidden Ecstasy

1) Ecstasy Unbound

2) Ecstasy Claimed

3) Denying Ecstasy

4) Tempting Ecstasy

5) Piercing Ecstasy

6) Binding Ecstasy

7) Searing Ecstasy

8) Divine Ecstasy

9) Storm of Ecstasy

Eternal Ecstasy

Setta Jay

A Guardians of the Realms Novel

Copyright:

Disclaimer:

This book is a work of fiction. Any resemblance to any person living or dead is purely coincidental. The characters and places are products of the author's imagination and used fictitiously.

Warning: Take one possessive, dirty talking Warrior God and one smart, no nonsense Healer; combine and shake things up for explosive results and scorching content meant for mature audiences!

Contributors:

Editor: BookBlinders

Proofreader: Pauline Nolet

Cover Image: Fotolia stock image

Acknowledgements:

First off a giant thank you to my editor and proofreader, Lindy and Pauline, for helping make these books the best they can be.

Thank you to my amazing husband for calming my crazy like only he can.

As always, thank you to all the Book Bloggers who have given me immeasurable love and support. Sending out big hugs to all of you!

Thank you to Emily with Social Butterfly PR for all the help.

I also want to thank those of you in the Setta's Sexies fan groups on Facebook and Goodreads. You make me smile every day! I love you all!

Thank you to all who post, engage or just watch from the sidelines in all my social media outlets.

And last, but definitely not least, a MASSIVE thank you to all of the readers out there. I wouldn't be able to do what I love without your support.

Eternal Ecstasy – Book Ten (The Guardians of the Realms)

As the ruling God of Thule, Hroarr's priority is the survival of his world. Gifted with the ancient ability of sjá, he has *seen* the birth and destruction of hundreds of worlds. This incredible power comes at an enormous cost, yet its toll seems to ease in the presence of a hauntingly seductive healer from Earth.

Sirena's life is comprised of duty. Duty to her Guardian family, to healing those of her world and, most of all, the overwhelming duty to right the wrongs of her secret and vile bloodline. With everything on her plate a ruthless warlord God from another world is the last thing she needs, no matter what fate and her heated body demands.

Will a dark Destroyer of Worlds bring upon the end of Earth and Thule or will two strong-minded beings fight and discover their own eternal ecstasy?

Author's Note—Starting the Series with this Title (Contains Spoilers from Earlier Books):

We've always done our best to make the Guardians of the Realms series as standalone as possible, but I do not recommend starting with book ten. If you decide to attempt it anyway, this is a little background that *may* help:

The twelve Guardians of the Realms were gifted with immense power and responsibility to watch over the four Realms: Earth (the Realm of humanity), Heaven (Realm of pure souls), Hell (Realm of tainted souls), and Tetartos (Realm of beasts and Immortals). They were also charged by the Creators with watching over the sleeping Gods, who would "one day be needed on Earth." The nine male and three female Guardians represent the strongest and most powerful of the different Immortal races, and all are telepathically linked along with their various other gifts.

Of the twelve sleeping Gods, only Hades, Athena and Aphrodite remained good, the others were tainted with evil and madness. Yet all were sent into sleeping chambers that were meant to purge the bad Gods of all the dark energies they'd consumed while feeding off the suffering of humans and once-enslaved Immortals instead of the pure energy of the Earth, which was the sustenance of Immortals and Gods alike.

Unfortunately the Creators hadn't sent Ares and Artemis' evil triplets, the spawn of their dark incestuous coupling, to sleep. The Great Beings had left them restrained to their prison in Hell Realm, not realizing that one day the vile entities would be able to cause chaos from their cage. So for centuries the Guardians have battled against demon souls the evil three sent out to possess humans while at the same time continuously destroying hell beasts dispatched into Heaven and Tetartos Realms.

As for the Immortal races, two of the most reviled Gods, Apollo and Hermes, captured, experimented on and callously bred any they could find before being imprisoned in the stasis of sleep. In their attempt to create a powerful army, they infused Immortals with animal DNA to provide added strength, instincts and in some cases the ability to transform into the very beast that had been forced on them.

One of the tormented Immortal breeders, Charybdis, eventually cast a spell using a portion of her own life force in the ultimate sacrifice. The spell ensured the Gods could no longer impel them to breed before ripping the young away to be sent to warrior camps. Because of her spell, no Immortal could produce young with anyone who wasn't their fated mate. After the Immortals were freed by the Creators and exiled to Tetartos, finding a mate turned into an exceedingly rare and beautiful occurrence. An event that made the pair more powerful and allowed for the possibility of children a decade after their souls had connected.

And so it had always been until something drastically shifted in the Realms. Guardians suddenly began finding their fated mates after millennia alone. The added power that came from the pairings made already powerful beings nearly as strong as the Gods themselves.

Months ago Apollo had been freed from his stasis unit by a now dead enemy of the Guardians. Before they could recapture him, the Deity was abducted by unknown warriors. Without a clue as to the God's whereabouts, the Guardians were forced to awaken Hades, the strongest of the just Gods, in the hopes that he could telepathically track his brother.

Hades hadn't been able to locate Apollo, but he did provide knowledge they needed, including the fact that they were dealing with a previously unknown ancient world... Thule.

Hades had once held a secret allegiance with the Thulian God Agnarr. The Deity told no one of the other world or of his ally as a way to ensure neither world ever learned of his son, Pothos' birth to a priestess of Thule. The long-dead female had warned Hades that the Gods of Thule would destroy Pothos if they ever became aware of his existence.

In light of Apollo's capture, Hades was forced to share the concealed information before attempting to contact his old Thulian ally by melting drops of a Thulian stone into a lake on a mystical island of Earth.

Following a tense face-off with the powerful Gods of Thule, Pothos and the Goddess Gefn mated, joining the two worlds.

Only after the Thulian Goddess' powerful pets were saved from near death by Sirena, the Guardian healer, the massive lynx-like cats decided to play matchmaker. The celestial beasts swept Sirena away from Earth, leaving her in the ruling God of Thule's bathing chamber, directly in the path of the wildly powerful overlord God, Hroarr.

Prologue

Thule – Moments Ago

Warm water slid over Hroarr's hot flesh as he took his shaft in hand, hefting the weight before roughly stroking from tip to root on a harsh grunt. Another harsh pull tensed his muscles on a growl. Dim torchlight flickered against the wall before trailing over his deep bathing pool only to disappear into the shadows beyond.

He ran his other hand over his soaked beard before moving it to yank the long strands of his hair back. Closing his eyes, he focused on the raw need clawing at him and hissed in a breath as he braced that palm against the stone wall.

He was the ruling God of Thule, millennia old, and he could not remember the last moment he felt anything at all, much less lust. Even then he knew it could never have been this savage. Nothing had ever threatened his control.

Each harsh pull tore another grunt from his lips, drowning out the sound of the water as he violently stroked his aching shaft, the water and his own need slicking the way.

He nearly snapped when the hunger swelled out of nowhere. The need reached out and gripped him, tensing the muscles of his shoulders, his stomach. Nothing existed but desire pulsing in his ears until he finally threw his head back on a harsh roar, his body rocked with pleasure. Hot seed jetted against the stone until it slowed, flowing over his knuckles before being washed away.

The moment his breathing evened, he stilled. Instant awareness pulled his muscles tighter.

His head snapped toward the shadows on the other side of his bathing pool. No one dared enter his private space. Yet someone had, he felt it.

He stalked from the water, growling, "Who. Are. You?"

There, against the far wall, was a nude female he'd never seen. His narrowed gaze took in the sight of her soft bare skin. Her hands were braced against the stone, and even through the shadows he could see her flushed golden flesh and the hard nipples tipping heavy breasts. The wet strands of her long pale hair clung to those mounds even as her chest heaved with each breath.

His nostrils flared as he inhaled deeply, swearing he could scent the female's desire, and animalistic need shot through his veins as some unique power slid over his skin. In that moment he was hit with recognition. "Healer?" His fury at the blatant intrusion into his space was momentarily replaced with another blast of the same lust that had led him to the bathing chamber in the first place.

Her power wrapped around his re-hardened flesh and he nearly growled with the intensity of what she was doing to him.

He might never have set eyes on the female before him, but he'd encountered her power... once. When the female had been in his palace days ago to heal his sister Gefn's beasts. The celestial creatures had been near death when *this* female was brought forth from Earth by Gefn's male. The consort had blocked the healer from Hroarr's sight then, yet here she was now, seemingly entranced by the hardening of his body. "Have you come for payment?" he demanded while hefting the rigid flesh.

If she wanted her reward for saving the beasts in the form of his seed, then he would gladly give it to her. He would lift her up and take her there against the stone.

He narrowed his eyes when hers flashed with something akin to panic… and then she was gone. He roared in displeasure when she disappeared in the way of her people. Barely a moment passed before she reappeared in the same darkened corner, biting off words he did not understand.

His massive shaft jerked, causing him to growl, "What game is this?" Moving with the speed of a Thulian God, he caged her bewitching frame against the wall, towering over her as her power caressed his hot skin. She had done this to him.

A hammering at the heavy door to his chambers distracted him. Clenching his jaw, he watched her, intending to demand his brother Dagur cease and leave.

One look into the powerful flashing eyes of the small healer stilled him. He tensed, not liking the fear and anger that muddied the succulent scent of her arousal.

The warmth radiating from her dewy skin and the mixed emotion dragging air from her lungs distracted him while her powers stroking over his aching flesh ignited a fire in his veins.

Before he could demand answers to her presence or command Dagur to stop pounding on the door, it slammed open, causing him to whip around in fury. "Get out, Dagur!" he snarled, placing his body in front of the nude female, who'd yet to utter a decipherable word. He growled, furious at his insolent brother's invasion, while primal rage surged through his entire body at the mere thought of anyone seeing her bare. Dagur's kilted form stood tense in the doorway, hard golden eyes meeting Hroarr's.

"It is urgent," Dagur bit out.

His brother's tense stance told him this was indeed important, forcing a curse from Hroarr's lips and rage to infuse him when he felt his female disappear again.

Had she returned to her world this time?

A muscle in his jaw ticked under the beard as his brother frowned, gazing around, instantly alert to a change in the air. "What is this power I feel?"

Hroarr had his brother by the throat, pushing him against the wall with little thought. "Never enter without my permission, Dagur."

His brother sputtered incoherently until Hroarr dropped him to his feet. "It was urgent," Dagur growled while rubbing his neck.

He battled back the new fury and possessiveness she'd evoked in him, yet he craved the ability to *feel* anything even if it was raw and untamed.

"What do I feel in this room, Hroarr?"

Hroarr let the flames inside him dry his skin as Dagur's questions persisted.

"I sense Spa and Velspar's power, but it has been drowned out by different magic."

His brother was correct. His sister's powerful beasts had been in his space. He had been far too focused on the female to have noticed it, and he *should* have sensed them.

"Is Gefn here?" he demanded, sending flames to the torches

against the walls. He fully intended to have answers from his sister. Spa and Velspar were the Guardians of Thule for a reason and they had led the healer to him, he felt it.

The magical black creatures had been gifted to Gefn by their sires before the powerful beings left their world. He and his siblings had been instructed to heed the beasts' instincts if they had any hope of Thule surviving the *ófǫlr*, the Destroyer of Worlds, that would eventually descend upon them. They had also led Thule into an alliance with Earth by way of his sister's desire to take a half-Earth, half-Thulian male as her *maðr*, her consort. A first for any Thulian God.

Dagur gritted out, "Gefn is not here. At least not that I was made aware of. Though, with her new ability to appear and reappear without the use of a portal, she is free to come and go without warning. *Anywhere* they please without any warning..." His sister had gained a great deal of power and new abilities with this bond to her male.

"Enough," Hroarr growled. He was fully assessing everything in the space. The healer's power had dulled, she'd gone from Thule, yet her effect on him remained.

His brother would not stop. "The power in here came from someone of Earth, did it not? Hroarr, you must tell me if there is someone else able to breach this palace!" Dagur's own power roiled through the room in frustration.

"That is none of your concern, brother." Hroarr's eyes flashed as his own potent energy surged, easily smothering his brother's into submission. "What was so urgent?" There was warning in his tone that clearly stated Dagur had better have a good reason for his intrusion.

Dagur clenched his jaw before opening and closing his mouth, seeming to debate questioning Hroarr further. Hroarr sent him a hard glare that his brother wisely heeded. "There is something calling the Darkness to Earth."

Hroarr stilled at his brother's ominous words. In their efforts to safeguard Thule and their battle ties to Earth, Dagur had been using his skill with spells to detect when the *ófǫlr*, the impending darkness, a plague that preyed on all worlds, would find its way to Earth.

Hroarr's already tense muscles pulled impossibly tighter as he thought of the Earth female who'd been in his chambers. "Explain this," he demanded as he moved through the open doors to his bedchamber. He had already intended to hunt down the healer; this situation only gave him one more reason to go to Earth immediately. Opening a portal to the other world served as a signal to Gefn wherever his sister and her consort might be.

The ability to mentally communicate with his siblings, as the Gods and Guardians of the Earth could, would have been useful at the moment. The Deities might have lacked his power, but he would admit they held unique abilities that could be an advantage during the upcoming battle.

A battle he anticipated with renewed relish now that he intended to take something for himself in return. He would have the seductive healer writhing in his bed, her power making him *feel* something beyond the darkness and shadows of his numb soul.

What was her name? His sister had given it to him. It had been something seductive, like her power.

Sirena.

Dagur's next words tore him from his thoughts. "I've never seen the *ófǫlr* move through the ether at this speed. The Earth Gods will have little time to save their world."

"Do you know the cause?"

Dagur shook his head. "I cannot tell what this beacon is that is drawing it."

"How long?" Hroarr did not bother binding his long hair, taking only the time needed to don leathers and boots. His brother's continued presence at his back seemed enough to calm his shaft so he could contain it within his breeches.

"A year..." After a discontented pause Dagur went on, "If they are fortunate... I know Gefn intends to fight this battle with her male, but the majority of their Gods are still sleeping. If the God Hades and these Guardians release the rest of the Earth Deities, will they be of any true use in the fight? *Our* siblings would have been a liability. I cannot believe *theirs* will be any different." Dagur scoffed. "I do not see them defeating the Darkness. Earth has *four* Realms to our two. Even with all of their Gods *and* their Guardians, it does not seem likely. You will relocate them here. Their power can help us win when the *ófǫlr* comes for Thule," Dagur demanded as he crossed his arms over his bare chest.

This was the reason Hroarr ruled Thule, not only was he more powerful and stronger than his siblings, but Dagur's words once more proved the other God's recklessness. He did not think. Hroarr did not respond as he waved a wrist, sending power to sweep the door to his chambers wide. He knew well the need to protect one's world, and he knew it would be no different for the Earth Gods and Guardians. They would not abandon their Realms easily, especially if it meant leaving nearly all their mortals behind. Even if their pride would allow them to live under Hroarr's rule, the honor he'd sensed in his sister's male would force them to defend their world to the end. If he'd judged them well, he would guess they would only send their females away. Or attempt to.

His sister and the few other females he'd seen of the other world would not likely leave their males' sides should it come to that.

Hroarr sneered to himself. They needed him.

Warriors rushed down the hallway, readying for his planned return to the Northern Lands. He barked orders to find his *þrír* immediately and be ready to depart the moment he returned from Earth.

"Hroarr?" Dagur growled as Hroarr ignored him.

"You will tell Hades of their issue and help them detect this... *beacon*."

Assisting Earth had always been a tactical advantage for Thule. The *ófǫlr* devoured all worlds, but Thule was more prepared than those that had fallen before. Hroarr's unique power allowed him to see the birth and destruction of hundreds of worlds destroyed by the *ófǫlr*. No others had the knowledge he held, nor had he come across other Gods who could portal to different worlds like the Thulian Deities. By the time Gefn had declared her intentions to fight for Earth as well as Thule, he had already decided to ally himself with the Earth Gods.

He would help them. But he would take something in return.

They stalked the torchlit hallways of his palace with two of his most trusted warriors silently shadowing them.

Once out of the palace, they bounded down the stone steps with a view of the icy seas beyond. Hroarr lifted a hand to summon the wild power he harnessed and opened a portal to Earth, anticipation burning in his veins.

"Stay here," he commanded his warriors. With bows they stepped to the side of the watery air, with their golden dragon staffs raised beside them. Only he and Dagur would travel to Earth for this task. His guards did not need to know the details of the arrangement to come.

Hroarr stepped through the thick power, with Dagur at his side. After being pulled through to the other side, he instantly scanned the banks surrounding the lake he and Dagur descended to. Dew-covered forest lay beyond the sight of his sister Gefn, her powerful *maðr*, Pothos, and both mystical felines that never left her side.

Power emanated from him in restless, furious waves that howled through the trees and rocked the waters beneath his and Dagur's feet. Gods of Thule ruled all the elements around them, which meant the water beneath his boots would only give if he wished it.

He took in the massive black felines, their pointed golden ears turned to him as they flanked his sister. He assessed them, noting their golden eyes were just as intent on him. The powerful beasts not only championed Gefn's male, Pothos, but they had led the healer to Hroarr. He could feel it.

After a moment his eyes moved to Pothos. The male's bright blue eyes were a match to that of his father, Hades, who appeared at his son's side, with the calm beautiful female, Sacha. The God's black wings flexed out behind him as he looked at Hroarr. The dragon, Drake, appeared next, with another female whose feral magic was as wild as her glowing eyes and dark red hair.

Winds whipped at Gefn's long pale hair as serious green eyes met his. "What is it?" she asked in the old language, that of the Creators. A universal tongue remembered by all Gods.

Dagur answered their sister's question, "You have a serious problem in this world."

He paid close attention to those facing him, even as he wondered where his female was. Had she indeed come back to her own world?

Gefn snapped, "What did you find?" The tension in her frame was apparent as was that of the other five, who represented Earth.

Dagur explained, "Something exists in this world that is calling the Darkness here."

Hroarr noted that Hades' massive black wings flared and his demeanor grew harsh at the announcement.

He wasn't sure who said the words, "The Tria," but the others stiffened and cursed.

"You know the cause?" Hroarr demanded.

"Yes," Pothos gritted out as Hroarr's sister shook her head in shocked silence.

As soon as his sister came out of her stupor, she explained, "The Tria are incredibly evil triplets born of a coupling between two Earth Gods. They were fed the energies of death and destruction from the womb." Hroarr's own disgust was mirrored on his sister's face as she continued, "They were imprisoned in one of Earth's four Realms millennia ago. They cannot leave their cage, but are powerful enough to send beasts and tainted souls out to the other Realms."

"You believe they are calling the *ófǫlr* here?" he demanded to know.

His sister nodded. "It seems the most likely possibility." A second passed before she continued, "They are apparently indestructible...

And the three have recently been taunting Hades, using mortals of Earth as their mouthpieces. They said that something was coming, demanding to be released in order to *help*." It was obvious to him that no one believed the beings meant to assist in any way. He narrowed his eyes, not liking what he was hearing.

As Gefn had been sharing information about these "Tria," her male had been discussing the situation with Drake, Hades and their females. Hroarr half listened to the male's strategies in between his sister's words, hearing enough to know they indeed had a plan for these beings.

His sister's male spoke of the sleeping chambers Hroarr knew all the Earth Gods had been banished to by the Creators of Earth. It seemed the chambers had been designed to purge evil energies from a God. If the Tria were pure evil, it might kill them outright and solve the problem, but it would cause a huge elemental impact on their world. He knew the damage firsthand when his evil siblings had killed one another millennia ago. "You will need more than you have to survive this." Hroarr allowed his words to cleave the crisp morning air.

He did not pause long, only enough to let his words sink in. They were enough to cause Hades' black wings to unfurl and twitch with agitation. The Earth God's power rippled through the air currents around them as Hroarr began again, "We can provide the prisons that will help your world, but I demand something in return." The cylinders that were both confinement and weapon for Thule would be Earth's best chance at surviving, and he knew they were aware of that fact. Pothos held Gefn's knowledge of the battle strategy Hroarr had long since created for Thule.

He would give them what they needed to battle the scourge slithering through the ether in their direction. Yes, he would save their world... for a price.

Hades' eyes flashed a violent blue as he demanded, "What do you want?"

Gefn protested, "Hroarr!" but he ignored her appalled tone.

Hroarr's lips curled as he demanded with finality, "Your healer."

Chapter 1

Mystical Lake, Earth Realm

Dangerous silence met the building power violently thrashing through the trees and sending glittering waves over the banks of the lake as Gefn and the others processed Hroarr's demand for Sirena. Cool morning air slid over his arms as he waited.

Hroarr expected it to be Hades who spoke, but it was Drake, the Guardian leader of this world, who growled, "I better have fucking heard you wrong." Smoke filtered from the male's lips as he continued snarling, "Because Sirena is *not* a fucking payment for anything. If you have need of assistance healing your people—"

Hroarr brought a hand up to stop the next words. "Give me *Sirena* or defend your world without my help."

Dagur's intake of breath sounded like a hiss as he accused, "That was the power I felt in your bathing chamber? The healer was with you!"

"Bathing chamber?" Drake growled. "You're wrong, Thulian. She is here."

Dagur snarled, "She may be back in your world now, but you obviously cannot keep track of your people."

His sister glared at their brother. "Stop it, Dagur. You are mistaken. Sirena has not been in Thule since she *saved* Spa's and

Velspar's lives. I would know, as neither Pothos nor I teleported her." The two beasts in question had not taken their glowing gaze off Hroarr since the moment he arrived.

Dagur spat out, "Interesting, sister, as your beasts' power signature was there as well."

Gefn's flashing emerald eyes were a match to Hroarr's, but at the moment they were full of anger as she glared at the beasts, who did not so much as look up at her. "Hroarr?"

"We will discuss this later," he ground out before adding to the others, "You have my price."

A variety of harsh nos came from the others of Earth. Even Drake's quiet female made her opinion clear as wild power roiled from her, lifting her dark red hair and flashing in her gold eyes. Hades' Sacha narrowed her eyes, assessing him closely.

Gefn practically growled in frustration. "Sirena is not a possession, brother. And it is not the way of Thule to demand a person as a... reward," his sister snapped. "She is not some kind of battle prize. She is a being with her own thoughts and desires."

Dagur added his own protests, which Hroarr ignored.

Sacha calmly asked one word, silencing everyone, "Why?" The God's consort was quiet, but she was no less powerful than her furious male. Power lashed through the trees, and the ground rocked under their feet as each male's fury grew. The dark female continued when he did not answer, "If she was indeed with you moments ago, did you ask her or gain the impression that she *wished* to stay with you?"

He raised an eyebrow. He was the ruling God of Thule.

Sacha continued, "What *exactly* is it you want from Sirena?"

"It is none of your concern," he dismissed.

"Yes... It is." The dark warning from Drake's feral female was filled with magic. There was a great deal of primal strength in her.

Hades' tone was filled with sharp finality when he addressed the others. "It doesn't matter what he wants." To Hroarr, the Earth God bit out, "We don't need your help, Thulian."

Hroarr cocked a brow in challenge. "You have no idea what you are facing. Once you realize how poorly equipped you are for this battle, you will know where to find me. Once Sirena is at my side, I will help you save your world. Do not wait too long."

His siblings were still protesting his actions when Sacha spoke again. "At your side? Or in your bed?"

The males of Earth snarled and snapped their fury at the thought of Sirena warming his bed.

Hroarr threw up a hand to silence them all. "Enough. You can take the chance of freeing your Gods and hope they are of use when the Darkness arrives. But even that will not be enough to save your world." He challenged, "In time you will learn I am your world's only true chance at survival."

He did not wait for more blustering and conversation; instead he turned and stepped through the portal at his back.

The tiny healer had ignited something inside him. For once in his long existence he felt... anticipation...

Dagur was growling at his heels the second they were back on the steps of his palace. "What was that?"

He stilled his brother's incessant questioning with a quelling look as he released the power of the portal, allowing it to disappear into nothingness. Without a word, he bounded up the steps, his warriors moving to follow him and Dagur through the halls to his study. He had much to plan.

*****

The second the portal closed, Gefn turned to the others, wishing to throttle her brother, but needing to deal with the fallout of his madness first. "I swear my brother is not the monster he seems! This is not how things are done in Thule. I will fix this," she assured Hades, Sacha, Drake and Era. Pothos remained at her side, shaking his head. "I need to go and speak with him," she admitted.

There was absolutely no excusing demanding a person as payment for his help! A female who had saved the Guardians of Thule. Not to mention the female in question was like a sister to Gefn's male!

"He's never acted this way before?" Sacha's calm words pulled Gefn from the anxious need to rip her brother to pieces. Before she could answer, Sacha asked, "How does he act with other females?"

Pothos squeezed her hand and sent her calming energies. The relationship between Earth and Thule was a new one and the last thing she wanted was for her *maðr*'s family to gain a terrible view of her world. A world she loved and was proud of. A world ruled by two Gods and two *Goddesses*. Females were not possessions!

She took a frustrated breath before answering Sacha's question. "He's never acted like this with any female."

She tried to actually remember when she'd last heard of her brother having kept company with any female. Hroarr did not take mortals to his bed, so that left only a handful of priestesses. Neither brother took pleasure with their own *þrír*... she guessed that was because of the emotional bonds Thulian Gods shared with their priestesses.

"Did Sirena and Hroarr come in contact when she healed Spa and Velspar?" Drake asked, glaring at Pothos.

Pothos gritted out, "No. Hroarr came to the room, but I blocked her from his view. They didn't interact at all..." Her male paused. "She did seem off afterwards though, but she just said she needed to replenish her energies."

"She *never* admits to being depleted," Drake growled.

Tension filled the space.

Sacha sighed. "I think we can all guess what's gotten into him."

Era shook her head before adding, "That's no excuse. Even if he is her mate, I don't see his arrogant demand going well for him when Sirena hears about it."

Pothos looked down at Spa and Velspar and glared. "I don't believe she would have teleported there on her own. If it were even possible, which I doubt. She had help... but was that what she *wanted*?" The last was ground out.

Had her beasts actually abducted the healer? Gefn pinched the bridge of her nose, knowing the beasts would do anything if they thought it was for the good of Thule. If it were true that Sirena and Hroarr were mates, then the added power of the bond would be good for both worlds.

Smoke filtered into the skies as Drake growled, "You need to control those damned beasts, Pothos."

Sacha stared thoughtfully down at Spa and Velspar as she

added, "The beasts were willing to sacrifice their lives to prevent a war while Gefn and Pothos finished their mating. It isn't a stretch to assume they were trying to do something else to align our worlds if they'd felt Sirena's connection to the God."

Gefn glared at her beasts, demanding, "Is that what you're doing?" She could feel their emotion through the bond they shared, but it would be far better if the animals could just speak.

Twin sets of golden eyes met hers as they started purring.

Pothos groaned. "I'll take that as a yes."

She was about to speak when both beasts disappeared into thin air.

"Gods damn it, Pothos!" The dragon was furious.

"What the hell do you want me to do?" Gefn felt her male's agitation through their bond, her own frustration and anger at the animals just as strong. She watched Pothos run his hand over his short hair.

"This is my fault. They are my responsibility," Gefn admitted as she mentally searched for their location. "Spa and Velspar are in Thule at the moment." More specifically they were in her brother's palace.

Turning to Sacha, she asked, "Do you truly believe they are mated?" She hoped that was the case. Otherwise her brother was being what her male would call an asshole, and she would not deal well with that.

Sacha tilted her head. "It would seem so. I will find out from Sirena after she's done delivering Alyssa and Gregoire's baby."

Hades changed the topic. "Right now we need to get out and

deal with the hell beast attacks and then focus on getting the Tria into stasis units." The attacks had started when they all felt the portal opening, signaling her brothers' arrival. That meant Guardians were out dealing with that now.

"I will go see my brother," Gefn said as she gazed into her male's bright blue eyes. *I think it better if I go alone*, but she needed to know what was going on with Hroarr.

She was preparing to leave when Hades smiled at her. "Your brother's demand is of no consequence, Gefn. *You* know as much as Hroarr does about the Darkness."

She had knowledge, yes, but there was much more to it.

They really would need Hroarr.

She did not get the chance to admit that fact before Drake growled, "Hades is right. We need to deal with the last of the attacks and then start developing a plan to stop the Tria from calling this shit here." Wafts of smoke were filtering from his lips, and she felt guilty for the hard look the dragon was sending to her male.

Pothos leaned in and kissed her head before sending through their telepathic link, *Everything will be fine,* thea mou. His Goddess. Her heart filled with sweet emotion at his words and the love she felt coming through the bond.

"We will all meet in a few hours," Drake added. "Sacha, take your male and deal with the attacks in Earth Realm."

Hades shook his head, scoffing, "Is it so difficult to ask for my help, nephew?"

The others had disappeared, leaving Gefn and Pothos alone with the sun slowly rising, sending a glitter over the trees and smooth waters of the lake.

Pothos sent soothing emotions as his eyes took her in. *Go. We don't know for sure he's Sirena's mate yet.*

She firmed her lips. "Trust me. He'd better hope that's what's addling his mind. I will not defend him if he isn't being affected by the mating." No, she would be the first to rip him to pieces for acting like a barbarian.

Pothos smiled before pulling her into his arms for a deep kiss that left her breathless and dizzy.

When they broke apart, he kissed her head. "Give your brother hell. Call me if you need me."

And then he was gone.

Chapter 2

Guardian Manor, Tetartos Realm

Sirena's heart was still pounding in her chest. The last tense minutes of Alyssa's delivery had been like waging battle, but they'd all made it through to the other side. Gregoire, Alyssa, their precious newborn daughter and Sirena had survived the whirlwind of power surges that had left them in a nearly demolished room. The air was still charged with energy as Sirena's bruises healed. She smiled as she quickly finished running tendrils of healing ability to assess the warm bundle in her arms. There was no doubt in her mind that those sweet little bow lips and curious pale green eyes were going to rule them all like they ruled her emotional parents.

Only a moment had passed since her birth and Sirena was moving through her tasks as quickly as possible, knowing Alyssa and Gregoire were anxious to officially greet her.

The dark, once cozy suite had been destroyed around them. The seating area was a mess of overturned furniture crashed against the wall and stone fireplace. They'd met a better fate than the double doors leading to the balcony; those had been relegated to a mess of jagged glass shards and charred wood. A situation Gregoire had immediately resolved by spelling a barrier into the opening so that none of the cool morning winds or snow flurries could invade the space. There'd been no time to move Alyssa from the room, not after the baby's power started wildly rocketing through the room, signaling her immediate entrance.

"Is she okay?" Gregoire's impatience and anxiety was a living thing in the room, and she knew without looking that a muscle was ticking beneath his auburn beard. Sirena's nearly seven-foot Guardian brother had nearly lost his mind at the end, but he'd still managed to be incredibly gentle as he'd held his tiny mate. There'd been no mistaking how much Alyssa's pain had nearly destroyed him, but throughout there'd been an intensely raw and beautiful connection between the two.

The soul bond.

"She's absolutely perfect," Sirena assured them both as she quickly cleaned the warm bundle in her arms. She heard the rush of relieved air that left both parents before a glance showed Gregoire kissing Alyssa softly.

Energy and love had flowed through the pain of labor as the two held each other. Sirena wouldn't have blamed Alyssa if she'd snapped at the big oaf, but the chestnut-haired beauty had been strong and incredible. It had been enough to wrench Sirena's heart the entire time she'd been busily using all her power to pull off the delivery.

She felt Gregoire stir after several whispered words to his mate. Telekinetic power lashed out, righting a big chaise with a clank before a mountain of pillows flew to it. All the while the big male focused on painstakingly playing nursemaid for his female, blatantly ignoring Alyssa's soft protest. Sirena smiled. The female had healed almost immediately after the birth, far more rapidly than any mother Sirena had seen. She chalked up part of the speed to Alyssa sharing Gregoire's Guardian abilities, but even those enhancements wouldn't have led to these near instantaneous results.

It had been incredible. Maybe a gift from their very powerful child? Sirena wanted to look into it, but that was for another time.

Sirena shook her head when Gregoire ignored Alyssa's protests and enfolded his female in a clean blanket before carrying her to the lounge he'd arranged for her. There was no missing the way his hands shook as he knelt at Alyssa's side, kissing her forehead reverently.

She finished wrapping the babe securely in a cozy champagne-colored blanket Alyssa had for this purpose, noticing Gregoire's tenderness toward his female as he whispered again softly, words meant for his mate's ears only. Alyssa's eyes sparkled with love and unshed tears as she accepted his kiss. Sirena forced her gaze to the baby as she moved to the new parents.

Inquisitive eyes twinkled up between long dark lashes, the shade was a match to her mother's, and tiny bow lips curved into a smile that shot right to Sirena's heart. The efforts to contain her arms had proven useless against the tiny escape artist.

Immortal babies were more advanced than mortal ones, but Sirena was still in awe at how alert and fidgety her niece was. She chuckled as chubby fingers clenched and grabbed while a sweet, kind power radiated from the child. There was no mistaking the demand for Sirena to hasten in the direction of her parents. She chuckled. "Apparently I'm not moving fast enough for her."

Alyssa smiled brilliantly as Sirena bent, handing over the child. The female eagerly cradled the babe against her chest and Gregoire's arm tightened as he watched with a reverence that was beautiful to behold. One of his massive hands came to stroke his thumb over a tiny rounded cheek as Alyssa spoke. "Hello, my impatient little Lucia."

Sirena's lips tilted as tiny hands reached toward mother and father.

It was a damned good thing Alyssa's healing was so rapid because she had a feeling the two were going to need all their strength to keep the baby's power in check. Fortunately, Gregoire had quickly learned to harness and subdue Lucia's power blasts once the baby was free. The massive male had been too worried to attempt anything like that while the little bundle had been causing the same kind of havoc from the womb.

"Welcome, princess," Gregoire rasped.

As if her thoughts conjured the action, an untamed blast came as the sweetest melodic giggle trilled through the room. Sirena braced for impact, but Gregoire's power unleashed and he gently absorbed the impact and eased it back down. The sheer warmth of the unconditional love that slipped from him and Alyssa as they gazed down at Lucia was incredible and she had to swallow back tears at the beauty of the family.

Gregoire smiled down. "Papa's got you, princess. I'll watch over you and your mama. No need for shield blasts now, my little warrior." He leaned down and kissed his daughter's questing hands.

And that quickly, the tiny infant wrapped her grumbly warhorse father completely around her little finger.

Sirena stifled a laugh that bubbled up as she moved toward the door. "I'm going to go."

Gregoire's hazel eyes shot up as he demanded, "What if they need you?"

With a smile she assured him, "They are both in perfect health, and I'm only a telepathic call away." She paused before adding, "You have this under control. You both know to feed her personal energies." Immortals' nourishment came in the form of Earth's healing energies, but Immortal babies needed to be nourished by both parents through their new telepathic familial links. In the early stages it would serve as sustenance as well as bonding. They already knew this, but they were new parents and Gregoire was anything if not overly protective of Alyssa.

And now Lucia.

Alyssa eased out a breath. "Thank you, Sirena." Tears of joy threatened to spill free of the new mother's eyes as she cradled and kissed her baby. There was absolutely no mistaking the sheer gratitude and joy filling the room.

Sirena nodded. "It was my pleasure. I'll be back to check on you in another hour. Your parents are likely waiting outside," she reminded them.

Sirena had sent the grandparents out when they came rushing in before the birth. It was as much for their safety as it was to give Alyssa and Gregoire privacy during the delivery. Adras and Ava were likely pacing the hallway at that moment.

Gregoire and Alyssa nodded, but her brother Guardian was the one who ground out, "You can send them in to meet their grandchild."

Gregoire and Adras, Alyssa's father, had once been friends, but that had changed when Gregoire took a look at Alyssa as a baby and knew she'd one day be his mate. The two males had suffered a very tense and awkward relationship ever since. Sirena only hoped they would bond over their mutual need to protect Lucia. Though she felt sorry for any male who thought to get close to the baby once she was of age.

"I'll send them in, then."

The second she slipped from the room, Adras and Ava were in front of her, demanding answers to the safety and health of their grandchild and daughter.

Sirena raised her hands and smiled softly. "Alyssa and the baby are perfectly healthy. You can go in and meet your grandchild."

Ava gave her a quick anxiety-filled hug before practically running into the room.

The second the door clicked shut behind them, Sirena let out a breath filled with relief.

That relief proved short lived.

Now that the baby was safely born, she felt the niggling worry in the back of her mind. She hadn't had time to think about her abbreviated abduction by P and Gefn's meddling cats. She'd had only moments after they returned her to her rooms before Alyssa had gone into labor while at the same time the air charged, signaling a portal from Thule.

So what had happened?

Sacha's appearance at the end of the hall added to Sirena's anxiety. The beautiful dark-haired Guardian was her friend, and even with her serene expression, Sirena knew somehow this wasn't just a visit to check on Alyssa and Gregoire. Sirena's ears started ringing and her mouth seemed to dry up. Had Hroarr told Drake and the others about her naked intrusion into Thule?

She could happily skin those damned magical cats. Teleporting her, *unclothed*, to that damned Warlord God's bathroom had nearly sent her into the mating frenzy. She'd once saved the ungrateful beasts' lives, but now she was incredibly tempted to reverse the favor.

"The baby?" Sacha asked.

She nodded. "Born and perfect. Both mother and daughter."

"And Gregoire?"

Without thought Sirena turned and her sister Guardian walked at her side. If they were going to talk, she was going to need a drink. She needed energy and some sleep, but wine would have to do. She answered her sister as they neared the door to her own suite. "He's better now. Though I have a feeling Lucia is going to keep him on his toes. She's immensely powerful."

Sacha smiled softly. "Lucia? I like it. And I'm thrilled for them."

"I still need to let everyone know," she said. The others had been called out to fight possessed or hell beast attacks during Alyssa's labor. That was, everyone but the handful that went to greet the open portal from Thule... like Sacha.

"What did the Thulians have to say?"

Sacha glanced over with a look that seemed to see all of Sirena's secrets. "Quite a bit, actually."

Damn it. Her sister knew something.

And Sirena needed that drink, sooner than later.

Chapter 3

Guardian Manor, Tetartos Realm

Sirena sent out a telepathic message through the Guardian link about the baby, smiling at the excited whoops and questions that created a reprieve in the upcoming conversation with Sacha.

She led Sacha into her suite, the sound of the door clicking shut behind them seeming overly loud, almost drowning out the harsh thumping of Sirena's heartbeat. She immediately veered left into the small kitchen area, heading straight for the wine fridge at the end. Morning light streamed through the glass doors leading to the balcony and she barely noted the snow flurries settling on the railing beyond. She sent a thought to turn on the small lights over the stone island. The rest of her space was a mix of mostly white and bright red, with black-framed pin-up art on the walls. It might not be her primary home, but with Alyssa's wild pregnancy, she'd made the space hers in order to be close.

"Wine?" she offered, holding up the dark bottle, cocking a brow in Sacha's direction.

Her sister Guardian nodded. "Please." It wasn't lost on her that they both seemed a bit eager to start drinking when it was still technically *morning*.

Screw it, she had a feeling she was going to need fortification. Sirena usually worked until she fell into bed or had to head to a cavern to feed her energy levels with Earth's healing balm. If ever there was a time for her to start drinking in the morning, it was now.

Within seconds the bottle was uncorked and being poured into two glasses. The sweet red wine was a magical concoction made in the Immortal Realm, and the vintner had taken Immortal biology into consideration when blending it. Mortal wine wouldn't intoxicate her, but a few glasses of this would be enough to calm her nerves.

Sirena took a deep pull, not even pretending to savor the sweet warmth as it slid down her throat.

Sacha didn't say anything as she casually leaned a black leather-clad hip against the cream stone countertop. The fact that her sister was wearing spelled fighting gear meant she'd likely been out dealing with possessed or hell beasts. Sirena's bet was on possessed since Sacha didn't reek of hell beast blood.

When the door burst open, Sirena's head snapped in that direction to see Brianne whisk through like hellfire, complete with the scent of sulphur. *She* had been battling hell beasts.

"You better not have fucking started without me," their wild sister snapped as she sent a warning look in Sirena and Sacha's direction. Sirena mentally groaned, it seemed Sacha had an intervention planned because this obviously wasn't a chat about Alyssa and Gregoire's new baby. Sirena cocked a brow in her dark-haired sister's direction.

"We haven't," Sacha offered.

Sirena lifted her own glass as she offered, "Wine?"

"Fuck yeah," Brianne said with a smile in her tone. With barely a movement Brianne released her blade harness and tossed it on the counter with a clank of metal. Sirena stepped aside so Brianne could get to the sink and wash off the beast blood sending smoke from her tanned skin. Her sister's wild red curls were up in a braided ponytail and her long toned body was clad in brown fighting leathers. The top was her usual halter style as opposed to the sleeved version Sacha wore. It offered little protection for Brianne's upper body, but Geraki, as half bird of prey, hated to have their backs covered.

Brianne twisted to grab a hand towel and Sirena caught a glimpse of the brown, umber and greens that made up the tattooed wings flowing down her sister's back to her butt. They were a color match to the very real wings the warrior was able to release at any given moment. It wasn't just the wings that drew Sirena's attention, it was the markings hinted at beneath the waistband. A mark taken by mated pairs. Brianne's version was different. As different as the female herself. The traditional mating symbol of twin dragons entwined in figure eights held together by their tails was drawn into fine lines that made the shape of jagged claw marks on her sister Guardian's ass. Every single Guardian and their mate had some version, and Brianne's fit her and Vane's relationship, so much that her sister's male had the same claw marks on his ass.

She couldn't see herself doing the same with that damned God of Thule. She refused to think about his raw masculine perfection holding a brand that said he was hers. He *wasn't* hers and likely couldn't be. His very nature would likely drive her insane.

Her hand was shaking when she pulled a glass from the cabinet and started pouring the wine. She'd never even considered having a male of her own. There were no options for her on Earth. But finding one in another world was far worse, because she had no intention of leaving her home. Her duty. Her *life*.

It was her identity. And she could more than guess that the asshole Warlord God would do everything in his power to rule her if she let him. If she were to *ever* accept the male, she would need to be convinced that he would not try to run her life or prevent her from doing her job. She mentally snorted at that. There wasn't an ounce of compromise in that God. He would be a nightmare as a mate

Handing over Brianne's glass, she awkwardly stated the obvious just to say something. "I take it you were stuck with hell beast attacks?"

Brianne smirked as she answered, "Yep, I left Vane with cleanup duty." Sirena had no doubt Brianne's mate was grumbling about having been left behind with that task. "Now, spill. I got here as fast as I could."

Sirena shucked her high heels, losing three inches as she stalked to the seating area. She was shorter than her sisters, but it wasn't anything like standing around her brother Guardians, whose shortest male was a foot taller even with the boost of her high pumps. Even if she hadn't loved fifties fashion and high heels, she would have worn them just to prevent neck strain with all the males around.

Sacha and Brianne took the couch and Sirena curled up in a club chair as Sacha spoke. "Drake is going to call a meeting as soon as the possessed and hell beast attacks are wrapped up, which I'm guessing will be any time now. I asked him to give me a minute first... The Thulians' news was... unsettling."

Sirena's shoulders instantly tensed at her sister's ominous tone. "How so?" Was this about her naked visit to Thule, or was it the news they'd all been waiting on regarding the Darkness?

"Dagur said we'll have about a year before the threat reaches Earth."

Sirena felt her heart stop in her chest and then it pumped triple time to make up for the stall.

A *year*?

They'd all known something had been on the horizon, the Creators had said the Gods would one day be needed in this world. That was why the bastard Deities had been sent to sleep millennia ago instead of being more severely punished for the destruction and chaos they'd caused during their rule on Earth. The Guardians had always known something would happen, they just hadn't known any details until Pothos mated with Gefn and was given her memories and knowledge of the threat that came for all worlds.

Brianne started cursing. "What the fuck? A year is nothing."

Sacha nodded before continuing, "Dagur said there's a problem. Something's calling it here." Before either she or Brianne had a chance to say anything, Sacha added, "We all assume it's the Tria's doing. They've been taunting Hades since he was awoken from stasis. And we knew they had ramped up their attacks. We just hadn't known why."

"We still don't know why," Brianne snapped. "They're powerful, but fucking sending some message to something that destroys worlds? Why?"

Sirena suddenly felt like she hadn't slept in years. Her mind wasn't processing the way it should be. Granted, her energy levels were not the best after all she'd expended with Alyssa's delivery, but she needed to try to think clearly. "Is there a plan to stop it? And will that delay its arrival?"

"I'm sure that's what Drake plans to talk about in the meeting. P suggested putting the Tria in the God stasis units."

Tension filled the room.

Brianne practically growled, "Son of a bitch. That's only a partial fix. One that releases two more Gods and keeps Apollo in his current prison cell. But, fucking hell, we have a year to figure out a way to fight an enemy we don't *really* know dick about. Only that Thule had weapons they hoped to use to try to stop it."

"The Thulians' knowledge is more than we had before," Sirena pointed out, her fingers gripping her glass a little too tightly as her world started crumbling around her. As much as she didn't want to think about having a damned barbarian as a mate, Earth was going to need all the power they could get for the upcoming battle. The extra power of her mating a God was an advantage they would all need. As long as the bastard God's power actually strengthened hers as opposed to causing some other reaction. She was likely grasping, but they *were* beings of two different worlds. There were no certainties. Yes, P and Gefn were able to bond and share power, but Pothos was born of both worlds.

She knew Gefn had succumbed to the mating frenzy though, which was a traditional reaction for Earth Immortals.

Would Hroarr? She needed to talk to Gefn and P immediately. Suddenly her head was throbbing behind her eyes, causing her to rub her temple.

"Sirena?"

Damn it, she hadn't been paying attention. "Sorry. I was thinking."

Both her sisters were staring at her closely as Sacha spoke. "Dagur said that he sensed you in Hroarr's room this morning. Along with the cats' power signature."

Brianne demanded, "What the hell happened? And why didn't you tell us?"

So Dagur had essentially ratted out her presence in Thule? "Hroarr didn't demand to know what I was doing there?"

"No. But you were there?"

"Yes." She groaned. "As I got out of the shower, I was ported into Hroarr's bathroom by Gefn's beasts. I tried to teleport back here but couldn't get out of that world."

Brianne was shaking her head. "Why? The furry bastards are menaces, but I never got the impression they were cruel or evil. Dropping you off as some kind of offering to their God is fucked up." Then her sister paused, trying to make sense of it, before continuing, "Unless... Holy shit, Sirena! Is the God your mate?"

Sirena blew out a breath and nodded, feeling as if her world had been upended just by admitting that fact.

Both sisters were silent for long minutes as Sirena drank more from her glass.

"Are you okay?" Sacha asked softly.

Sirena admitted, "I'm still processing it."

Brianne was shaking her head now. "We should have seen this coming. That world is obviously compatible with ours. Hence the birth of P." Who was born to a Thulian priestess and Hades.

Then Brianne's lips started twitching. "I'm guessing you were naked when they dropped you off. And yet you're back and don't *seem* to be in the frenzy? So what'd you do to him? And do we skin the furry assholes now, or did you have something else in mind for their torture?"

Sirena tilted her head back on the couch as her cheeks heated. "No torture. Not right now at least. And, yes, I was naked."

Sirena sighed before proceeding to explain every detail of her arrival and then her porting to a room in the palace where she'd healed the cats. Spa and Velspar had been waiting there, and after several threats, the beasts returned her home. She'd even shared the fact that she'd watched Hroarr jack off in the shower before he caught her. Just the thought of his powerful body was enough to heat her blood. She felt her cheeks flushing brighter.

"Well, damn. He's arrogant as shit, but I have no doubt you can handle him." Brianne smiled encouragingly. Fate could be such a bitch, but there was no fighting it, and they all knew that fact very well. She supposed it was best to look at it all from Sacha's long-held theory that only good beings found mates. If so, that meant Hroarr wasn't all that bad.

Sacha finally asked, "Did you know he was yours when you went to heal the cats in Thule?" It was a question she could tell Sacha already knew the answer to.

"Yes."

"That was days ago! Why the hell didn't you tell us?" There was no missing Brianne's affront.

Sirena didn't have a good excuse, other than shock. That and the fact that she'd wanted to avoid it. Possibly forever. Now, with the threat to Earth coming so soon, she likely didn't have the luxury of avoidance for long. If at all. The cats' meddling had been a pain in the ass, but Brianne was right, they weren't malicious. They were powerful and intelligent, and she forced herself to remember that they'd nearly died while expending power to ensure that Thule and Earth kept the peace during P and Gefn's mating. As much as she wanted to skin them, they'd likely been doing what they thought best for Thule. The ancient creatures were Guardians of the other world, but damn it, she'd saved their lives. Would they completely throw her under the bus purely for Thule's benefit? Or was their matchmaking for the good of both worlds?

Her mind was reeling.

Sacha added softly, "You know we would have been there for you."

"I know that. I just... needed time."

The end of the world definitely made her dedication to avoidance seem... selfish. Maybe cowardly. Damn it and damn him.

First and foremost, they needed to deal with the Tria. But a year wasn't a lot of time. In reality it was the exact time it generally took for the powers of a mated pair to meld completely. She doubted there was a coincidence in that.

A glance at Sacha was all it took to see the other female was contemplating something. Sirena narrowed her eyes. "What haven't you told me?"

Sacha took far too long to answer and it added to Sirena's anxiety.

"Hroarr said that if we wanted Thule's assistance, he wanted something in return."

Sirena's heart felt like it was thudding in her head now.

He wouldn't.

Sacha waited only a beat before saying, "He demanded you."

Of course he fucking did.

Brianne was spouting expletives on the stupidity of males and threats to his genitals. There was mention of using copper to a very sensitive part of his anatomy. They'd learned that the element had draining effects on Thulians. The double entendre wasn't missed on Sirena.

Sirena's vision bled red as she ground out, "Let me get this straight." She paused to take a deep breath in order to battle back her fury. "He said he would only help us fight this if I do *what* exactly?" If the God actually demanded that she fuck him as payment, she might let Brianne find the copper. The whole thing was degrading, infuriating and mortifying. P and Drake had been her family since before they were ever Guardians, so knowing the arrogant bastard had demanded that from them only pissed her off more.

Hroarr couldn't just ask to speak with her?

Of course not, he was a God. A big arrogant demanding fool of a God.

Sacha shook her head. "He technically said he would build the prisons the second you were at his side. But, yes, we all assume he wants you in his bed."

Sirena closed her eyes as she imagined ripping that damned God to pieces.

"His demand was denied. Vehemently."

Sirena could imagine how Drake and the others had reacted. "Gefn's in Thule right now. She was shocked and mortified by her brother's actions. She swears he's never acted this way and that they do not treat women as possessions in Thule." Sacha paused. "It was her and Dagur's blatant shock that probably kept it from getting bloody."

Now she needed to think about how to deal with an asshole.

Maybe Dagur was wrong about the year. Maybe she had more time to develop a plan that didn't include bloodshed.

"I need to talk to Gefn," she bit out.

A resounding, "Yes," came from both Sacha and Brianne.

Chapter 4

Hroarr's Palace, Thule

Hroarr felt a rush of icy wind whipping through the wide stone hallway of the palace, a blatant signal that their sister Kara was close. She was known in Thule as the Ice Goddess, less for her skill with chilling the waves, but for the cold façade she wore like armor. Dagur groaned deep when she arrived before them in a rush of pale blue silk that had torchlight flickering in her wake. Her black hair was tied up in the formal style she seemed to prefer, and she was scowling in his direction.

He raised an eyebrow until she moved aside as he continued to his study. More cold filled the space as she demanded, "Where have you been? Were you in Earth?"

Her mouth snapped shut the second he sent her a hard glance. She knew better than to challenge or demand things from him, but the Goddess lacked control of her temper. A fact that made her less than welcome in his palace, yet at this moment he had questions for her.

He commanded, "With me."

Kara's chest might have heaved, but she wisely kept her mouth closed.

The second he neared his study, the massive spelled doors split wide, allowing them entrance while his guards stopped before the opening. He could feel his sister's tension as the door clanked shut behind them.

Kara had finally returned to full strength after suffering the effects of an attack that *she* had initiated on Earth. Even though her body had thoroughly healed, she refused to return to her own palace, choosing to remain in his space while making it clear she was not pleased that he'd forbidden her to return to Earth. He did not care. Her altercation with Hades was of her own making. She'd allowed her temper to reign free and she'd suffered for her mistake. He'd made it abundantly clear that if she chose to seek retribution for losing that particular battle, there would be severe consequences. Thule was allied with the other world and Kara would need to get used to that fact or return home.

He ignored Dagur's low curses at Kara's presence, along with the icy glare she sent in their brother's direction.

Hroarr was more interested in the presence of Spa and Velspar perched beside his massive carved desk, directly in front of the two-story wooden shelves containing ancient artifacts.

Tension charged the room as all three of them stared at the beasts who rarely left Gefn's side. Twin golden eyes assessed them in return, regally watchful.

Kara bit out, "What are they doing without Gefn?"

The creatures were not to be taken lightly. They were powerful, but their instincts were heeded well within Thule and he wondered what they were about at the moment.

Before he could say a word, the doors whipped open to allow his sister Gefn to whisk through. He could feel his blonde sister's fury and the cats immediately prowled over to flank her.

The doors had barely shut before her green eyes flashed at him. "What were you thinking?" Her power was a living breathing thing that whipped her pale hair around her shoulders. It was interesting how much her magic had grown after she'd bonded with her half-Earth, half-Thulian male. A male who was not currently at his sister's side.

"Tread carefully, sister." He growled as he leaned against a high-backed chair. Gefn was indeed his favorite, if there was such a thing, but as the ruling God of Thule, he not only commanded respect, he demanded it.

"Hroarr, Sirena is my friend. A female my *maðr* considers a sister. If you want her, you do not demand her as some kind of payment for fighting alongside the Earth Gods. You court her."

Kara gasped and her icy blue eyes bored in his direction. "You want one of their females? It is bad enough Gefn has taken one of them. And you wish us to *fight* beside them? That world has already betrayed us once!"

Gefn's furious gaze speared her sister. "Cease! The Earth Gods did not betray you or their alliance with Agnarr. They were sent to sleep by their Creators, imprisoned and incapable of extending assistance when Tyr continued to destroy our priestesses and siblings. Your anger is misplaced and you know it. I know Hroarr and Dagur told you everything we've learned." Gefn sucked in a breath before continuing, "Do not think you were the only one to suffer a loss all those millennia ago." Gefn had lost her priestesses to the destruction of their brother Tyr and his allies. Priestesses shared a bond with the God they served, and Gefn would likely have suffered madness had it not been for the added empathetic connection she had with the powerful beasts at her feet. Without the cats, Gefn could have turned just as sociopathic as their malevolent sibling Tyr and the others who'd massacred their own priestesses in an effort to steal their Immortal abilities.

Kara's fury seemed to flicker at Gefn's words, but Gefn was not finished. "We have *all* suffered from Tyr's destruction. But your recklessness and anger regarding the past ended with the loss of dozens of your own warriors. It was a terrible waste when we have so few births. But not only that, your actions put a strain on relations with a world who could help defeat the *ófǫlr*. If you choose to hold onto the past and misplaced anger, do not fight at my side. But I choose to fight and end this Darkness before it comes for Thule."

Kara clenched her teeth as she seethed, but as furious as she appeared to be, she did not defend her actions or refute the truth of Gefn's words.

While Kara flexed her fingers mutely, Hroarr crossed his arms over his chest and spoke. "Kara may choose to fight at your side, but it will not be enough." He raised a brow, allowing that to sink in before adding, "I will not waver, sister." If she thought to convince him to give up his prize, it would not happen. The healer would be his.

Gefn turned to face him and he saw her gaze flash to Dagur for a brief moment as she admitted, "I know that."

He easily assessed her intentions and growled, "Dagur will not help you build the prisons. And even if he used the material we have, it will not be enough. And you already know I am the only one who can find more."

Dagur threw up his hands when Gefn sent a look in his direction. "I cannot understand why he demands her, but you know I will not go against him, sister. If it were up to me, you would bring the Earth Gods here and we would have plenty of power to defeat the *ófǫlr* in Thule. Earth is too large to defend."

Kara narrowed her eyes. "What does all of this mean?"

Hroarr was eying Gefn, letting her see that he would not be swayed as Dagur explained to Kara what had happened during their trip to Earth.

Gefn hissed, "Would it truly have killed you to offer for her? If you truly want her, then do not be disrespectful and treat her as some kind of possession." When he did not answer her ridiculous thoughts, she growled, "I have been busy convincing my *maðr* and his family that we are not monsters who use females as property in Thule. We would never allow our mortals to behave the way you have."

He cocked a brow. "I am no mortal." And then he added, "She will want for nothing here. They will give her to me, or they will fight the Darkness without my help."

"You would leave me to fight and die on Earth when it makes far more strategic sense to battle the *ófǫlr* there? To defeat it before it even has a chance to come for Thule?" she gritted out with a hand on her hip. Both Kara and Dagur were watching, and the cats flanking his sister had not so much as twitched.

He growled at his sister, "No, you will *not* die there," letting his power lift into the room, flames flaring in the fireplace and torches crackling against Gefn's winds. "I will remove you if it comes to that." His voice rumbled with finality.

*****

There was no doubt in Gefn's mind that her brother would remove her bodily from Earth should it start to fall completely. He was not a male to make false statements. He was also not known for being stupid. It made far more sense to find a way to defeat the threat when it came for Earth than to wait for it to come to Thule.

But her argument had meant nothing to him. It was blatantly obvious that her infuriating brother would not budge.

After a tense pause in which Kara and Dagur stared at them, Hroarr spoke again. "Heed me well, sister. They will have no help from Thule until she is here."

Gefn watched her brother carefully. He'd closed off any potential assistance other than allowing Kara the option of fighting beside Gefn. He knew it would force all their hands. Dagur would never go against Hroarr's wishes, if only for the sheer fact that Hroarr could make Dagur's life miserable without even actually harming him. Taking away Dagur's female entertainment, in the form of Hroarr's priestesses, would likely be their wild brother's worst nightmare.

What is happening there, thea mou*?* Pothos' voice was a balm she needed. She had no doubt he'd felt her agitation and now her resignation even as she was trying to shield her emotion from her male. The last thing she needed was for Pothos to show up and be party to her brothers' and sister's power plays. This was not the time, though she'd give anything for Pothos' warmth against her skin. Her tension eased when she felt him sending her soothing energy through their bond.

At the same time Spa and Velspar stood and rubbed their massive bodies against her leg. She shook her head with a smile as she looked down at their twitching golden ears. They were definitely conniving if they'd abducted Sirena, but she couldn't deny feeling comfort and love from the meddling creatures.

A knock at the door sounded in the tension-filled room.

Hroarr growled, "Enter." Gefn could not miss his displeasure at the guard's interruption, but he was wise enough to know his warriors would only do so if it was truly urgent.

She listened to the exchange before mentally sending back to Pothos, *I'm fine. Hroarr is getting called away to our northern lands.* She also needed to see to her own territory soon. She'd been lax in easing the elements, and soon the air would tear through their world in a violent frenzy if she didn't calm the currents.

Right now she needed to tell her *maðr* what was happening, *There is no way Hroarr is going to budge on giving his help.* She felt her stomach clench, trying to decide how she would fix this. She hated admitting, *I don't have the knowledge to help Earth. Not like Hroarr. And he has forbidden Dagur to help. He is adamant that he have Sirena. I will find a way to... do something. He is being completely unreasonable.*

Do you want me to come there now, love?

No. She could feel Pothos' anger at her brother, and it would only increase tensions having her *maðr* there. This would be up to her to fix. Somehow.

I will come to you, she sent with a smile touching her lips. Her fingers threaded through Spa's and Velspar's fur, shaking her head in frustration at what they'd done. She would need to find a way to insure they no longer caused havoc with her new family.

She ignored the last of Hroarr's orders to his warriors and looked at Dagur and Kara. Dagur shook his head and lifted his hands. She frowned, wondering if it would help to confront Hroarr about the possibility of his being Sirena's mate, but she wasn't sure it would help anything. Nor was she in any mood to give her brother any warning of the frenzy to come if Sirena was destined for him.

Hroarr turned a hard stare in her direction. "I will return in two days. I expect Sirena to be here."

And then he was gone.

Chapter 5

Guardian Manor, Tetartos Realm

It took all Sirena's self-control not to throw the blood sample against the wall. She ripped off her latex gloves and tossed them in the trash instead, but it didn't have the same effect she'd been looking for. Shaking her head, she glared at the sterile white cabinets, attempting to clear her mind of the endless thoughts rolling around like pinballs in her head.

She wasn't even supposed to be in her lab. After her brother's interruption of her and her sisters' talk and then the Guardian briefing, she'd had every intention of going to refuel her energies. That was where everyone else was, after their detours taking turns to meet the newest Guardian.

In the days to come, they'd all need any strength they could get, and she was already depleted, but the thought of sitting calmly in her cavern with her mind running rampant wasn't possible.

With a groan she paced back and forth behind the high counter before finally slipping into her adjacent office. The space consisted of black and red furniture, while vibrant pin-up girl paintings and glass display cases filled an entire wall.

"Damn it, I need that Warlord God's blood!" she snarled to herself. There was no one to hear her. Her busts of horror icons merely sneered back at her. Looking around at her collectables used to make her smile, but they were doing nothing for her current mood. Even the terrifying scarred doll and his bride couldn't drag a smile from her lips.

Gefn's soft voice filtered from the cracked door. "Am I interrupting?"

"No." She breathed and bade her enter. "I'm actually glad you came." A glance told her that P was not with his mate.

Gefn nodded as if understanding her unspoken thoughts. "I left Pothos to greet the newest Guardian. The others had already gone and he was anxious to meet the baby." After a pause she added, "This is a time for family, not strangers."

That Gefn understood and didn't find offense in that particular fact was just another reason to like the Goddess. The female added, "The child's power is everywhere in the wing. It's so incredibly pure and beautiful. I've never encountered anything like it. Spa and Velspar have perched outside the room. I believe they are smitten and hoping for a look at her."

When Sirena stilled at the mention of the twin menaces, Gefn lifted her hands to assure her, "I have warned them to stay away. And both Pothos and I are taking turns watching their every movement through the mental bond."

Sirena smiled at that.

"They will behave if it kills us both to keep watch over them."

"I think that's a good idea, considering. I for one am tempted to turn them into rugs," Sirena replied, shaking her head. "But Gregoire has always been possessive and protective, and I doubt he's in a place to allow the cats or anyone he doesn't know near Alyssa or Lucia."

"Yes. And you were right to insist no one share the news about the Darkness or the Tria with them." Drake had agreed with Sirena's insistence that Alyssa and Gregoire be spared that knowledge until tomorrow. The new parents deserved to have at least one night to enjoy the beauty of their new daughter without the weight of impending danger on their minds. One night to love her and not worry how they would protect her a year from now. That thought alone made Sirena's heart clench. The baby was just one more reason for her to deal with Hroarr and the mating quickly. They were running out of time and she would need the year for his power to meld with hers. She could hope it happened rapidly with him being a God, but how could she justify taking that kind of chance?

Gefn's face lit for a second and she smiled. "Pothos is in love with his niece." The two were obviously communicating mentally and the way Gefn's already beautiful face changed made Sirena's heart ache a little. She couldn't imagine sharing that with a male who thought of her as only a possession.

The Goddess cleared her throat. "We didn't get much time to talk when I returned from Thule."

Sirena scoffed, "You mean when Drake, Hades and your mate were busy demanding I never see the male without them being present?"

It was a rhetorical question and Gefn's lips twitched for only a moment. "If it helps, I believe you handled it well."

"You mean when I told them where they could keep their protective tendencies and reminded them I was not helpless or a fool." It was about that time their mates had ushered them out of the room to the Guardian meeting while shaking their heads at Sirena. Brianne had told them all they needed to shut the hell up and wait until Sirena actually asked for their opinion. Sirena smiled, thinking there might have been mention of hell freezing over along with a reminder of the fact that Sacha, Gefn and Brianne were fully capable of having Sirena's back during any meeting with the God. That hadn't gone over any better with her brothers, but thankfully Sirena had been able to convince them all to keep their mouths shut during the Guardian briefing. She wasn't ready to tell the rest of her brethren, especially not when they had the Tria to focus on.

"Sirena, I will do everything in my power to get the information we need without you feeling trapped into mating with Hroarr."

She sighed. "I appreciate that. He and I need to have a heart-to-heart at some point." More accurately Sirena needed to squeeze his heart until it stopped beating or until he acknowledged the fact that he'd been an asshole and agreed instead to respect her and ensure she had the freedom to pursue the life she already had on Earth. After, of course, he helped her save the world.

She mentally snorted at the sheer ridiculousness her mind had conjured. He was a Warlord God through and through. There was no give in him, not in his hard body or his attitude. She had zero illusions of it being easy to bring the male down a peg or fifty until they had a reasonable relationship that didn't end with his murder at her hands.

"You will meet him, then?" Gefn raised an eyebrow.

"Once I have more information. I sure as hell will not be summoned like a dog," Sirena pointed out before asking the Goddess, "Can you get me some of Hroarr's blood to test against mine?" She couldn't take the chance that there would be some unforeseen complication in their compatibility when she and the God made it to the blood-bonding portion of the mating.

The odds were slim anything bad would come of it. The cats were apparently all for this mating and she knew where their loyalties lay, so if her and Hroarr's mating benefited Thule, it seemed likely it meant they at least thought Hroarr would become more powerful. An advantage if he was fighting at her side.

Sirena had already analyzed all the blood she could think to combine before Gefn had gotten there. Testing Pothos' and Gefn's the most, but she'd even used the Thulian Goddess Kara's, Hades', some of Conn's, half-wolf, in laws, and all of the Thulian mortal warrior blood she'd collected in different combinations to assess general compatibility between Earth and Thule. They were compatible every—single—time, and it actually seemed that the Immortals of Earth were *more* compatible with Thulian mortals than they were with humans, or even Mageia, the magic-wielding mortals of this world. It was almost as if the two worlds were made to be joined.

Fucking fate.

All that information should have made her ecstatic. A major part of her life's work had been finding potential mates for the Immortals of Earth and it was still so very rare all these millennia later. But now... Now, with the world on the brink of destruction, *now* they had the potential of destined mates and Immortal children. She fisted her hands against the need to toss something.

Her emotions were all over the place.

And worse. Her blood was showing more advanced signs of mating than it should be. Immortals able to change forms had always been more impacted by their mate's scent. She barely had any beast blood and she could *not* shift. His scent shouldn't have affected her this way, but he hadn't touched her and that was the only other way for her blood to have reacted this way.

While delivering the baby, she'd been able to tune it out. Even with her sisters it had been okay, but since then... All she could see was all that chiseled naked flesh, the feel of his incredible animalistic power and warmth sliding over her flesh when he'd been inches from her.

He looked like a barbarian, yet he hadn't tossed her over his shoulder as she'd half expected.

And he'd shielded her nudity from his brother when the other God had barged in. She mentally tore into herself for trying to turn him into something he obviously wasn't. He hadn't been being *nice*, he'd been exhibiting possessiveness of his prize. That meant she could look forward to dealing with Gregoire times two with more arrogance than Hades, if that were even possible.

Wonderful.

Alyssa couldn't even pet Uri's damned hellhound without Gregoire getting all bent out of shape. Alyssa handled her male diplomatically, but Sirena was not that kind of female.

Sirena frowned when she realized Gefn had been silent while she had been lost in thought. A glance showed the Goddess was staring at the glass cases with a look somewhere between confusion and morbid curiosity. "What... are these?"

"They are replicas of bad movie villains." Very expensive and realistic replicas that had provided Sirena a great deal of amusement over the last two or three decades.

"Has Pothos shown you movies?" Sirena asked the other female. If not, there would be no way of explaining anything in her office. Brianne called it Sirena's twisted sense of romance. She saw smiles and kissing and cuddling up with popcorn when she looked into these cases. Serial killers in lakes and ugly comical creatures shuffling around with big teeth and knives while females gasped and jumped into the arms of their lovers. Simple sweetness. And only Sacha and Brianne knew that about her. There was no way in hell she'd admit that out loud.

"He has... but none with these..."

Sirena smiled. "I can imagine. The movies are silly."

It looked like the Goddess was shaking off her confusion, but she was currently studying the one with a burned face sneering behind a hand of blades.

"What else do you need? I can go to Hroarr tonight and get the blood you need."

"He'll give it to you freely?"

Gefn's gaze hardened. "I will get it. Is there anything else I can do?"

"I'm not sure. I'll need to confront him. But not on his terms and not until I've tested his blood against mine."

Gefn nodded. "Hroarr is cunning and powerful, but he rules Thule well. He would never allow the mortals of our world to treat a female as a possession. He would not tell me why he insisted on treating you like this, but it's not acceptable."

Sirena sighed. "It's not okay that he's acting like an ass, but I will deal with him."

She wasn't technically in the mating frenzy, but it was close and she wondered how it was going to progress over the next days. The damned Warlord God apparently had extra-potent pheromones if her blood was already affected. It begged the question as to what else was super strength.

Contraception wasn't something she'd been able to create for Immortals. Images of Alyssa and Gregoire slid into her mind. If she got pregnant on her mating night like Alyssa, Sirena would likely kill the God. The absolute last thing she needed to worry about was pregnancy during the end of the world.

It was just one more thing to stress about, and right now she was all full.

Unfortunately she didn't have the luxury of time to process everything.

She needed to confirm what P said about his mating to Gefn. "Can you tell me everything you experienced after Pothos touched you?"

Gefn moved from the glass and her movements flowed as if she were the air itself. The power she held was immense, and Sirena was actually a little entranced by the grace of it. The Goddess was regal without being pompous, and she actually cared about others, so Sirena wasn't surprised the female answered easily, "I felt arousal like nothing I'd ever known and experienced pain when we did not join our bodies quickly enough. Pothos said it progressed much the same as other matings, except that the arousal was apparently more demanding." Gefn's brows furrowed for a moment before she continued, "I believe that may have to do with his mother's blood. Priestesses of Thule are very sexual beings."

That was an interesting insight Sirena hadn't been told before. She'd known about the accelerated arousal, but not that there was a potential reason for it. She could only hope it was P's priestess blood and not something to do with Gefn's Thulian blood.

"What does Hroarr know about your mating?"

"I believe he knows everything. The priestesses kept showing up in Fólkvangr when we were in the middle of it."

"Do you think he would change his mind about keeping me if he knew it involved a permanent soul bond?"

Gefn firmed her lips while shaking her head. "I have never seen him change his mind about something he was this certain of. It's more likely he will assume the rules of mating will not apply to him." It was like Hades all over again, damn the arrogance of Gods. At least Hades treated Sacha differently than he treated everyone else; the God truly adored her sister Guardian.

"And you said he will be gone from the palace for days? What is he doing?" Sirena was curious why he would not just return to his palace using a portal. What would make him stay away from his home for days at a time? Was he not so all-powerful?

Gefn took a moment. "It has to do with the prisons for our Gods. The magical material and spells that were used in creating the holding chambers filter the Gods' power through Thule and back. It has strengthened our mortals and given them longer lives, but sometimes areas are tainted with the evil of our brothers... It infects the mortals and causes strife and war when not destroyed with Hroarr's flames." The female shook her head. "It is against our laws for clans to war. We have far too few mortals in our world to squander lives senselessly."

It seemed the male's primary element was fire. It hadn't been a secret that Thulians were far more elemental than those of Earth.

"And this process takes days? Does he sleep?"

"Hroarr chooses to conserve all his strength when burning the venom all the way back to the source. If it's not done quickly, it only advances again. He will take time to sleep for short spans during the process."

Sirena thought about this. “He will build the same kind of prisons for our Gods?” The Earth Gods were in stasis units designed to purge dark energies from the Deities. Did that mean Earth would not have the same problem of toxic power slipping out and causing problems in their world, or would they be tasked with doing what Hroarr was doing in his world?

“It’s the best weapon we’ve come across to use against the Darkness. For us it was also a way to imprison our terrible siblings. Once your Gods are in the chambers, you will be able to access their power and energy in the form of a contained weapon of light against the Darkness.”

“And the Gods won’t die?”

She shook her head. “No. It would upset the balance of Earth to kill a God of your world. We would need to drain them, but not so much that it kills them.”

Sirena felt too tired to ask another question. “I need to refuel, but I’d like to discuss this more when you bring me his blood.”

“Yes. I will have it for you by tomorrow.” There was a determination in the Goddess that Sirena wished she felt in that moment.

Instead she felt like this was just the calm before everything went to hell.

Chapter 6

Northern Lands, Thule

"I will not be disturbed," Hroarr ordered Ivarr and the other three guards. They silently moved closer to the doorway, safely distancing themselves from what was to come. The cave walls shimmered with minerals that flickered light through the underground streams and lakes inside the mountain. Outside, the snowcapped peaks led down to the villages on either side, where his *þrír* were currently dealing with the mortals affected by the toxins he was tasked with burning away.

Tossing his leather shirt on the flat rock he used to rest on, he sat before lying back in only his leather breeches. When charring the pestilence sent out from his brothers' prison confinements, he chose to stay within the mountains to be close to his task while leaving his priestesses to deal with the clansmen in the villages.

He had already wasted entirely too much time in this place without eradicating the problem. Each time he'd started over the weeks, he'd been called away. And each time he returned, the tendrils of hate and discord had grown back at a larger rate, infecting most of the mountain now. He clenched his jaw, readying for a brief sleep before returning to it. He'd made the cavern system safe enough for his warriors, for the moment, but things would not stay that way for long. He needed to drive the disease back to the bowels it had come from.

Once his guards were away, he called forth his fire, freeing the waves to create a protective blaze encasing his temporary sleeping area. His warriors would watch over his rest, but he never left it to them alone. The blaze would not damage anything unless someone dared touch the flame, and then the suffering was far worse than a burn. It would engulf them and render any being a pile of ash. His warriors and all those of Thule knew to keep their distance when the fires of the ruling God of Thule arose.

Closing his eyes seemed to invite the healer to him. She was there above him, purple eyes flashing with heat as she straddled his thighs, naked, setting her fingers to his chest before leaning in letting her pale hair trail over his chest and neck. He growled against her lips and flipped her beneath him, his weight trapping her against the rock. His shaft rose hard in between her creamy thighs. A gasp escaped her and then she arched for him, mewling against his lips. She was just as eager, her tongue sliding along his, igniting his blood.

Was it dream or sleep? Before his dreams were of her power and a shadowy figure driving his body wild. Now he had a face to imagine as that same power slid inside his skin. He growled as he devoured her mouth, wanting to taste her entire body. The flames shrouded them, hiding them from his males, if she were truly there, but the blaze would not muffle her sounds of need or his grunts as he touched her warm flesh. His breeches were a barrier that displeased him. He could scent her wet sheath as she writhed beneath him.

He released her lips to command, “Release the fastenings.” And he bit her lip as he thrust his leather-covered shaft between her thighs. His palms gripped her hips before sliding to her breasts, into her hair, tangling and pulling the soft strands as she moaned into his mouth.

He lifted away. The bright light sent a golden glow over her small, perfectly shaped body. He growled his demand once more, "Do it." Her eyes were glazed with lust and something defiant even as her cheeks flushed with need. His healer did not wish to obey his commands.

She would.

He smirked before taking possession of her swollen lips once more. He'd never wanted a female like he wanted this one. She tasted of sweet honey mead, and the second she freed his staff, he would have her, right there enclosed in his flames. He ruled them and their heat would never mar her tempting flesh.

He tugged her hair, arching her neck back for his teeth and tongue. Even her skin was sweet and the moans she issued vibrated against his stomach and chest. When she arched her back, hard little nipples stabbed into him and he snarled, wishing to suck and bite the nubs until she screamed for him.

Her fingers moved between them and he growled his approval as he slid his beard over her neck and nipped a small earlobe.

"This feels so good in dreams," she said and his shaft throbbed when he heard her melodic voice. Her fingers were not freeing him quickly enough. They seemed to be only teasing him through the fabric. "But I am no possession in real life."

A rush of air seized from his lips as he stared down at her in surprise. She was doing things to his lungs, his heart. His shaft. His neck arched in equal parts pleasure and pain.

When it cut off, he knew she was gone.

Hroarr's eyes shot open and he growled, willing his breath to ease before lowering the flames that surrounded him, revealing the dank cavern walls. She hadn't really been there.

"Leave me," he commanded his guards as he sat up, the remnants of his dreams making his hard shaft ache. His elite warriors slipped silently out to the tunnel, giving him privacy. He adjusted his hard flesh in the tight leather while breathing in the cool air.

Had she been there physically? He didn't smell her on his skin, but he swore he tasted her on his tongue. He rubbed a thumb over his lip. Had the little healer somehow visited his dreams? Had she not said as much?

His heart still twinged with aftershocks of what she'd done to it. She'd tempted him and then actually used power *against* him. He should be enraged... yet he wasn't.

He felt oddly alive in a way he'd never been. At least not in centuries.

She infused him with pleasure even when she was being defiant and fiery. Sirena had challenged a God she had no hope of winning against, and he felt his lips curl, thinking about it. All his prize had accomplished was making him that much more determined to have her.

He was just fastening his leather shirt when he felt a disturbance. He turned as Mist, Reginleif and Geiravor swept in on a rush of air. "What is it?" he growled.

Reginleif's golden eyes flashed bright, her dark features taut. "There are many infected with the toxin and they insist on trying our tempers." Her upset was enough to cool his need. He felt hints of his priestesses' ire, though he never allowed them to feel anything from him.

He narrowed his eyes. "I will deal with the clans."

"No," she insisted, raising a hand in his direction. "We only needed a moment away. We have handled the worst of it," she assured him. "They are not themselves, Hroarr. This infestation has gone on too long. We only need you to clear the rift. We will do our part with the clansmen." The mortals knew better than to offend any of his *þrír*; he did not care that they were suffering the ill effects of the toxins. The females represented him; they were to be respected.

"If they do not desist, you will come for me," he commanded. He should have brought them with him on past visits, but too much had been happening with Gefn and her beasts. Not to mention the issues with Earth Gods and his reckless siblings' infuriating machinations. Now they were paying the consequences.

"It will not come to that. Though our task is days from being met," Mist replied, her white hair flowing out wildly in her annoyance. Geiravor was the calm one of the three and even her moss-colored eyes had stayed hardened. They obviously weren't telling him everything regarding the clan's behavior. The green-haired priestess had yet to utter a word, but the look on her face said she was less than pleased.

He needed to fix the problem here, but he would not allow mortals to defy his *þrír*. "Take Ivarr and Ranulfr with you."

Mist shook her pale head. "Laire is with us, we do not need more warriors." Laire was Gefn's private guard on loan to his priestesses while his sister and her male traveled between worlds.

"Take them," he ordered, "and inform the clans that if I have to leave the caverns, they will not like the way I deal with their warring."

His elite warriors would probably jump at the opportunity to do something other than stand at attention as Hroarr tirelessly scorched the pestilence streaming through these mountains. He knew the males were restless.

They nodded almost in unison before whipping away in a rush of wind that pushed his long hair back. He ruthlessly tied the mass back to begin his task again.

After a moment, Hroarr lifted his hands and breathed in the power he needed before sending it to seek out the strains of malicious energy beneath his booted feet. It had already moved and grown in the time he'd rested. This was definitely the worst infection he'd seen in centuries and would take his full concentration.

Barely an hour had passed when he felt the power of his sister and snarled, "This is not the time, Gefn." He did not wish to hear more badgering where the healer was concerned. She knew him and was aware that he would not change his mind.

"Make time," she demanded. Only his sister would dare talk to him thus.

"This had better be urgent. Otherwise you try my patience needlessly, sister." He growled. Torches at the entrance to the room blazed with his annoyance.

"I need your blood."

He stilled and narrowed his eyes. "For what purpose?"

"To see if it will be compatible with Sirena's."

Just the sound of the healer's name made his body react. It was odd, yet he wanted more. Now, however, was not the time to lust after the tiny female.

Compatible?

"Our blood does not need to be compatible for her to be mine." The Earth God Hades had obviously had no difficulty indulging in the company of a Thulian priestess or Gefn's *maðr* would never have been conceived.

"It does if you are her mate, like I am Pothos'."

Mate. The animalistic word they used in Earth for the bond his sister held with her *maðr*.

His sister sighed. "She needs confirmation or she will not come to you. Do you wish to have the healer, or do you not?"

He raised an eyebrow. She'd had no trouble coming to him in his dreams. Yet it was interesting the female thought they would have a bond like Gefn and her male. He would have scoffed at that if he were willing to show his sister his thoughts. He was the ruling God of Thule. Even his bond with his priestesses was not like that of other Gods. He felt their emotion, but they were cut off from his. And even they could never mesmerize or use their power to calm him, as a priestess was usually able to do with their God.

He was more than tempted to demand his healer come for the blood herself, but he had an important duty to see to. She would be a distraction that he could not allow himself at the moment.

He also would not have the healer use this as an excuse to delay coming to him. "You will oversee this test personally. I will not have her playing tricks with my blood." He could not be controlled, so he doubted she could truly do harm with simple blood, but he was not ignorant enough to take the smallest of chances with the female who'd come into his dreams and actually been able to cause him pain.

Gefn was frowning. "I will oversee it." And then she sighed. "Can you not at least try to treat her with the same respect you would Regin and the others?"

His temper flared. "Do you believe she would be treated any

other way?"

"Yet you demand her as a payment for your assistance. She is a being with feelings and duties of her own on Earth. She is well respected there, and I will tell you, brother, that Hades and the others have demanded she not go to you."

He narrowed his eyes. Gefn continued, "They did not take kindly to your demand and neither have I. How would you have reacted to the same demand for Reginleif? Or myself?"

He did not respond. He didn't need to. She knew the answer.

Yet his sister would not cease. "If Sirena decides to come to you, you will give me your oath that you will do nothing she does not agree to in your bed."

He eyed his sibling and the fires flared brighter in his annoyance. "This is none of your concern, sister."

"You are not acting like yourself, Hroarr. Admit it. You're powerful and stronger than she is. I will not have you force her into anything she does not wish."

He crossed his arms over his chest before growling, "You think I would take the female against her will? Choose your answer carefully."

Her shoulders relaxed. "Give me your blood and swear an oath that you will protect her even from yourself."

A surge of malicious toxins slithered out of the rock beneath his feet and he growled in annoyance. He had no time for any of this. He conjured a dagger from the air and sliced his hand. Drops of red dripped free and he wrapped them in air and sent them soaring to his sister. "I will not force Sirena to give of her body unwillingly." He would not think about how he had agreed so quickly, not when the magic of the blood oath settled heavily around them. "Watch over these *tests* of hers. And I expect her in my palace two nights from now."

With a thought the blade was gone and his hand was healed. His sister looked ready to argue, but a hard glance shut her mouth and she was gone by the time he turned back to his task.

Chapter 7

Guardian Manor, Tetartos Realm

Sirena's eyes shot open as she worked to pull air into her lungs. The blankets slid across her oversensitive flesh when she moved to sit up at the side of her bed. Sliding a hand over the back of her neck, she groaned. How was it possible to still feel his hands on her skin, his weight and warmth holding her down, when it had only been a dream?

Swallowing, she tried to tune out erotic images of the damned God above her, devouring her lips. His tanned skin glistening with the golden glow of the fire that had surrounded them. She had no idea why there were flames in the dream, but the effect was fitting, as he'd lit her on fire.

She bit off a curse. It had been real in a way. He'd been in her dream. She turned her mind inward and cursed. There was a mental link. It was faint and not entirely formed, but definitely new, and she'd bet her ass it went to the damned God. They were already forming a telepathic bond. Her breath heaved as she attempted to block it from sharing her private thoughts. She wasn't sure it was necessary this early, but she wasn't taking any chances.

Well, if it had been a real shared dream, she'd officially thrown down a gauntlet and then proceeded to smash it with a sledgehammer for added effect. Teasing him and then letting him feel the bite of her power would have been a challenge to any average alpha and he was far from average.

She had to give herself some credit, though. Considering she'd never experienced a male's touch in the sexual sense, she'd met his passion equally. It had felt like the most natural animalistic experience of her life and she loved every second. Including the power in teasing him.

She smiled. She was indeed playing with fire, but at least she'd appeased her pride after having been rendered mute during their first encounter.

She groaned as she got out of bed on shaking legs. Her heart was still beating too hard and her body ached with need she didn't have time to take care of on her own. If it could be that real in some kind of shared dream, what would it be like when they truly touched for the first time?

Explosive.

With a telekinetic thought, she turned on the water in the shower. She needed to calm down, and a glance at the clock said she needed to get to Alyssa and Gregoire's room in the next twenty minutes.

She tied up her hair and stepped into the steaming water. After rushing through the steps of washing and drying, she dressed in black fitted capris and a white halter top. She whipped her hair into a high ponytail, hopping from one foot to another to don her red pumps. She barely slipped on matching lipstick and mascara before she was out of her suite and into the hallway in record time.

Spa and Velspar were flanking the door outside the baby's room. She put her hands on her hips and stared at the massive beasts. This was not going to go over well with Gregoire.

With narrowed eyes she warned, "Keep your distance. I will not hesitate to skin you for rugs, and that's kinder than what Gregoire will do if you get near his females."

They lay down with their heads on massive paws, golden ears turned and matching eyes looking up in such a ridiculous display of innocence she snorted, "I'm not buying it."

She'd never gotten a hint of maliciousness from the beasts, but they were too damned powerful and they did whatever the hell they wanted. It wasn't good. She eyed them, ready to defend herself from unwanted teleportation, but they stayed put as she cautiously stepped by them. With a sigh she gave them one more warning, "Seriously, you two, Gregoire is possessive of his females. He doesn't even like Havoc getting near his mate. He will not be okay with unknown powerful beings near his baby. You should not be here." As if her mention of the hellhound conjured the pup, she heard a deep excited woof and turned to see the slick black beast with Alex and Uri. The pup's bright red eyes and flopping tongue made her smile. The red flame-patterned harness signaled to the staff that he was Uri's and not a hellhound to be killed.

One of the cats hissed as both beasts moved to sitting positions at her side.

"Are we late?" Uri asked, eyeing the felines. Uri was Gregoire's best friend, showing up to support Gregoire when the male heard the bad news about the Darkness and the Tria.

"I just got here." And she hadn't rushed to go in, because in reality she was dreading it. She wanted to check on the new parents and the baby, but she didn't want to tell them about the impending attack or the fact that they were waking up Athena and Aphrodite, along with the mates that shared their current homes, in order to have stasis units to contain the Tria in. The two Goddesses and Hades had been the only good Gods when they'd been awake millennia ago, and it made sense the Goddesses would be the ones released to provide the units.

None of the logistics truly mattered.

Her heart hurt just thinking about how Alyssa and Gregoire were going to feel when they knew a battle for Earth's survival was set for a year's time.

The look on Alex's and Uri's faces mirrored her current feelings. Though the two also had the added tension that one of the Goddesses they were about to wake was Alex's mother, Athena. Before Sirena could knock, she saw Rain and Dorian coming down the hall. Where Alex and Uri both had dark hair and light eyes, Rain and Dorian were all light hair and bright eyes. As colorful as they were with Rain in pink and Dorian wearing a bright orange Aquaman tee shirt, they still managed to look like they were heading towards an executioner.

"Well?" Rain asked anxiously.

"We haven't gone in yet," Sirena answered. Rain and Alyssa had been friends since they were children and she'd also asked to be there when Drake told the couple the bad news.

Havoc whined a little at one of the cats, and the feline turned its head haughtily in the opposite direction. The silly interaction between the animals eased some of the dread filling the hallway.

P answered her knock at the door. He, Drake and Era were already inside. Era was smiling down at the baby, and the tilt of her lips transformed the female's face to something even more beautiful. Her golden eyes flashed with pure delight when Lucia reached a hand in her direction.

With a sigh Sirena turned, taking far too much petty amusement in shutting the door on two curious meowing faces. The fact that Havoc had trailed in with Uri was not missed by the felines, but they did not teleport inside as she'd almost expected the beasts to do. She could only assume they were actually obeying orders from Pothos and Gefn.

"Where is Gefn?" Sirena asked P.

He smiled at the mention of his female and she swore she'd never seen him so at ease. Their bond had given him control over his power to enthrall and the female herself made him happy. It was written on his face. "She and I were out on some early morning tasks in Thule. When we finished, she went to ask Hroarr something while I came here."

"Tasks?"

"She was teaching me to help calm their weather systems." The slightly proud look on his face said he'd done well. The fact that he was finding a way to be a part of two worlds gave her some optimism that she would find a way through this too. She wouldn't consider the fact that she had to tame a barbarian to do it; she'd find a way. That was what she did. She solved problems and healed people, but she could be ruthless and deadly when the need arose.

The Warlord wouldn't find it easy to rule her.

Gregoire and Alyssa had moved to a room that didn't have a hole in the balcony doors. They were giving Lucia a couple of days before teleporting with her, so until they could take their little girl home, they'd be staying in the manor.

This was a room done in bright yellow and white and it felt... fresh and peaceful with light streaming in from the open curtains. Gregoire was dressed in a green tee shirt and jeans as he sat on the bed with Alyssa sideways in his massive lap and baby Lucia in their arms. Lucia was in a pink onesie that said something about girls ruling and guys drooling scrolled across the front. Sirena was pretty sure it had been a present from Nastia. The baby had a million clothes and toys, most already at Alyssa and Gregoire's home.

Sirena smiled when she saw the beautiful frilly white bassinette beside the bed. It obviously hadn't been used. She doubted the child would get a chance to move from her parents' arms for a while. Lucia seemed pleased, as her tiny feet kicked absently in front of her father's chest as she lay in her mother's arms while everyone gazed down at her.

"How is she doing?" Sirena asked softly.

Alyssa smiled. "She's only slept for a few hours. It's almost like she's worried she'll miss something if she sleeps. And Lucy and her father have developed a terrible game where her powers are concerned. The shield has a telekinetic application that she's already learned."

Gregoire growled, "It is not a terrible game. Using her powers is how she will learn."

"Yes, but now she has learned to pull things to her. That's asking for trouble," Alyssa ground out. And as if on command, the baby giggled and her power filled the room. The next thing they all knew, a bubble of magic developed around a stiff-looking Havoc and lifted him in the air directly high enough for the baby to see him.

"Son of a bitch," Uri said, moving to grab the hound and getting jolted by the powerful bubble's apparent shield. Gregoire sent his power out to lower Havoc and release his daughter's hold.

"Language," Gregoire snapped.

Uri's eyebrows snapped up over his swirling silver eyes. His mate, Alex, covered her smile with her hands.

"Really?" Uri groused. "Language? When your little baby actually lifted a two-hundred-pound hellhound in the air with something that shocked the... crap out of me?"

Alyssa groaned. "No, Lucy. You could have dropped him!"

Gregoire scoffed. "I would not have let the pup drop. And she did not want to hurt Havoc, she simply wanted to see him. She's curious and smart." The pride in his tone was unmistakable.

"This is trouble," Drake growled, but there was no heat in the words. "She's more powerful than any Immortal baby I've ever seen."

Her power was almost soothing. It was pure and beautifully innocent and for the moment they were all silent. The feeling of family and sheer peace was something none of them seemed ready to disturb.

Alyssa ground out a lecture to her mate, "We are not going to cave in and give her everything she wants, Gregoire." The small female was shaking her head in exasperation. "We'll need to set rules and boundaries or she'll be rotten." Alyssa sighed down at her daughter. "Little one, you cannot just pick up living beings like that."

Sirena and her healer heart ached when she saw the uncertainty in the new mother as Alyssa softly sent a telepathic question through their bond, *Do you think she understands? We get her emotions, but they are simple. I'm worried I'm doing it all wrong.*

Gregoire leaned in and kissed Alyssa's forehead, having obviously heard her private conversation with Sirena.

I'm not sure she'll understand anything complex for a while, but I can just about guarantee she loves the sound of her mother's voice, so say anything you'd like. She beamed at you when you did it.

Alyssa released a heavy breath and gave Sirena a bright smile. *Thank you.*

I believe it's normal to have doubts. You'll be a perfect mother and you have all the support you could ever ask for. Your mother will probably be able to give some insight on all of this.

She has offered and I plan to talk to her more in the days to come.

After a second Alyssa admitted, "Lucy wants to touch everything. She called the painting off the wall. And then she saw the stuffed dolphin from Rain on the nightstand and decided she needed that as well." That made Rain light up with delight.

Gregoire gazed down at his child. "And Papa's princess can have anything she wants. Except boys. She can never have boys."

Everyone chuckled, but they all knew that Gregoire was dead serious.

The child would be spoiled rotten, but any boy wanting to speak to her would deal with her seven-foot-tall solidly muscled Guardian father. And then they'd likely run for the hills.

Uri shook his head. "Soon you'll decide she needs a baby pony, just so she has something her size when she first shifts." They all found that amusing. Thankfully, she shouldn't be walking or shifting for a little while. Though first transformations varied with each child, it usually happened when they started walking. Sirena smiled, imagining the tiny toddler shifting into her horse form. It was going to be adorable.

“If she wants a pony, she will have one. What is wrong with that?” Gregoire groused, but now everyone was laughing even louder, but Alyssa just shook her head as she cradled her daughter.

The child was beaming up at her father as if she understood everything he’d said.

They all stayed for nearly an hour, teasing and talking to Lucy, who remained just as wide awake as she’d been when they all arrived. When the baby learned to open the door, it was even more apparent they were all in for a great deal of trouble with her. Two golden-eyed beasts stared in every single time. And Gregoire actually told his daughter no for once.

After the second time the baby opened the door and sent her power out to the cats, P admitted, “If it helps, Spa and Velspar would never harm her. They seem to be drawn to Lucia’s power. Their emotions are very protective toward the baby.”

“You can feel this?” Gregoire growled. He didn’t want his daughter near the powerful beings, but the word protective had him narrowing his eyes at the door.

“I can.”

Gregoire grumbled from his place as he lifted Lucia to lean against his chest and sent the door open. “If you want to see the cats, you can see them from here, princess.” Her chubby little hands went straight out and she smiled brightly when she saw the beasts. They both purred loudly as they stood and gazed at the small baby.

The exchange felt oddly magical, but the beasts did not enter the room. They were being very respectful.

P was shaking his head. “They love her, G. It’s odd to feel. Your little girl has systematically wrapped everyone around her tiny fingers."

"That's enough for now, princess," Alyssa said with a breath. It was Alyssa's power that shut the door on the cats this time. "I'm not ready for them to come closer to her yet."

"She is your baby. You make the rules; they'll stay out there," Pothos said with a wink.

After another minute, Drake finally decided it was time. The dragon grew serious and Gregoire felt the shift instantly.

Gregoire visibly tensed and growled, "What's happened?"

"The Tria need to be contained." Sirena was more in tune to Gregoire and Alyssa's reactions than to what Drake was sharing. Their worry and fear seemed to affect Lucia and her powers surged. The new parents tamped it down and stared down at their daughter with such fierce protectiveness that Sirena felt her heart wrench painfully.

Sirena interrupted Drake, infusing her voice with her calming Siren power as she shared the worst with Gregoire. About the Gods being awakened, the Tria sending out a call to the Darkness, all of it. No one spoke as Sirena shared, and she soon felt the drain on her energy, but it was worth it. Her tone was the Immortal version of Xanax and the new parents needed it. Even Lucy had stilled her movements and seemed to be calm and content now.

After telling them everything, she assured them with feeling, "We will win this. I have found my mate and he is the ruling God of Thule. He has power that's let him see how the Darkness works and he will help us defeat it."

Uri's, Alex's, Rain's and Dorian's mouths dropped hearing that information, but they didn't say a word about it. Likely because Sirena was still using her powerful voice throughout the room. She had noticed the way P and Drake had stiffened, but again, not one word was spoken. They knew better.

"You, Alyssa and Lucia will be completely safe. You can stay in Thule during the battle."

Sirena didn't care what anyone said, she'd tie them up there if she needed to. They were a part of her family, and if she could keep them safe and their family intact, she would move heaven and hell to do it. Drake could growl if he chose, but she doubted he wanted them anywhere near the battle either, because the dragon hadn't uttered a word.

The Guardian leader finally issued a nod and she eased a little.

"I will not allow anything to happen to her, Gregoire." It was a vow and they all felt the magic of Sirena's oath settle into the room around them.

"You will all be sent away. I will not bend on that," Drake growled with finality. "For now, you stay here. Era and I are going to wake my mother and father."

She wasn't sure anyone could have spoken if they wanted to. The dragon was waking Aphrodite and Ladon. And soon after he would be waking Alex's mother and father, Athena and Niall.

It was a turning point for their world and she only hoped it was a good one.

Chapter 8

Guardian Manor, Tetartos Realm

The door to Alyssa and Gregoire's room had barely clicked shut behind them and Sirena already knew what was coming.

"My office. *Now*," Drake snarled as smoke lifted around him.

Rain, Dorian, Uri and Alex had stayed with Gregoire and Alyssa. It was a wise move considering how irritated Drake had been. The dragon might have avoided saying anything about her revelation regarding Hroarr, but he'd been two seconds from having a dragon meltdown.

Sirena lifted her chin. "Good idea." They were about to go through a battle regarding her decision to go to the Warlord God.

Just because she planned to go to the God as he'd demanded didn't mean she was going to be easy on him. Hroarr had a lot to learn about the type of female she was.

Without another word she passed P, Drake, Era and the cats, maintaining a mental watch on the two curious beasts as she moved in the direction of the other wing.

She couldn't shake the yawning pit in her stomach. The looks on Gregoire's and Alyssa's faces would haunt her until they were able to end the threat. She knew without a doubt that Gregoire was struggling and she felt for him. Yes, he was a warrior and a Guardian, but he was also a mate with a newborn. Sirena fully intended to cage Gregoire with his family when the threat came and she didn't care what Drake thought. Although, so far the dragon seemed on her side about that. If they only sent Alyssa and the baby away and something happened to Gregoire, it would be immensely tragic.

Soul bonds weren't like a human marriage. Sirena had seen what happened when a soul-bonded pair lost their other half.

The one left alive went mad.

This was the last thing they needed to be doing, but she knew Drake and P wouldn't let up until they'd had it out with her again about this. In all reality Drake needed to be waking the Goddesses and getting the ball rolling where the Tria were concerned instead of lecturing her.

Gefn appeared at the end of the hall and the cats suddenly flanked her; the bastards were getting quite good at teleporting. Too damned good, Sirena thought as she narrowed her eyes at the animals. There was no doubt in Sirena's mind that the felines understood every detail of what was going on. They might not speak the language, but they had no trouble deciphering it.

"What's happening?" the Goddess asked, though Sirena could see by the flash of her eyes that the Goddess and P were already communicating telepathically.

"We're on our way to Drake's office," Sirena informed her without missing a step. "Were you able to get what I asked for?" Before doing anything with that damned Warlord, she planned to check her blood against his.

Drake was snarling at P about the cats' running rampant all over the damned manor. She was barely listening to the two as P said it was better to have them where he could watch them.

Gefn ignored the growling males as she answered Sirena softly, "Yes. I have what you asked for."

She caught sight of Hades and Sacha the next wing over. The God's chest was bare and his massive black wings trailed to the ground. He wore black slacks whereas Sacha was in her black fighting leathers, her hair in braids. Sirena wondered if the outfit represented Sacha's feelings about going to wake Aphrodite. She'd definitely dressed for battle, which made Sirena's lips twitch. The look on her sister's face said they were there for more than the task of waking a Goddess. Drake had likely called the duo there. Did the dragon feel he needed backup where she was concerned?

Probably.

It was definitely going to be a party. The kind that held the appeal of an event with maggot-covered appetizers and knife-wielding clowns.

Are you okay? Sacha sent telepathically.

Yes. Drake's furious that I made the decision to take Hroarr's deal.

Sacha nodded. *Did you think he wouldn't be?*

No, she answered with a self-deprecating tilt of her lips. *But I will handle it.* She'd spent millennia dealing with overprotective males and she refused to back down now. No matter how edgy the decision made her, it was hers to make. Not theirs, and she was intelligent enough to gain assurances from the Warlord before ever entering his bed. Fitting since the ass had turned this into a *business* transaction.

Sacha nodded. Sirena knew her sister Guardian would support her in anything, but Sacha would also let Sirena deal with her issues in her own way. It was nice to feel not only her sister's support, but that of Era and Gefn as well.

It wasn't long before they arrived at Drake's office. The door swung wide with the dragon's telekinetic power. Before it was even closed behind them, Drake had already rounded to lean back against his desk. "You will not serve yourself up as a damned bargaining chip."

P was at the dragon's side, both of their stances matched as if choreographed. Two angry males with thick arms crossed over their chests as they glared at her. She lifted her chin, barely aware of Hades smirking off to the side as if he were watching a show. She noticed Sacha nudging him with her elbow and all the winged Deity did was pull her into his side, one black wing curling around his mate as the male continued to watch.

"It's not as if she won't have control of the situation." Hades grinned and shook his head.

P rounded on his father. "How do you figure?"

"First of all, she's the God's mate. Can you think of a better female to bring that bastard to his knees?" Hades' grin widened, apparently delighted with that particular fact. Sirena wasn't sure if she should be offended or flattered. She was nudging towards the former. "And as much as I don't like him, I don't believe he's an idiot. He has to know that if he dares harm a single hair on her head, we would know. Pothos can get into his palace easily. If anything happens, they will bring me there." Hades said the last with a deadly smile.

Sirena shook her head and noticed Sacha's lips twitching. Hades was nothing if not subtle, she mused sarcastically.

Drake wasn't having any of it. "He's too damned powerful! What if things don't work the same? If your powers don't actually combine? What if something goes wrong?"

Sirena took a breath, fully aware of the two golden-eyed beasts avidly watching the entire interaction, "Look at the benefits. If the mating goes the way it should, a mighty God fights at our side, he and I are *both* more powerful, *and* I also have his knowledge." Sirena moved both hands to her hips before continuing with logic. "If for some reason our powers don't connect, he will still fight with us and help us with the prisons slash weapons for our Gods. I'm not an idiot, Drake. I would get his promises the second I discussed my potential arrangement with him." She'd prefer not to think of it as whoring herself out, but in truth she would do far worse if it meant protecting those she loved along with the world she'd dedicated her entire life to.

And if she didn't gain the ability to teleport or portal from Thule, she knew Gefn or Pothos could come and get her anytime she wished. She wouldn't be trapped with the Warlord. As far as something going wrong... that was why she would test their blood. Even Vane and Brianne's hybrid mating had eventually worked when everything she'd ever known warned races couldn't mix. The Thulian had no beast to cause trouble with their mating and all the other blood tests indicated an unsettling overall compatibility between the worlds.

"You are not a damned possession, Sirena!" Drake snarled.

She ached for his upset. The dragon was worried about her and it was blinding him to all her arguments. She softened her tone a fraction. "I know you're concerned, but this is not your choice to make. It's mine and I've made it."

"You don't need to make this choice at all! Not so soon. Take time to think about this."

This was going nowhere.

"He has given me his blood to test against Sirena's," Gefn offered.

Drake was too infuriated to listen and bit off, "That's only part of the issue."

The entire room stilled at the Goddess' next words. "I also have his blood oath to not force Sirena to do anything she doesn't... physically want to do."

Sirena fought back her mortification that Gefn would share that information in front of her brothers, because the Goddess had meant well. She'd just rather have heard this anywhere else.

Gefn sent, *I'm sorry. I should have told you privately, but they were so worried that I thought it would help.*

Hades recovered first with his lips twitching. "Good. See, Draken, problem solved. Nephew, you really need to give Sirena credit. She faced off with me easily enough since I was awakened. I have complete faith in my niece's ability to bring the Thulian to heel."

Sirena raised her eyebrows not only at the fact that the God truly believed she would be able to control the God, but that he mentioned their familial bond, which had been masked by Aphrodite when she was a baby and never spoken of.

Drake had already turned to growl at Hades.

She shook those thoughts off to answer Gefn. *Just, please never mention my becoming physical with your brother. Not to Drake. We'll either all die of smoke inhalation or Drake will lose his damned mind.*

Era's the only reason he's as calm as he is. Sirena could actually feel the powerful female's power in soft tendrils in the room, wrapping around Drake. It was so... intense. Sirena wanted that kind of connection. She wasn't sure it would come with the barbarian, but she could think fancifully in the safety of her own mind.

A second later Hades flexed his wings. "Now, we need to wake my sisters so we can take care of the Tria." There was a hint of seriousness that rarely came from the arrogant God.

She knew they planned to awaken Aphrodite and her mate first. And they were all hoping Hades would be able to keep his favorite sister under control until she got over the fact that her son had been partially responsible for her imprisonment. Add in the fact that Drake was the actual key to her prison and he was in for a potentially volatile family reunion. One Sirena was thankful as hell Drake hadn't expected her to attend. P was going to be there with the dragon, Era, Hades and Sacha. That would be plenty of support for that particular task, and if it wasn't, Sirena was only a telepathic call away.

She just hoped to hell that didn't happen. Being around Aphrodite's power over inhibitions was the last thing she needed when she was so close to falling into the mating frenzy. When she lived in the palace, it had never been a problem for her, but that wasn't the case now. She wasn't ready for the wild lust fest that would hit as soon as she touched the God and wouldn't relent until they completed the steps that led to a soul bond.

She was so caught up in her own thoughts she jolted a little when Gefn responded. There was no mistaking the regret in the Goddess' tone. *I promise I won't mention it again... It's truly wonderful how much they love you.*

It is, Sirena agreed. *They've been brothers to me my entire life, and I love them, but their protectiveness can be frustrating. They won't see logic any time soon.* Sirena mentally sighed. *But, thank you for what you did with your brother.*

She glanced over and saw that Gefn's features had softened. *I am completely on your side in this, Sirena. If you go to Hroarr, you will have me as an ally; you wouldn't be there on your own. Both Pothos and I will be a mental call away. I have to admit that I love that particular ability... I also want you to know that Hroarr wouldn't have harmed you even without an oath. My asking for it offended him greatly, but I felt it was needed, not just for your peace of mind but for Pothos and Drake as well.*

She wasn't sure how she felt about that information, so she stored it away to think about later. In all reality he was likely offended that Gefn thought any female wouldn't automatically jump at the opportunity to jump into his bed. He was a God, after all.

Drake was glaring in her and Gefn's direction while silently fuming. P was more thoughtful and Sirena had a feeling he'd heard every word she and the Goddess had shared.

Drake bit out, "The fact that he needs to make a damned oath is reason enough for you not to be with him."

"You've made your point," Sirena ground out. "But right now we're getting nowhere. I have blood work to check and you have Goddesses to wake."

Drake warned, "*Sirena*, don't do anything rash. He didn't touch you, so we have time to figure it out later."

She wasn't about to tell Drake that it didn't seem to matter that the God hadn't touched her and started the process. She and Hroarr were forming a bond already. And she had a bad feeling she could easily slip into the mating frenzy without his laying a hand on her.

Sirena clenched her teeth, uncomfortable at the slowly building arousal. She needed to make plans for exactly what she'd do and say before she was too needy to think straight.

What is it? Sacha asked. Sirena's expression must have betrayed her.

Nothing. Just making plans. Get them out of here. And good luck waking the Goddesses.

Sacha mentally sighed. *I don't think I should be there, I don't want to be there, but Hades is insistent that his sisters meet me immediately.* Sacha looked like she'd rather attend her own execution than go with her mate. After having been a slave to Apollo and Hermes millennia ago, Gods weren't a favorite of her sister Guardian. Hades gazed down at Sacha before tucking her even closer to his side while smiling down into her eyes as if she were the only female in the world. It was incredibly sweet how he was with her.

"We are not done with this conversation," Drake growled, but moved in the direction of the door, which was a good sign.

Hades winked at her as he and Sacha moved to follow Drake. The God was far too pleased to be waking Aphrodite.

Era added, *We'll support you in anything you wish to do, Sirena.* The female rarely spoke much, she was far more watchful and assessing unless she was assisting Sirena with patients. In those cases Era was caring and soft spoken, and as much as Sirena hated the idea of someone taking her place as healer, she couldn't deny the female was skilled and needed to use her healing power.

Thank you, she sent to Era, and then it was only Gefn, P, their very still beasts, and a blood sample Sirena was anxious to test.

"I need to have Drake's back when he wakes his mother." P

seemed torn, looking like he'd much rather stay with his female. Sirena understood. She didn't envy him the task to come.

Gefn gazed up at her male and there was a hint of regret in her tone. "Go. I gave Hroarr my word I would be there when Sirena tested the samples. Be with your brother and I will be here."

He sighed and kissed his female fleetingly. "Don't take Sirena to Thule." He said the words to Gefn, but he had turned to eye Sirena. "Sleep on it. We're already going to have our fucking hands full with our damned aunts."

She raised an eyebrow that he'd mentioned they were Sirena's aunts too. It appeared everyone was mentioning her bloodlines today. The Guardians knew and had never faulted her for it. Aphrodite knew... but the Immortals of Tetartos didn't.

Her life had been full of lies. Omissions.

It had started when she was a babe. Her history was fabricated by Aphrodite so that Apollo wouldn't find out Sirena was alive and find a way to come for her. When she'd become a Guardian, the lies continued for what she felt was the good of the Immortal races. Nearly every single Immortal had suffered at her father's hand, having been abducted, enslaved and bred like animals to build the bastard's army. She'd never wanted them to know his blood ran in her veins. She'd always been ashamed and she'd wondered if they would have refused her skills because of her vile parentage.

Her brethren might not care or fault her for the circumstances of her birth. But she did. That was part of her drive. She worked hard to fix all the torment he'd caused.

P shook his head at her and then did something out of character. He leaned down and kissed the top of her head.

Her mouth gaped open as she watched him leave. He'd hugged her after she'd healed the cats. And now this? She had to swallow back the emotion at the action. Until Gefn, he'd never gotten physically close to any of them. His power to enthrall had always kept him at a distance, even when they were children.

She forced herself to take a deep breath and was snapped back to reality when two massive beasts rubbed against her arms. She looked down at them. When they purred up at her, she tried hard not to forgive them. "You're really working it, cats, I'll give you that."

When she glanced at Gefn, she saw the Goddess smiling.

"Let's go see what your blood does with Hroarr's."

Chapter 9

Guardian Manor, Tetartos Realm

Sirena was feeling jittery by the time she and Gefn made it to her office. Taking deep breaths wasn't doing anything to calm her nerves.

Before Spa and Velspar attempted setting their paws in her clean lab, she stopped them. "Not gonna happen. No fur in the lab, guys." To Gefn she added, "They can stay in my office."

Both beasts huffed before planting their asses on her office floor, their curious golden eyes looking up to stare at the display cases, and she wondered how they saw them.

"Do not break anything in here," she warned them as she and Gefn slipped through the door leading into her private work space. She moved around the high counter with the Goddess at her side.

"Okay, where's the sample?" Sirena asked while attempting to will away the shaking of her hands. Why was she suddenly a thousand times more nervous than before? Nothing bad could happen in combining blood on a glass slide. She turned to get supplies out of a cabinet, then opened a drawer for some latex gloves.

But what if they weren't truly compatible?

What if the blood didn't combine?

What if her blood rejected his or vice versa?

That was likely doubtful, considering the link already building between them. Destiny had decided, and she doubted it would be so insistent if this wasn't meant to be.

She mentally scoffed at that before turning back to the high sterile counter and... she stilled, just staring at the Goddess. Gefn was holding her palm out with something hovering just above it.

Sirena cleared her throat before asking, "Is his blood being held in an air bubble?" She felt a little ridiculous for stating the obvious. Yes, she was aware that she was dealing with a far more elemental being, in theory, but... really? She couldn't have just put the blood in a jar?

Gefn tilted her head. "Yes."

Sirena hesitated only a moment before turning back to the cabinet. After taking a deep breath, she retrieved a glass vial and stand before turning to set them on the counter. She took out the stopper and handed the vial to Gefn, who was looking on curiously.

"Can you put his blood in this?"

"Of course," the Goddess intoned helpfully as Sirena shook her head slightly. She was still processing the fact that the Goddess had been traipsing about Thule and then the manor with blood in an air bubble this whole time. It seemed like far more work than just putting it in something, but who was Sirena to determine what made sense for Gods of another world?

Hell, she could heal an organ without ever making an incision. To them, her powers might seem odd.

"May I ask where you were holding this?" she asked. Sirena

hadn't seen it when they were in the office.

"In the air."

"You can *hide* things in the air?" After Sirena had healed the cats, Gefn had produced a blade out of air to use in the act of gifting Sirena with a blood debt for saving their lives. At the time she'd assumed that Gefn had called it from somewhere in the room with telekinesis.

The Goddess smiled, her emerald eyes lighting up with amusement. "You can't?"

"Do I get to know what else you have hidden about? Is this power like a bottomless handbag?" The magic-bag bit was a joke, but in reality she was curious.

Gefn's laughter filled the air in a musical way that made Sirena smile. A second later the Goddess lifted a hand and with a surge of power a dagger of glowing blue appeared in the female's palm. Probably the same one she'd given Sirena the oath with? A second later the Goddess flicked her wrist and the small blade disappeared, only to be replaced with a shimmering blue sword with a gorgeous carved hilt. "Just these at the moment. My sister, Kara, has such skill she can hide several warriors in the mist she commands. The limitation is that things hidden must stay within close proximity."

Sirena had only seen Kara when the Goddess had been knocked unconscious after a battle with Hades.

It truly was mind-boggling how much had happened between their two worlds in such a short span of time, and it seemed there was a great deal they still needed to learn about one another.

She and her brethren had a lot of knowledge of Thule's history after Pothos saw Gefn's memories in their blood bonding. The problem was those memories were personal and prominent and wouldn't necessarily share details of everyday life.

Like the ability to create hidden air bubbles to store things. For Gefn, hiding things in the air was normal. It was possible that Pothos had already learned the skill, or maybe he would acquire it during the year it usually took for mated pairs to share power, but it definitely highlighted the differences between their worlds.

Sirena was caught by the desire to understand more about Hroarr and what made his power so special that Gefn and the other Gods would follow him. He could supposedly see the birth and destruction of worlds. How had that started? Hell, how much power and control would an ability like that even require?

Her curiosity was killing her. It was a byproduct of being a scientist. She always wanted to understand how things worked.

Gefn's lips were still tilted as she moved the blood into the vial. Sirena stilled when the bubble surrounding the blood dissipated, allowing the exposed power to filter free and slide all around her, caressing her skin. She sucked in a breath, shocked. She could feel power in his blood alone? She'd never felt anything like that in a blood sample.

Never.

Even the scent was different, completely unique from even Gefn's blood samples. Immortal blood wasn't as metallic as a human's; it was vaguely sweet smelling. Hroarr's was like wine.

Seductive.

Suddenly she worried this was a bad idea. She hesitated a moment before finally shaking her head. "I can't touch it. Just close the vial."

"Do you want me to do the test for you?" Gefn offered with a slight frown. But the Goddess had capped the vial as she'd asked.

"You're really being great about all of this," Sirena pointed out, her mind spinning.

Gefn looked at her for a moment. "I would say that it has to do with this being my brother's fault, but it's more than that. I enjoy this. Being a part of this family." The Goddess smiled at that.

Sirena nodded. "I'm glad you're comfortable with us. And I'm grateful for the help." She didn't get the impression that Gefn and the other Gods of Thule were all that close, so the Goddess' life had consisted of just her and the cats. Though there was also a mortal guard, Laire, that Sirena had only briefly met, but according to P, she was very fond of the male. So much so that Pothos had insisted she test Laire's blood for compatibility as a mate to an Immortal of Earth. Her brother Guardian had become determined as hell to find the male a mate. Looking at Gefn, she realized it was because P didn't want his Goddess to lose her friend one day. She was warmed at the beauty of the two's mating, of all her brethren's pairings.

She shook off those thoughts and focused on her current problem. Should she test the blood or not? On the one hand, she really needed to know how her blood reacted with Hroarr's. Yet on the other hand, her heart was beating nearly out of her chest just from being this close to the power of his exposed blood, and that was not normal. She sucked in a deep breath.

The real question was whether she truly had the luxury of waiting. A link was already building between them. And even though P and Drake thought there was time, she felt *anxious*. Something was coming to destroy the world in a year. She'd need all that time for her power to meld with the God's if she and Hroarr's mating progressed like any other. If it wasn't going to do that, she needed to be prepared.

The test held answers she needed.

She had to know what his blood did when mixed with hers, and this was the safest way.

These were samples. If she kept her distance, it would be fine.

Sirena firmed her lips and asked, "Would you mind handling it?"

"Of course not," Gefn agreed.

With a thought Sirena used her power to split the flesh of her palm. It felt as if time slowed when she fisted her hand and let the drops fall onto the glass.

She took a deep breath and healed the cut before instructing, "You'll need to use this dropper." Sirena handed her the tool and showed her how it worked as she continued, "Just one drop in the center of my blood and then put the other piece of glass on top before sliding it under the scope." She pointed to the piece of equipment that was stationary on the back counter.

Before she could stop herself, Sirena backed up until she was against the edge of the Formica. She wasn't sure why, but she needed the space as much as the support.

Gefn was cautious, yet fluid in her movements.

Sirena hadn't realized she'd been holding her breath until she watched the first drop of his powerful blood pool and fall.

The world suddenly felt like it stopped moving; the air currents charged just as she felt something snap into place, not just in her mind.

Her power surged through a brilliant and complete telepathic bond to the God.

It shone in her mind as a blinding light, and magic flowed straight through until she was seeing flashes of a torchlit cavern. Flames. Warriors.

She gripped the counter behind her. It was wild and out of her control, and when an animalistic growl slipped into her mind, she nearly came from the pleasure already running free inside her.

The flames she'd seen? She'd been looking through his eyes, she was certain of it.

The God knew she was there in his mind and he was furious. She could hear and feel his anger, *Get out.* But she couldn't. Her power continued to lash out uncontrollably. It moved deeper even though she fought it.

It was intoxicating.

I can't stop, she snapped back at the furious male. It wasn't as if she were trying to do this.

Through her half-drugged stupor, images flashed in her mind. She was slipping deeper into the male's psyche. Panic ripped through the desire, but she couldn't let any of it stop her seemingly futile battle for control.

Gefn was suddenly in front of her, her hands on Sirena's arms. "What's happening, Sirena?" She felt the warm fur of the cats against her legs as the Goddess demanded, "Are you okay?"

"Do not call P. Just... give me... a second." The words were choked out by sheer strength of will. Her brothers couldn't do anything for her, and she didn't want them to see her like this. She was far too consumed with wanting more of the God. If she couldn't find her way free of the God's mind, she'd call Alex before she'd call P or Drake. Alex had power over the mind.

That was when she realized she couldn't see or feel any of her other links. She was completely encompassed within the bond to Hroarr. It was if nothing else truly existed. That fact scared some of the desire out of her. Then she was so lost to it that she couldn't even feel or hear Gefn or the cats.

Nothing.

She felt a blast of raw anger and heard Hroarr's fury.

She sucked in air, thankful that his fury yanked her out of the terror at being trapped there alone. "Damn it, Thulian. Why not try helping me get out!" she snarled back, hating to even ask for his assistance, but couldn't he feel her struggle for freedom?

She was spiraling out of control into a dark abyss, where she finally saw what was pulling her in. A dark shroud covering… pure brilliant power unlike anything she'd ever seen.

The God roared, "Do not get near the power!"

It was his ability of sight, she knew it. And as much as she wanted to know what it meant, how it worked, she had no intention of touching it. It was far too strong beneath its covering.

There had to be a way out… but she couldn't find it.

Just as she found a way to slow down, his power rushed forward like a solar flare, bringing her into all its warmth. She might have screeched in shock, but she hoped not.

Then everything changed.

In a blink she was somewhere else.

A different world.

A different time.

A memory. If it were possible to hyperventilate in this state, that horrifying fact would do it. She couldn't even hear his anger anymore. She was alone, and she'd never felt anything like the panic that filled her. The isolation was terrifying. She'd had the comfort of her Guardian links for millennia and now they were gone. Everything was!

She stood in a forest of brilliant green and yellow. Primitive beings moved around with ancient weapons. Hunters. Flash after flash showed the world evolving and changing around her. Cities were built up into the skies.

And then came torrential winds and rains ripping through foliage, violently crashing into glass and bending metal. Seas overtaking islands, dragging homes and mortals into the depths. Mountains erupted with glowing lava that scorched paths into streets.

Screams.

Death.

Then the entire world shook with the impact of Realms crashing into one, nearly suffocating her as the air compressed and the bright lights of souls flitted everywhere. Wild beasts ran free and tore into mortals with sharp teeth.

Just as suddenly it was like being thrust into a post-apocalyptic movie. One filled with desolate dark clouds eerily lowering over the land, blacking out the sun. It was like the thickest of smoke. Mortals breathed it in and she watched as their bodies seized like they did in horror movies, bones cracking in a far more terrifying version of a human demon possession. They were being overtaken by something. Black eyes looked out. Not just the irises, even the whites were gone. Consumed with black. Their skin turned gray as suddenly man turned against man. Immortals were next to battle one another. Males and females with jewel-colored eyes and hair, they fell much the same way though they fought it longer.

Then she was faced with Gods whose skin glowed with golden marks. They wielded magic curved blades and flew into the skies without wings. They attempted to use magic spells and power against the smoke, but it didn't change. One by one she watched the massive Deities' bodies seize, twisting violently in the air, shaking until they stilled eerily.

The powerful beings turned on each other one by one. And as the battles ended, their bodies turned gray and gaunt, their power leeching away as they became nothing more than shrunken shells. Gray and lifeless like the dirt and trees around them. The sick feeling of death slid over her skin, inside her mind, through her body until she felt too heavy to stand. The weight brought her to her knees. To his knees, because it was like she'd seen and felt it all through Hroarr's eyes and body.

Lives and magic were gone, the lakes and seas dried up, and the trees and bugs were dead. Every bit of life had been sucked away until finally the black cloud lifted back into the ether. It simply floated up as if it hadn't just left a desolate world lifelessly spinning in its wake.

Her stomach turned violently with fury and anger.

Then the power flowed lovingly over her and soft numbness invaded her mind, taking the sickness and rage with it.

Chapter 10

Northern Lands, Thule

Hroarr roared with a fury that shook the cavern walls with the rage pulling at his muscles. His warriors rushed in and he snarled, "Leave me."

The healer was in his mind.

He clenched his jaw as he tried to get her free. It wasn't just his mind though, whatever she was doing was making his shaft ache.

Get out! he commanded her. It was if she were under his flesh, not in his mind, and his powers were raging out of control. His flames lashed out against the walls.

Damn it. Try helping me! she'd cursed. The healer had trespassed and now she demanded *he* get her free? These mental skills were *Earth* abilities, not Thulian.

He snarled when he felt her moving closer to his very power, his sjá, and it surged wildly for her. The beating in his chest nearly stopped.

"Do not get near it!" he demanded as a foreign emotion hit his gut. Panic. Sirena's mind was not equipped to handle the sheer power he was infused with.

He instantly pulled power to open a portal in the middle of the cavern without considering the damage. He needed to get to her. To get the infuriating Earth God to fix this before his magic killed her.

Before he released his ability, Spa and Velspar appeared, and he hadn't time for thought before he was breaking apart, moving through the air, out into the ether. It was different than moving through a portal, and he did not like the sensation.

And then he felt it, the raw waves of sjá flaring toward her, pulling her into it. He roared his fury before his body had fully reformed in a stark room. The ground shook beneath his feet. Items crashed to the ground in his fury. He couldn't feel her mind sliding against his.

Gefn's eyes widened. Pothos was holding the healer and the sight did something to Hroarr.

"Get your God. Now!" The male's fierce blue eyes narrowed and Hroarr wasted no time in sending power to tear the male from his female. If the male hadn't fixed this, then it meant only his God could. He didn't look as Pothos went crashing into a wall. Hroarr lifted a hand, sending flames to cage him there as he caught the tiny female up in his arms. He had no time for battles and he was furious with her and *worried* about what his ability was doing to her now. She wasn't speaking and her eyes were closed, but her slight body jerked in his arms and she was growing paler.

He couldn't feel her panic. Her anger. Or even her seductive mental touch teasing and tempting him as she had been.

"Hroarr, no! You cannot touch her," Gefn yelled. His sister's ire was too late. He already had the female.

He turned on his sister. "Get Hades now! She found a way inside my mind. Inside my *power*."

He gazed at her shaking body. How long could she survive inside the sjá? This should not have been possible. And he could not use the sheer power inside him to attempt to free her, he wasn't sure what the sjá would do to the female's mind.

When Pothos appeared next to him, Hroarr growled, "I do not have time to battle you."

"My thoughts exactly!" Pothos snapped as he gazed at the female in Hroarr's arms.

The dragon and Hades appeared next with their mates. Drake's golden-eyed female commanded, "Lay her on the counter."

He snarled until Hades snapped, "Era is a powerful healer, Hroarr. Let her figure out what's wrong!"

He glared as he laid Sirena's shaking body down. The female could touch her as long as she fixed this. Era didn't even look at him as she released power through his female, running her hands above the healer's body. The dragon was at her side, rapidly firing questions at his sister's male. He cared not how this happened. He heard something about their blood touching and his female having instructed Gefn not to call them. Gefn obviously hadn't followed that instruction, as her male was there.

Her body contorted and it ripped at his soul, and his power flared again, lashing flames along the walls.

"What the fuck kind of power is this?!" The dragon was furious.

"It is far too strong for even *your Gods* to wield, dragon!" Hroarr snarled.

"She is your mate. She can wield anything you can," Hades snapped, the male's wings flexing in agitation.

"She cannot wield this! If you cannot free her or heal her body, show me how this mental power of yours works and I will get her out of it myself! Hades, I command you to fix this, now!" Hroarr roared. The healer was doing nothing to stop the shaking, and Sirena's mind was not back touching his.

She was his!

And he was forced to seek the inferior God to fix this because he was not skilled in mental powers. He would change that. Once she woke, she would show him all the skills. He hated this sensation.

Helplessness.

Drake's power unleashed to diminish Hroarr's flames as Hades' power surged in the room. The males wings unfurled and his eyes glowed until Hroarr felt the God's power inside him and roared in fury. He felt the Deity pulling at his very essence until it was suddenly caught up and he snapped together with another's. *Sirena's* soul was leashing to his with intense finality. His entire being jolted and swelled with raw pleasure and a blinding rush of new power. With it came fury at Hades' insolence added with a blinding possessiveness toward his female. All the emotion slamming into him after millennia of numbness was hard to decipher.

He felt her being released from his power and reveled in the feeling of her mind sliding alongside his until finally her body slowly relaxed.

A wave of her confusion came next as he watched color infuse her pale cheeks until he was racked with relief.

In the next second he was in front of Hades, grabbing the God by his throat to lift him before the male could move. "You bound my soul to hers without my permission, Hades?" The words were said in a deadly growl and then he suddenly understood why the male had done it. He felt the new power, *his* power sliding through Sirena's body. The God had tied them together to strengthen her enough for her to handle his sjá. Though he could not believe it could happen this way, yet his power released her after they were connected.

This was indeed like the bond Gefn shared with her male.

The other Deity's lips split wide before he broke Hroarr's hold with more power than he'd ever given the male credit for. "I fixed it." And then he smirked harder. "You're welcome."

The sound of his female's groan made him turn. Her mind was against his, turning him inside out, and the sensation of her relief was unnerving. It soothed the fury that demanded he rip the God to pieces for binding him to her without his permission.

When her eyes opened, he sucked in a breath to growl because he was pleased with the other God's machinations. She was indeed his, forever. The seductive creature sat up and stared at him, narrowing her eyes. "How long was I gone?" He felt her emotions. Confusion. Worry. And then shock. "We're soul bonded." Her eyes shot from his to Hades'.

The others were talking, yet he ignored them to claim his prize. "Leave us!" he commanded the others.

When the males all snarled and snapped that he would not be alone with her, he pulled power into his fingertips. All the while his gaze never left his female's.

Gefn yelled, "Hroarr, no! A portal will destroy everything in here."

Sirena suddenly stood before him with a flash of speed he'd never seen from the Earth beings. "No," she said with enough power and force that it surprised him into momentary stillness.

Oh, yes, if he was tied to this fiery creature, he intended to have every inch of the body and mind that now belonged to him. Her eyes flashed with heat and ire, providing him with no doubt they would battle in the best way before she lay beneath him.

And then for the second time that day he was breaking apart and flying away. The healer's doing this time. He growled at the pleasure of their bodies combining and pulled her tighter into him until her moan filled his senses.

He would allow her to do this again if it always felt so pleasurable.

Chapter 11

Hroarr's Palace, Thule

Sirena ported out of Hroarr's range the second they reformed. She took only a moment to assess her surroundings.

The infuriated God had taken control of their direction during the teleport and now she was standing in what was obviously his bedroom. The Deity-sized bed at one side was a dead giveaway. Torches flared against the dark walls and flickered light along the carved wood of his headboard. The wall opposite the bed held a floor-to-ceiling jagged stone fireplace flanked by two bronze dragons. The wall to one side was lined with high shelves holding what looked to be ancient tomes with the odd archaic object mixed in.

There were two dark chocolate leather chairs and a table with more books spread across it. What really caught her eye was one entire glass wall leading to a balcony with stone dragon statues and chairs that overlooked an icy sea. Twin moons were soft against the midafternoon sun and she swore she saw a pirate ship in the distance. She begrudgingly admitted it was incredible, the view as well as the comfortable room that was more masculine than ornate all the way down to its thick comfy rugs over gray stone floors.

He was stalking her, she felt it in their connection. Her heart was thudding in her chest and she ached with arousal, and the new power surging in her veins only seemed to be adding to it. Her skin was oversensitive with the need for his touch, but she was also pissed. “A little arrogant, don’t you think?”

Sirena had been teleporting them to Heaven Realm, somewhere without a convenient bed or her brothers furiously attempting to protect her. This was the last place she could focus on the conversation they needed to have before she ended up on her back, and she would.

He’d created the need, and now that she was irrevocably bonded to him, she’d better get something mind-blowing out of it.

“Arrogant?” He wasn’t really asking her for clarification, just trying to distract her before he pounced. She could feel it. Could even see it in the flex of his muscle as he prowled toward her.

“I was leading us somewhere else. You directed us to your bed, so, yeah, arrogant and also presumptuous,” she said with hands on her hips, watching him. The God was a walking fantasy come to life. Her eyes took in his midnight hair, which was long enough to be tied in a knot at the back of his head, and moved lower to the leather covering his chest, leaving his wide shoulders bare. When he flashed her a feral smile, his white teeth where set off by his dark beard and tanned skin. He was ruthlessly magnificent and he knew it. Their emotions were one massive combined sex fest at the moment and she was struggling to focus.

He lifted a hand and her clothes incinerated. The only thing left was ash carried on some magical current to the fireplace. She took in a deep breath at how quick and easy that had been for him. She didn’t even feel the heat of the flames, but she felt his power as if it were her own.

She was furious, but so damned turned on she didn’t know what to do with herself. He wouldn’t listen if she railed at his actions, so she turned to the power that was running rampant through her. After a moment she accessed it, and with a shift of her hand, she set blaze to one of the massive chairs, igniting and incinerating it within seconds before focusing to move the ash to the fireplace. It might not have had the same *finesse* as what he'd done, but she was pleased with herself. And impressed that she'd shown restraint, because something far more vulnerable could have been incinerated.

He barely spared the furniture a glance as she chastised, "It's not nice to destroy people's things, Hroarr."

He smiled and tossed away his shirt. The dark dusting of chest hair and the line that led from his navel to beneath his pants completely derailed her and he knew it. Now that she could see how his chiseled body flexed as he moved, she was done. She forced her eyes up to his face and noted a hint of amusement there. Her point might have been better made by setting the bed on fire, but in all reality she'd shown her hand when she hadn't. It had been a sure sign that she planned to get in it.

She didn't dare look away from him. She was too vulnerable in only her red high heels. Not with his eyes on her like that. They were roving over her bare pussy and hips at the moment, and his desire was so incredibly intense she felt it spiking her own. They wouldn't last long upright at this point.

The mating frenzy usually came before a soul bond, but, like Sacha and Hades' mating, that didn't seem to be the case here. She was nearly in pain she wanted him so much.

Once they started this, there would be no interruptions. She'd sent a telepathic command to her brethren to give her space before leaving with him, and then she'd masked not only her telepathic thread, but Hroarr's connection to her as well. She couldn't trust Drake or Pothos not to come after her.

He toed off his boots next. He was towering over her when she spoke. “We do this after you vow two things.” She hissed with pleasure when he lifted her up by her thighs, spreading them to wrap her legs around his hips. She felt dizzy with all the sensations hitting her at once. His need was slipping into her mind through their bond, and the warmth of his body pressed against hers was making her crazy. The vulnerability of her legs spread with the only thing separating them being soft leather over a very hard erection. It was nearly unbearable.

The growl he uttered made her nipples ache, and her harsh intake of breath only stabbed them against his chest, tormenting her as he spoke. “Why would I do that?”

She was having difficulties remembering the question and shook her head in an attempt to clear it.

“I’ve seen what’s coming.” She was serious. “Your power showed me.”

He’d stilled at her words and then snarled, “It showed you what, exactly?”

She sent him the images in her mind like a short movie.

He growled as he processed that information and it didn’t please him.

They were both too needy to go into any more conversation about that, yet she still needed his vow before succumbing completely. “You were the one who made this a business transaction. Me in your bed for the prisons to help Earth.” She was having a hard time breathing as she spoke. He sent her a dark glare as she added, “I want you to vow to keep your part of the bargain. I’ll go *willingly* into your bed if you build the prisons *and* fight for Earth.”

"You are already willing to enter my bed, Sirena. Do you deny how slick you are for me?"

She shook her head. They seem to be understanding each other's languages easily enough. "No, I don't deny it." She breathed. "But I can take care of that with my own fingers." Then she leaned in and whispered in his ear, "And you gave your sister your oath that I would not be forced."

His fingers tangled in her hair and he pulled her back to face him. There was raw heat in his eyes, but also a hint of irritation and... amusement. "You believe you have maneuvered me to do as you wish?" He tugged her head back further and set his lips to her bared neck. It took all her will not to moan at his heat on her skin. She was losing her mind, but she fought it, forcing her mind to what she'd seen in his memories. Seeing the death of a world was bone chilling, yet even that didn't completely cool her arousal.

A part of her knew he would not force her into anything. He wouldn't have to. Soon she'd be begging to get into his bed, but she didn't voice that; instead she fought with all her will.

He growled against her hot skin, "You invaded my palace. My dreams. Entered my mind, and then endangered yourself by seeking out my very power. And now you're connected to my soul, Healer. The question is... what will *you* give *me* for saving you from your own curiosity?"

She swore she felt his smile against her throat. He was challenging her, but there was something more. Teasing? No, it wasn't just that.

She ripped the tie from his hair and tangled her fingers in it to pull his lips from her throat when she figured out what she was feeling from him. "You always planned to fight on the side of Earth.

You were bluffing?"

His gaze hardened. "I do not *bluff, völur minn*." His witch?

She glared at him. "You did not just call me a witch."

He tilted his head. "I did."

The bastard thought it was an endearment? That was exactly how he'd said it. She shook her head, leaving that battle for later.

She was too focused on the fact that he'd been confident that she'd come to him, and the bastard had been right.

The heat in his eyes told her they were done talking. "You have your vow. Now show me what I pledged my sword for."

She flew through the air and found herself splayed on her back in the middle of the bed. She was panting because, put that way, it was far more hot at the moment than offensive. It was a matter of semantics, but she didn't care. Suddenly she felt a thousand times more powerful and too wet to care about anything else. She lifted up on her elbows, slowly spreading her thighs for him, tempting and tormenting the God as he'd been doing to her.

His power surged around them as he stared. She didn't even see him remove his pants, but she felt the air shift before a massive naked God appeared on top of her. There was a purely animalistic glint in his eye as his mouth descended on hers.

One of his hands was in her hair, the other on her swollen breast. She arched against his palm and groaned when he plumped and then plucked at the taut tip of a nipple. Lust, pure and blinding, rode her until it felt like a battle to touch and taste each other. Her fingers wrapped in his hair as she met the demands of his tongue. He tasted even better than he had in their shared dream.

Her back bowed as he rocked his hips, sliding his cock along her clit, slicking him with each carnal thrust. Her heart was racing as she fought for air, close to coming already and they'd just started.

She ran one leg up along his narrow hip until her ankle was against his flexing hip. She lost all ability to think as her hand moved down so she could grip his ass. She had to reach because he was so much bigger, but it was completely worth it. She protested when he broke her hold to slide down and torment her neck and suck her nipples. Her entire body was a mass of jagged oversensitive nerve endings. His cock wasn't riding her clit anymore and she thought she'd die without friction. She writhed against his chest, denied what she needed most.

He lifted up, towering over her to demand, "Guide my shaft."

Her ears were buzzing and she suddenly realized this was really happening. She slid her fingers over his hips to his cock and circled him, or as much of him as she could. He groaned and thrust into her palm. "Do not tease."

She wasn't teasing, she was savoring the moment, the feel of him. She was also realizing his cock was going to be a challenge when she'd never accommodated a man. Hell, she'd never wasted time on toys either, but her healing ability would solve any problems.

His eyes shot to hers and then he cursed as if in pain, so much emotion was riding through him into their link, and the raw pleasure and animalistic possessiveness rocked her and pleased some deep part she'd never felt. It had to be the finite amount of the beast blood inside her going insane for his wildness.

His chest was rising and falling hard as he demanded, "No male has touched you?"

"No, I've never been with anyone," she admitted.

He growled, but his emerald eyes were full of sheer masculine triumph. "This pleases me." And then he leaned down and arrogantly devoured her mouth.

One second she was grateful that she didn't need to respond, the next she was falling into the intoxicating haze of the God whose hands, lips and mind were turning her inside out.

He nearly hurt with the need to be inside her and she knew it. The desire flowing between them was only heightened by the fact that she could feel how out of control he was.

A harsh growl slipped from his lips before, with seemingly great effort, he tore his body from hers to sit on his knees. She had only a moment to protest before her hips were lifted high, his hands gripping her ass, bringing her pussy to his lips. His emerald eyes were blazing with heat as she gasped and writhed, the position leaving her head and shoulders on the bedding, putting her off balance and in his control.

She cried out, having never imagined how incredible a hot mouth and wet tongue could feel.

He snarled into their bond and then sucked her clit. *Your pleasure is mine, Sirena.*

His mind sliding into hers added another element that sent her over the edge. She cried out as her channel pulsed, but he was relentless. He growled against her, *Give me more.* Her shoulders dug into the soft bedding and she held her breath as her fingers clenched handfuls of material.

"I can't come again so soon," she protested on a groan, but instead of letting her go, he rubbed her thigh with his beard and then nipped it.

"You will." His tone was commanding, but she could hear and feel the strain in it.

"You will thank me for my patience." Before she could say a word, he flicked her clit with his tongue and she gasped, apparently she wasn't finished. His fingers gripped her ass as he buried his face in her pussy, his heated gaze never leaving hers.

She screamed to the ceiling as her body jerked. She'd never been vocal on her own. Then again, she'd never come so hard in her entire existence. She felt his arrogant smile against her thigh as he slid his beard against the sensitive flesh, marking her skin.

And then he was over her again, his weight bearing her down into the blankets, her thighs splayed wide around his hips. He was so much bigger in every way, a fact that should have made her feel trapped, threatened, with him pushing her into the bed, but she only felt need.

His hair brushed over her neck and she couldn't help but slide her fingers over his beard and through the heavy waves. It was rugged and sexy.

Her assessment seemed to please him as he rode his shaft back over her clit, taunting her before finally notching his massive cock at her entrance. She swallowed against the raw need to have him inside her. To know what it was like to feel full of him.

His gaze bored into hers as he growled, "Your body belongs to me now, Sirena." And then he thrust his hips, breaking the barrier and making her neck arch. It only stung for a split second before her healing power left only warmth in its wake. Warmth and supreme pleasure.

"So good." She moaned.

"Yes," he growled and started moving inside her. Her nails dug into his hair, his back, her eyes trained on the tight tendons at his neck, the pained need in his fierce eyes.

He hadn't stopped looking at her the entire time and she saw such primal satisfaction in his gaze that she'd swear he had a beast inside him. The raw possessiveness that streamed through the bond only added to the need already riding her. She pushed her hips against his and felt him flexing, thrusting deeper.

Her eyes nearly crossed when he slid out slowly. She clawed at his back until he thrust back, harder, deeper. He gauged every emotion until he was powering in and out of her greedy body. She needed more of what he was giving her. His cock was hitting some deep hidden spot that made her head thrash and her vision blur.

She was panting, trying to meet each powerful drive, but he was holding her firm, controlling each and every ounce of rapture he forced on her, each push grinding her clit against him, adding even more pleasure.

She thought she'd die when she finally came. Her entire body tensed and she knew she drew his blood as her climax tore through her and kept going until she forced him over with her. She felt him holding back, and she reveled in the moment he roared in pleasure. The entire room shook with it and her eyes shot wide when the sensation of his hot come forced tremors of release to pulse through her all over again.

The door shot open and flames erupted around the bed, shielding them from view as he snarled for his guards to leave them.

She closed her eyes, lying there with him still throbbing inside her.

It had been perfect.

The barbarian might be arrogant as hell, but she had to admit he'd earn that right. She felt conquered in the best way.

She sighed, but he didn't move. And she didn't want him to. She felt comfortable and warm beneath his weight.

Safe.

Chapter 12

Guardian Manor, Tetartos Realm

"I can't see her mental link. She's cut off from us!" Drake raged.

Pothos pulled Gefn into his side in the destroyed room. She relaxed into his warmth while silently watching Drake pace over broken glass. It wasn't her place to try to calm the furious dragon and she had a feeling this was the subdued version, because she could feel the power Era was sending to calm her male.

It was Sacha who calmly pointed out, "She said she needed time." They'd all heard Sirena's mental request before she'd teleported away with Hroarr.

"I don't care. I want to know where they are right *now*," the Guardian leader gritted out.

"For what purpose exactly?" Hades drawled while crossing his arms over his bare chest. "So you can barge in on them having sex? Then what? Tell her to leave her mate?"

Pothos shook his head. "Don't help, Father."

Gefn found her lips twitching at her male's dry tone. It would have been different if she was as worried as Drake, but all she felt was relief that Sirena was physically well again and safely soul bonded to Hroarr.

Sirena was exactly what her brother needed. And he just might be what Sirena needed, once they were done battling for control of one another.

Sacha sighed. "Sirena will call us if she needs help. And Hroarr was worried about her. He demanded we help her, Drake."

"Because he thinks she's his fucking property," Drake snarled. Era tucked into her male's side, and he finally took a breath, the room was thick with smoke even with the fans in the ceiling.

Era spoke softly. "She can take care of herself even more now that she has some of his power. And she knows we're here if she needs us." The female calmly added, "They're soul bonded; he'd only hurt himself if he attempted to harm her. She's safe, Drake."

Drake grunted in response, but it was obvious he still wasn't pleased.

Suddenly the Guardian leader turned in her and Pothos' direction, demanding, "How did Hroarr even *get* here? I didn't feel a portal open."

Sacha offered, "It wouldn't have been the first time a mate was pulled to the other when one was in danger."

The dark female's eyes were on Drake, but Gefn got the distinct impression that Sacha was offering her a way to keep Spa and Velspar's involvement to herself. Gefn wasn't sure how Sacha knew the truth, but she met the Guardian's eyes for the briefest of moments and it was enough to confirm Gefn's suspicion. It could have been simple logic that tipped the Guardian off. The beasts had been in the room up until Sirena teleported Hroarr away. The cats' quiet ejection from the room had been Gefn's doing.

Gefn inclined her head at Sacha before drawing Drake's

attention. "Spa and Velspar brought him here just as Sirena collapsed."

The Guardian leader didn't take his fury out on her, but he did snarl at her male, "Get those damned beasts under control, Pothos!"

Sacha pointed out, "Hroarr needed to be here for Hades to help Sirena."

Gefn didn't want to think of what the consequence could have been if Hades hadn't been there. His power with souls was truly frightening, but it had been all that saved Sirena.

Guilt surfaced for never having considered how dangerous Hroarr's power could have been to Sirena. The look on Sirena's face when she fell unconscious had scared Gefn. Without a thought she'd forcibly teleported her male into the room, but the cats had already acted. They appeared with Hroarr mere moments after she'd pulled Pothos away from waking the Earth Goddess.

Drake snapped, "The beasts can't just run free and do whatever the hell they want!" A quick telepathic check showed that the animals in question were currently outside the baby's room again. That information wasn't likely to improve the Guardian leader's mood, but for some reason Spa and Velspar had become infatuated with the child.

"I apologize..." Gefn started, but Pothos stopped her with a squeeze.

"They were trying to help Sirena," Pothos growled at his cousin. "It's not like they're out setting fucking fires or some shit."

Sacha thankfully changed the subject. "What I'd like to know is what power is so strong another *God* couldn't even touch it?"

Hades bristled. "Hroarr was being arrogant. I will admit he's powerful, but I could easily wield whatever he's capable of."

With a deep breath Gefn admitted, "Hroarr wasn't being arrogant."

Everyone turned to stare as she continued, "I had no idea Hroarr's power could be dangerous for Sirena." It was important they knew that before she continued, "I didn't even think about it when we learned she and Hroarr were mates, but... my brother was gifted one of our father's powers."

Pothos frowned down at her. "Your parents gifted him with their *direct* abilities?"

She nodded. "I don't remember them, but Hroarr does. The way he explained it was that our father relinquished a piece of *his* power to Hroarr. My brother was born stronger and more powerful than any of us, and our father was certain that if he was given an advantage, Thule had a true chance of surviving the Darkness." After another breath she added, "Hroarr's sjá is a piece of our father." The undiluted power of a celestial being who was too powerful to live in any one world.

The room fell silent for a moment.

Drake demanded, "What exactly does this added power do?"

"His sjá is the reason he knows so much about all the worlds that have fallen. He can use it to see and interpret any world's history leading all the way through to the present."

Pothos leaned down and softly reassured her, "You couldn't know what would happen. She's okay now; that's what matters." Her male wasn't happy that his sister wasn't telling them where she was. Gefn could feel his worry, but at least he didn't blame Gefn for her part in the mess.

You didn't do anything wrong, thea mou, he whispered into her mind as he sent soothing energies her way.

Hades groaned. "Enough. The situation is over. Sirena will call if she needs you. Now we need to wake my sisters. The Tria are a far bigger problem than Sirena's sex life."

"Hades!" Drake growled, but after a few moments he seemed to come to the same conclusion. "Fine, let's get this over with."

Murmurs of somber agreement filled the room.

Pothos rested his chin on her head. *Come with me to wake my aunt.*

She sighed in regret. *I should go see what's happening in the Northern Lands. Hroarr's priestesses and warriors are probably still there. He was supposed to be there for another day. I'm not sure what I can do, but as far as I know, there's still a problem.*

Go with me to wake Aphrodite. We only need to be there for as long as it takes for my father to calm her down. Then we can go to Thule together and I'll help you with the priestesses and whatever Hroarr was doing.

She smiled. *How long will it take?* In all reality she wanted them to enjoy every second they had together, because there were no guarantees that they would win the battle to come.

Hopefully less than an hour. My father will be in charge of watching over her, which means Sacha is on babysitting duty because Hades isn't all that capable. Drake won't need me to be there when he wakes Athena and Niall. He'll have Vane, Erik and Alex there to deal with their own parents.

Okay, she agreed, actually more than interested in meeting his aunt. Gefn had been welcomed into the Guardian fold, yet at times, like with the baby, she still felt like she shouldn't be there for certain events. That kind of thing would take time, but if he wanted her there, she would be there. They were partners.

He smiled down at her wickedly before leaning in for a fleeting kiss, and she sighed, wishing they had far more time to indulge.

Chapter 13

Hroarr's Palace, Thule

Hroarr woke with his female lying half atop him, surprised at having slept at all. Morning light streamed over her pale hair and skin. His *völur*'s nose was tucked into his neck and soft breaths slid over his skin. One of her hands had tangled in his hair and the other had somehow snaked its way beneath his. Her legs were tangled in the bedclothes at an angle that took up half the bed. Each time he'd allow her to rest, his healer managed to find her way back in this position. He'd never realized such a small creature could command such space, and he wasn't sure why he allowed it.

His shaft was ready for her again, even though he'd had her every couple of hours throughout the day and night.

He clenched his teeth when he realized there was no time.

Already he could feel the sickness in the Northern Lands growing even from a continent away. His power had indeed heightened since the Earth God connected their souls. He hadn't believed it possible, no matter what had happened with his sister and her male.

Once his duty was tended to, he could focus on the battle to come. There was much to do in a short span of time.

He stifled a growl when his female shifted in sleep. His body demanded he have her once more before he left, but it would have to wait because he could actually feel the toxins flowing out of the faraway mountains.

After untangling her fingers from his hair, he set her slight form aside so he could move from the bed.

He turned for one more look at her and with a thought increased the flames to warm the room. He liked the sight of her naked body splayed on his bed. He nearly growled knowing her virgin's blood marked the dark coverings. She'd done something to him. Everything seemed heightened, his power, his need, and he realized it was likely that he needed to get used to actually *feeling* intense emotion again after centuries.

Obsession.

He stalked to his bathing chamber, with images of her naked and writhing beneath him sliding through his mind.

He growled when he entered the spray of water and began washing her scent from his skin. He hissed when he got to his hard shaft. The temptation to take her with him to the north was biting, but she would be a distraction, and healer or not, her body would need to recover before he took her in the ways he wished. And he intended to have all of her, in every way he demanded, once he returned.

Before he left the palace, he would task his brother with preparations for the *ófǫlr*'s arrival on Earth. Dagur had no doubt been informed of his presence in the palace, but luckily for him, the other God had stayed away.

He washed quickly and was back in the room, donning clothes, when she woke. It wasn't a slow waking; no, his female shot up, looking around before remembering where she was.

When her eyes met his, he caught the heat that flickered there before she demanded, "How long was I asleep?" She shook her head and got up without waiting for an answer. A tug pulled the sheet away from the bed and he frowned when she wrapped it around her body.

"It's early morning."

She shook her head. "That means we've been in bed for nearly twenty-four hours?" And then she cursed. "I have to get back."

He narrowed his eyes and commanded, "You will stay here."

After picking up her shoes, she slowly turned to him. "I would choose your next words very wisely, Thulian. I have work to do and obviously so do you. I hope you are not going to tell me I'm a prisoner here."

"Your work there is done. You are mine, and your place is here."

He could actually feel her fury through their bond. "I am a Guardian of Earth, Hroarr. I have things to do there, and Drake and the rest of my family are likely worried."

"So speak in your mind with them, but you gave yourself to me."

"You're obviously leaving, so why would I stay here? Your demand is ridiculous."

He narrowed his eyes at her. "Female, you forget who you speak to. I agreed to fight for Earth for a price. That price is *you*. In my bed. Living in my home. Or at my side."

*****

Sirena felt her blood pressure rising. How could he give her the most explosive orgasms one minute and treat her like a damned piece of meat the next?

Suddenly he was in front of her, towering over her, easily a foot and a half taller with her bare feet. She glared up at him. "Correct me if I'm wrong, but it doesn't look like you were taking me with you now."

His eyes bored into her and all she could feel were waves of need and possessiveness coming from him when he responded, "I am not." He crossed his arms over his chest. She noted that he'd tied his wavy hair in a haphazard knot again at the back of his head like he was going out to battle, and as curious as she was about his destination, she was far too infuriated that he was being such an asshole.

When he didn't elaborate, she gritted out, "Then were you planning on fucking me right now?" That was number two of his contingencies for meeting their bargain. She wished she would have had the sense to define the terms, but it had taken all her focus to get his vow of help. It seemed he'd had terms in mind.

His eyes flashed with heat, but she could also feel that her words hadn't amused him.

"Living here means sleeping here, or am I wrong? Unless as your slave I'm required to wash your clothes and iron your damned sheets while you're away? Or maybe I'm supposed to clean up after your warriors and Dagur?" She glared at him, pulling the sheet tight around her when she really wished she could wrap it around his neck and squeeze.

A surge of anger ran through his connection to her along with a surge of jealousy. His eyes flickered and he ripped off the sheet before lifting her into his arms. His strong hands spread her legs to wrap them around his thighs as he spun them both to pin her back against the wall. Air slipped from her lips on impact. It hadn't hurt, but she felt caged and that was exactly the male's intent, she could feel it, and a traitorous part of her body responded to how much he wanted her. The evidence throbbed behind a layer of leather.

Lust, primal and wild, flowed between them as she dug her fingers into his shoulders while biting the inside of her cheek in hopes of calming her hormones. She glared at him. "I guess this means you require your fucking concubine now?"

She challenged him, "By all means, take your payment." His palms slid from her thighs to plump her aching breasts and she hated that his touch ignited her. She was beginning to truly hate the damned bond.

He could take what he wanted from her, but she refused to participate.

He snarled at her, "You take risks challenging your God, Sirena."

He was fighting a massive battle against emotion and logic. She felt his need dominate her, he wanted to rule her, yet his duty was demanding his attention.

He captured her lips in a taunting, demanding kiss before growling against her lips, "I will allow you to take care of your tasks on Earth, *völur*, on two conditions." His eyes flashed. "No one touches you. And you *will* return the moment I summon you." The warning wasn't just in his tone or words, it simmered through their bond, causing a thrill she resented. "Obey my wishes, Sirena. You will not like the consequences."

He set her back on her feet, but before she could respond, he was gone. He was so incredibly fast, the shifting air and slamming door were the only evidence he'd left on foot.

Her heart was beating out of her chest with lust, anger and beneath it all was something else. Irritation and disappointment. She refused to let it truly hit her that she'd finally found a mate who only wanted her as his sex slave, yet she had to remind herself that fate had done this to both of them. Not just her.

With a deep breath she sucked it up and did what she'd always done, she teleported home.

To bury herself in work.

Chapter 14

Guardian Manor, Tetartos Realm

Sirena was incredibly grateful to have the ability to move between worlds because she would have gone insane if she'd been stuck in Thule, always having to ask P or Gefn to teleport her out of there.

A shower was her first priority. His scent was already driving her nuts and her body felt like it was going through withdrawals, which wasn't a good sign. He'd given her so many orgasms through the night that if she were mortal, she wouldn't be able to walk, yet it hadn't been enough.

She cooled the water, but nothing helped diffuse the need. Her focus was shot and she couldn't put off dealing with her family any longer. They needed to know she was okay and she needed to know all that had happened while she'd been out of touch.

It was if time had slowed when she'd been with him.

Shaking her head, she quickly dressed in a soft white dress with a flared bottom and leopard peep-toed pumps to make her feel better. Her mind was running in a thousand directions that all seemed to circle back to how the God had made her feel before he'd left her.

Later she would have to find a way to deal with the bastard.

Focus on work, that was what she planned to do. She could throw herself into her duties and drown everything else out.

She knew Era would have checked on Alyssa and the baby, who should be nearly ready to return to their home. If the new family even chose to leave the security of the manor; she wasn't sure what she'd do in their situation.

With a thought she reopened the telepathic bond to her brethren and slipped out into the hall, bracing herself for her check-in with Drake. *I'm back. What's happening?*

Instead of answering her mental call, Drake appeared in front of her, fuming. "Where the hell were you?" She'd hoped he would call her to him and give her time to see the baby before facing the firing squad. It was wishful thinking to dream that he'd be fine with just knowing she was there and safe.

"I was with my mate, Drake. I told you I needed time."

"In my office. Now," he commanded and then proceeded to teleport her with him. Something he'd never done and was an infuriating move indicative of how determined he was to start his damned lecture. The step only saved them the two minutes it would have taken to walk. And she could have ported her damned self.

She reformed, grateful that he'd pissed her off, because her other emotions had gone too far into areas she couldn't deal with right now. She faced off with her furious brother. "That was ridiculous. I'm in no mood for your overbearing shit right now! You know better, Drake."

Brianne and Sacha must have seen her telepathic link return because both were in her mind a second later. *How did it go? Are you okay?* More from Brianne than Sacha only because Brianne wanted details about the sex. Sirena mentally snorted. Hearing their voices was exactly the balm she needed, but not one she had time to enjoy.

I'm with Drake. Give me a minute, she responded. And for a split second she wondered if Hroarr could hear the communication. He would eventually share her mental links, but she didn't feel anything from him to indicate he was intercepting anything now.

Good luck, both her sisters uttered nearly in unison.

"Hiding your telepathic link and blocking my call was out of fucking line," Drake snarled as he stood glaring down at her.

She shook her head, knowing he was only worried, but she'd had a damned good reason for her actions. "You would have barged in. And it wasn't as if you couldn't find me if there was an emergency," she pointed out.

He didn't deny that he would have barged in or that he could have found her. She had a feeling he'd already known where she'd been. Hroarr's palace guards had been aware not long after they'd arrived, and P and Gefn could have found out easily enough. He was only angry that she'd hidden her location in the first place.

After long moments where he stared at her as if searching for chinks in her armor, he asked, "Are you okay?"

And her stomach sank a little, worried that she was that transparent. She wanted to lash out or do something because she wasn't okay, but she sure as hell wasn't going to tell him that.

He'd never fully believe she was fine, so she told him what she hoped would appease him enough. "We seem to be going through what Sacha and Hades did, which means I won't be staying away from him for long until he and I get through it. Now, how is the baby? That's where I was headed," she pointed out as a way to change the subject.

Pothos appeared a second later. “Are you alright?”

Neither of her brothers’ mates had appeared, so she knew the two were ambushing her, and she honestly wasn’t in the mental state to battle them right now. She told P the same thing. After they kept staring at her, she finally snapped, “I’m fine. Both of you, just stop it. I’m powerful as hell, but he and I need to get the bond straight and I’m allowed some time to process the last twenty-four hours. Please do not give me grief right now. I know you were concerned and I’m sorry, but you’ve both worried the shit out of me with your mates, so I guess it’s your turn to fret. If you promise not to interfere or interrupt, I won’t tune you out.” She gritted her teeth, knowing she was acting a little out of character, and they were sensing it, but hadn’t Sacha acted off as well after being soul bonded to a stranger?

Power slid under her skin and she had to force it back down. It was intense and seemed to be getting more demanding the longer she stood there.

She had no idea what abilities were running inside of her now, or how to wield anything but the fire, and that was something she’d need to figure out.

If only there were a way to stop the arousal so she could think clearer. Sacha and Hades had suffered this side effect after their soul bond because he hadn’t embraced her sister Guardian’s beast, or so they’d thought. In every other mating, the frenzy of lust ended when the souls connected. Going straight to the final act didn’t have any other precedent beyond what Sacha and Hades went through. She and Sacha’s races were those with the least beast blood, but if she were tracking with the same problem, it meant the animal wanted more. She groaned, knowing just what her beast blood wanted from them. It wanted a full claiming from the God and for him to prove his dominance. Damn it.

Drake snapped her out of her thoughts, finally answering her earlier question while he and P continued to dissect her like a bug. "Alyssa and the baby are doing fine. Era is with them now, so you don't need to check on them unless you want to. We have a Guardian meeting in an hour. A lot has happened."

She took in a deep breath. "What does that mean? Are Athena and Aphrodite awake?"

P snorted. "Yeah, they're fucking awake."

When smoke lifted from Drake's lips, it actually relaxed her a fraction because irritated Drake was something she could deal with. The dragon ground out, "They are and so are their mates. Hades gave them all the information they needed to be up to speed, and he and Sacha have been keeping an eye on my mother and father. Alex and Erik are taking turns with Athena and Niall. Uri doesn't think he got the better deal with helping Alex, but he fucking did. My mother is a damned menace."

Sirena stilled. "What has she done? And please tell me she's keeping her power under control." Her heart started pounding. The last thing she needed was Aphrodite destroying her inhibitions right now. "Drake, I can't be around her if she isn't controlling herself." She felt heat rise to her cheeks. Both her brothers looked uncomfortable with her reaction, but, fucking hell, Aphrodite's 'go to' inhibition was sex. "Damn it, Drake. She'd better not be in the meeting causing a damned orgy!"

Sirena's own power flared in her frustration. No. Not her power, the damned God's. Fire lashed out from her hands, sliding over the walls as she frantically did all she could to pull it back, worried it would strike out at her brothers. Pothos let his ability free in order to mesmerize her enough to calm her as Drake eased the fires. She sucked in air when Pothos released her from his hold.

Learning to deal with the fire just moved to the top of her priority list. "Thank you."

What is happening? Hroarr demanded through their mental link, and she hated that his voice felt good, a trick of the damned bond. He'd obviously felt her power surge. Or her frustration could have slipped through their connection; she wasn't sure and she didn't care. She was shaking and Creators only knew what was spilling over to him. She swore there'd been moments in her shower that she'd felt his irritation mix with her own, which probably meant his task wasn't going well on Thule.

She really didn't want to have to explain anything to him, but she wasn't sure if he could teleport to her. He'd had no trouble refocusing her direction when they'd ported together, but he hadn't left the bedroom that way.

Everything is fine, she ground out.

What did I feel! he commanded.

It has nothing to do with you. I was irritated with news and my power flared. I'm fine now, she snapped back. She could feel him fuming, but she could also feel him assessing her for the truth.

He shut the hell up, so she guessed he had what he wanted.

"Well, fuck," P snapped as they all stared at the charred plaster.

Definitely number one on the priority list. And seeing the baby was now out of the question, which only frustrated her more. Holding the child was what she'd been looking forward to.

Her hands were still shaking when she turned to them and pointed out, "Do you need another example of how much I can't deal with Aphrodite right now?"

Drake stared at her before pointing out, “She would leash her power with me there, Sirena. Now are you going to tell us what’s going on with you and that fucking God?” Both brothers crossed their arms and waited. “Why aren’t you there fixing this with him if you know what the problem is?” He was right on both counts. Aphrodite wasn’t so disturbed as to unleash an orgy with her son in the room, and Sirena should be in Thule, finishing her bond with the God. If their connection was solid, she wouldn’t have power surges like this.

“Hroarr had to deal with something in Thule.”

She was relieved when P nodded. “In their Northern Lands. Gefn and I went there last night, but apparently fire is what it takes to drive away the toxins there and our combined skills only kept it from building again. It wasn’t enough to completely contain the problem. We sent Dagur and Kara to take over in the middle of the night.”

She nodded. “Where’s Gefn now?”

He smiled. “She went to meet Lucy.”

Sirena was both envious and really happy that Gefn was being treated more like a part of the Guardian fold now; she’d been keeping away out of respect. And in reality Gregoire was possessive as hell, so it was good that she’d given them time.

P’s next words, “She’s there with Aphrodite and Ladon,” made her groan.

“Gregoire allowed that?”

Drake growled, “Good luck denying my mother anything. Gregoire is not pleased, but as long as no one touches Alyssa or his child, he seems fine with showing her off.”

"So far it's been fine. The baby is curious and seems to love everyone."

Drake smiled. They all did.

P cleared his throat. "Did you and Hroarr talk at all?"

She wished they had, but all they'd done was have sex, sleep, and repeat. At least until that morning. "No. Not much."

"Gefn said the power that nearly killed you was given to him by their father. Hroarr didn't think you'd survive coming into contact with it."

She stilled. "Can one of you show me what happened when I was unconscious?" She'd known it was intense power, and it pulled her in and held on, but it hadn't felt deadly, it felt like it liked her, if that made any sense. She hadn't felt in danger, more isolated and terrified when it started showing her its secrets.

"I will," Pothos offered as he sent her telepathic images. It was like watching a movie. A movie that showed her body seizing and losing color as Hroarr lost his mind. Then Hades soul bonded them. She hadn't felt any of that... By the time the power released her, she'd obviously healed.

She hadn't even told them what she'd seen. Everything had happened so fast after the bond. "I didn't know. I felt trapped, but not like I was dying. I was in the power, seeing what I believe was the first time he used the ability." She breathed out. "I saw exactly what the Darkness does to a world. It's far more terrifying seeing it happen than hearing about it from Gefn."

She started to share the details. "And it doesn't just destroy the world... It takes down all the barriers between Realms and turns man against man and God against God before it sucks the life out of everything. Everything is destroyed. Even the oceans dry up." She never wanted to see anything like that happen to another world. Especially not Earth.

Drake demanded, "Show me."

"Us," P growled as Drake nodded.

She concentrated on both links to her brothers and let them see.

Her brothers were silent until P added, "Mother fuck. Knowing and watching it happen are two different things."

Drake and Pothos looked at each other before turning to her. "When we woke Athena, she shared things the Creators told her before putting her in stasis. Not even Hades had been told any of this."

"But Hades was the most powerful of the Earth Gods. Why wouldn't the Creators share more with him?"

Drake nodded. "Trust me, Hades wasn't happy about it."

P groaned. "That's a fucking understatement. He's still furious. Especially when Athena told him all she'd had to do was ask the Creators and if Hades hadn't been throwing tantamount to a tantrum when their parents set about putting them in the stasis units, he would know as well."

That hint of arrogant attitude tracked with what little information Sirena had on Athena. The Goddess was a warrior, but she was also said to be cold and cunning, a strategist. For that reason, Alex's mother had kept her family hidden as she'd built her own armies against the evil Gods. She'd been an ally of Hades and Aphrodite since they'd been the only good ones, but she'd never visited Aphrodite's palace. Not once during the decades Sirena spent living there.

She hated thinking about those times. The only good part had been Drake, and P when he came to visit. They'd been children together, but she had fewer freedoms, and leaving the palace wasn't usually one of them. At least not without a great deal of secrecy.

She was curious. "What exactly did Athena know that Hades didn't?"

P explained, "Athena said the Creators instructed her to contain the Tria in the units as soon as she woke up."

"Which was exactly what we intended," Drake added.

"Why didn't they just do that to begin with?" Sirena asked. It had never made sense that the bastards had been kept awake. They'd been in a prison created by Hades, Athena and Aphrodite, but all the other Gods had been sent to sleep to purge all the dark energies from their systems, why not the Tria?

"When we do it, the bastards may die, and if they do, it will upset Earth's elements. Floods, earthquakes. The Gods and the rest of us will need to try to balance everything out," P said and then let out a breath.

Looking at her brothers, she saw something she didn't like. "What aren't you telling me?"

"Athena's not known for fucking subtlety," P growled. "She basically said the Creators had used all their power to champion Earth and they hadn't had anything left to contain the Tria. They used every ounce of their power to give us a chance at survival."

She felt like the bottom dropped from her stomach. The Great

Beings had said they would never return, but knowing they'd left powerless meant what exactly? Had they gone to die? That was the impression she was getting from her brothers and it was hard to swallow.

"They told her that Earth had a chance against the Darkness, but light and magic was the only way we had a fighting chance. They gave everything they had to make that happen."

She closed her eyes, remembering the day they'd called the Creators back. Remembering the warmth of that presence. The light.

And now it was gone.

Extinguished.

Chapter 15

Northern Lands, Thule

Hroarr seethed with fury as he concentrated his power into the dark poison, burning back the whirling tendrils that snaked through the mountain from his brother's prison. The heightened power flowing in his blood was making the task faster, but the bond that had created it was wreaking havoc on him. The connection to his healer was a damned menace.

He felt her constantly and it wasn't only her need, but her upset and anger.

This bond was nothing like the one he had with his *þrír*. Those had always been faint drifts of emotion, easily distinguishable and disregarded as his priestesses.

What came from the healer slammed through him with no warning and demanded his attention before cutting off only to do it again. And the need to have her constantly was relentless.

She'd made him crave her.

As it was, he'd been away from the palace for mere hours and his shaft throbbed against his leathers, demanding he go to her. A muscle ticked in his jaw as he sent his flames deeper, battling back the poison of his brother's power as quickly as he could.

If he hadn't stepped through the portal only to deal with

incessant questions about her from his brother and Kara, he would have already called his female to him. Upon learning Kara and Dagur had gone to the Northern Lands to assist, he'd been pleased that they had acted with thought, yet neither had brought their *þrír* with them, so Hroarr had been delayed the time it had taken to collect the females and portal them in himself.

Regin and the others would have been finished with the task without assistance had he already destroyed the core issue. Had he known it would flare to such a menacing degree over the weeks, he would have sent Dagur in his place far sooner.

It was a misjudgment that he would not make again now with his new ability to sense the growing pestilence from a distance. It was an added benefit of the bond with his female, but it had come at a price.

Need.

Obsession.

When he finally found the end of the tendrils, he sent one last surge of flames to sear the core, feeling the malevolent rage burst free before being contained once again.

Dagur strode in and Hroarr turned to face him and he demanded, "Did the clans cease their fighting?"

Regin had rushed in nearly a half hour ago, informing them that dozens of infected mortals who had been hiding away in the mountains had come back, intent on ending their feud with blood. She'd said the rage of the toxins had quickly seeped back into the village before the palace warriors could deal with the riders. He'd immediately sent Kara and Dagur out to put an end to the battle while he took care of the poison that had caused the mortals' feuding in the first place.

His brother nodded, but his muscles were tense, his fingers fisting at his sides. "Kara and I were able to cage the affected clansmen before any losses, but there were injuries on both sides. Laire and Ivarr took the worst damage."

Hroarr snarled, furious with himself for leaving his *þrír* and warriors alone to see his work through while he'd gone to his female. Meaningless loss of life in a world that already had poor birth rates and far too few mortals had always been unacceptable to him.

He gritted his teeth. Had Gefn not thought to ensure one of the Gods was there using their minimal skills with fire, the toxins could have spread out completely to the village again.

He would not allow this to happen again. He was already moving through the tunnels and out of the mountain, with Dagur at his side. "How bad are the injuries?"

"Mist and Regin are tending Ivarr's and Laire's wounds, but they are not faring well."

"Where are they? And how many others were injured?"

"I moved Ivarr and Laire to a room in the Inn. A dozen of the clans took injuries before Kara and I could cage all the fighters. The clans took less damage because your warriors were not looking to kill." Dagur's face said it all. The clans had been out for blood and death.

Come to me, he sent to his female.

He felt her displeasure at being summoned. *Where? To the palace or where you are now?*

Find me in two minutes.

Dagur was fuming at his side.

Hroarr gritted out, "Where is Kara?"

"Watching over the priestesses and scaring the mortals." Dagur snorted.

"Go to her. My healer is on her way. She will deal with Laire and Ivarr." The thought of his female's hands on another male tightened his body with fury. This seething jealousy raging through him was a new and unpleasant emotion that he needed to contain. Sirena was skilled, and if Regin and Mist were unable to see to the warriors, she was his best option, no matter how it angered him.

Dagur asked, "The toxins are gone?"

"Yes," he growled. Once this was done, the Northern Lands would be secure. And then he would bury his hard flesh inside his *völur* before demanding answers to what she'd done to cause this need.

Chapter 16

Guardian Manor, Tetartos Realm – Moments Ago

Sirena sat in her sterile lab, testing the blood samples from mortals they'd saved months ago. She'd have to thank whoever cleaned the place up. She'd been grateful as hell when she saw it was back to normal and the samples were waiting on her desk.

There were only so many hours in a day and she never found it to be enough. Fortunately for her, with all the Guardian matings, they'd accumulated an extended family of sorts. Conn's in-laws had been amazing. The female wolves loved going into the cities and were vigilant about visiting the Mageia homes, and since the wolves lived at the manor, it was simple enough to bring back blood samples after their visits.

The Mageia, mortals with elemental abilities, had been used as nothing more than experiments by a now dead enemy.

An enemy who'd shared Sirena's blood.

That was part of the reason she worked day and night. She had always been trying to atone for the sins of her twisted bloodlines.

Her demented half-brother had shown the same vile tendencies as their father, Apollo. Both manipulated DNA for their own sick purposes, treating living beings like pawns. Apollo had used his skill to create his perfect army by enslaving and experimenting on Immortals millennia ago. Cyril was more interested in finding a way to take any female he wanted as a mate in order to become more powerful.

She hated that she was connected to both males. A fact that had been well hidden from everyone but her Guardian family.

She groaned. Her mind had been wandering incessantly. Between her arousal, emotions from Hroarr, and thoughts of what her brethren were planning to do with the Tria, concentration had become a nightmare. Add in the end of the world and her mind had apparently hit its maximum capacity. She was actually completely useless for the first time she could ever remember and she hated it.

Brianne and Sacha had come in with updates whenever possible, and the distractions, though appreciated, added to her concentration issue. The last update was on the start of their plans to hopefully stabilize the world's elements if the Tria died in stasis.

Everyone in the manor had been busy in meetings or preparing for the aftereffects that could come after the Tria were eradicated. There was a lot to consider in keeping everyone in the world safe while dealing with the Tria as quickly as possible.

In a week, to be specific.

She shook her head.

Sirena groaned when a blast of jealousy rushed through her bond with the damned Thulian. She felt his mind on hers—he was thinking of her. The emotional link was becoming more detailed with each hour that passed and she could feel it binding them tighter. She'd been getting so much rage and frustration for the last hour and it was so defined she could almost see what was angering him. His thoughts had never come through, but this was almost as strong.

She knocked her head on the counter because she really

couldn't concentrate to save her life at this point.

The change in movement rubbed her bra against her aching nipples and she cursed. The arousal and the edginess attached to her new powers made hiding out in the lab her only real option at the moment, but she was tempted to go to Thule and have at the God just so she could think clearly again. Even if it was only a temporary fix.

Come to me.

She stilled when his voice slipped into her mind. She could hear the urgency and sought out his location. Even a world away she could see it clearly, a damned beacon.

Where? To the palace or where you are now? She hated being summoned like some pet, but this was part of their deal.

Find me in two minutes, he growled and she felt him on the move already.

She didn't bother responding; instead she sent word to Drake that she was going to Thule.

Call me if you need me there, he commanded.

Stop worrying.

She closed her laptop and took a breath before grabbing the small bag of things she'd packed before coming to the lab.

She breathed out as she broke into a million pieces and soared out through the ether. It was longer and far more intense than porting within Earth's Realms.

When she reformed in front of him, she had to stop herself from jumping him right then and there. The look on his face, his power and scent hit her like an anvil.

They weren't alone in what appeared to be a clean but old manor house room. The window was split wide to the cool air, and a view of snowcapped mountains lay beyond.

"Help them," he commanded, but her instinct and need to heal was already upon her.

Two females—one dark, one light—flanked the beds. The once brightly flowered quilts were blood soaked and held bloody warriors in kilts. She'd already dropped her bag and was assessing injuries, her power sliding over them from a distance. Her healing came easier than ever before and she reveled in the flow that told her which warrior needed attention first.

She recognized the white-haired female as, Mist, one of Hroarr's priestesses who'd been there when Sirena healed the cats. The priestess bowed a fraction as she breathed out, "We are grateful for your help, Sirena."

Sirena swore she could feel Mist's relief as she moved to the side of the bed. The other female with dark skin and golden cat eyes watched. She could feel their power in the room, but more she could feel the God's. His anger and jealousy as she knelt on the bed was raging all around them.

Her first patient was Laire, Gefn's guard. She smiled down as her power moved over him. "Let's see what we have." She kept her voice soft with only a hint of power to keep them all calm, but in reality she was trying to calm Hroarr. He was losing his mind and it was affecting her too damned much. Laire's bare stomach and leather kilt were covered in blood, but the bleeding had been stopped by something. That was a plus, but the damage done to his stomach was extensive. She filtered the blood out before sending warm healing power to mend the gash in the organ.

The big blond warrior smiled, but his eyes were cloudy, which she didn't like.

"Gefn will not be happy about this, Laire," she teased, easily accessing the Thulian language as if it were her own.

She resorted to softly humming with her power to soothe the tension as she let healing warmth flow through her palms in waves.

She could feel her mate's anger and it was causing his power to lick over her skin so possessively she was close to coming.

Stifling a moan, she demanded, *You need to calm the hell down and back that power off. I'm not actually touching him.*

Your power is. Everything you are belongs to me and me alone, Sirena, he growled into her mind and the vibrations hummed over her sensitive nerve endings.

She sucked in air, her body on fire for him as she demanded, *Why did you call me here? This is what I am. Who I am. If you bring me to the injured, I* need *to be able to heal them. And to do that I need to fucking concentrate, so stop using your power to get me off while I'm doing this.*

The room shook with his power as he commanded, *Just do it.*

He seemed to ease his power away, finally gaining a little control. Thank fuck for that. She breathed out as she finished repairing Laire's muscle and flesh.

After long moments Laire groaned, finally breathing easier.

"You are right, my Goddess will not be pleased," the warrior finally answered.

"We'll have to get you back to new before she sees you, then. I'll be right back, Laire," she promised him with a smile when she'd healed the most dangerous parts. Hroarr was attempting to hold back all his possessive reactions, but it wasn't going well. He wanted her to heal them, but it was torturing him. This was just something he'd need to get used to.

She ignored the God to kneel on the other bed. The priestesses were at this warrior's other side, using some sort of potion on his wounds. "This is Ivarr. Regin stopped his bleeding," Mist said by way of introduction.

She nodded.

Ivarr was watching the God as if wary of accepting her help. She shot the God a glare before speaking to the male. "I'm Sirena, Ivarr. This won't hurt."

He seemed slightly offended that she thought he couldn't take the pain.

"Ivarr, you will let my female heal you," Hroarr commanded, but she'd already started. She couldn't give a shit what he thought about it, because being a healer made it nearly impossible not to do this.

The male in question glanced to Hroarr before nodding sharply. "Yes, *þjóðann minn*." *His ruler.*

"What more can we do?" Mist asked Sirena.

Looking up, she asked, "Are there more wounded?"

Regin bit out, "Yes. About a dozen. The other *þrír* are doing what they can with them."

Sirena looked up. "Please make sure to stop what blood loss you can while I heal Ivarr and Laire. I will see them next."

Hroarr's anger at her assurance was palpable enough that the females hesitated for a second and looked at him like he'd lost his mind.

He had.

Just like that the priestesses were gone in a rush of air.

She moved back and forth between the warriors until they were completely healed. After letting her power slide over them from head to boot, she nodded. "There's no more internal damage and everything but the bruises are healed. You'll still feel sluggish from the blood loss." Sirena couldn't make new blood. Transfusions were the only way to deal with massive blood loss. These two had significant loss, but not enough for something that drastic, and with their advanced genetics, she had a feeling they would recover quickly.

You owe me for this, she sent to Hroarr, even though the bastard had turned this entire thing around on her. He'd wanted her to heal his people, but he hated it, and in the end she'd shown him all her cards. She'd shown him her *need* to heal and it made any bargaining useless at this point. She could leave, but she'd hate herself for it, which meant she'd likely have to demand to heal *his* damned people.

He didn't agree, just stared down at her with such possession in his eyes that she was forced to turn away or murder him.

Both males got up and bowed to her respectfully. Laire smiled when his head lifted. "Thank you."

She barely got the, "You're welcome," out before Hroarr lashed out, "No one touches her! Make it known." The power behind the order rocked the room.

Both warriors' eyes lowered. "Yes, *þjóðann minn*." Then the males were gone in a blast of speed.

She glared up at Hroarr. "Take me to the other wounded."

*****

"No." Hroarr refused his healer and then silenced her fury with a hard stare.

He paced to the window, needing air and a way to control the madness thrumming in his blood.

Sirena hissed, "You are un-fucking-believable!" He could feel her anger as she glared in his direction, "Then you go tell your priestesses why I'm not there. Or you pull your head out of your ass and do the logical thing."

"Enough," he commanded, the building shaking beneath their feet as he waged an internal war with the cunning and intelligent God he had always been and the male who violently demanded he keep all of her to himself.

Watching her work had been agony. The sight of her white dress covered in blood as she knelt beside his males had unleashed his power and his fury. Her healing strength had called to his fire and sjá, igniting every ounce of his being until he'd marked her with it, making her ache for him while she healed his warriors. When she'd had the gall to challenge him, it had only made him more possessive, more determined to brand her as his and his alone.

He breathed in the cold air, fighting his reactions because he could feel his priestesses' worry; it was dull, but there. Logic and duty demanded he make use of Sirena's skill to heal the rest of his people. They were his responsibility and they were wounded because he had not ensured his brothers' malevolent power had been burned away.

He turned and a part of him wanted to lift her skirt right there as she glared defiantly at him, assessing him, debating her next move.

Three steps and he was in front of her. "Your hands will touch no one. And your voice is mine and mine alone."

He turned and left the room that housed the scent of blood and his female. It had a deadly effect on him.

She followed and exited to the cobbled street below. Flowers bloomed in the wood outside the inn. When he saw her breath fog, he let his power warm her. He would burn the dress to ash the moment they returned to his palace. He hated seeing any blood on her.

She scented the air as she looked around the small village, and he did not take long wondering at what she thought of it. She had on high shoes that did not work on the streets, nor would her speed match that of a Thulian God, so he growled and lifted her into his arms, finding satisfaction in the moan of pleasure that slipped from her red lips. Her small body melted into him and his lips twitched at how much she fought that reaction.

The street lined with shops and pubs gave way to a massive clearing before the mountains soared with jagged paths and snow-covered rock.

They came to crowds of villagers fidgeting outside a grouping of icy cages holding males that were infected with the toxins. The prisons were obviously Kara's doing. The priestesses' colorful hair and light dresses billowed around them as they tried to heal the cursing mortals while ridding them of the toxins. His guards were standing at attention with the females, but the uninfected maintained a distance, as only wives or mothers would be allowed near the infected to try to calm the males as the *þrír* worked.

He moved to Mist, feeling her need was more urgent.

Hroarr set Sirena down with great effort, noting Mist's relief at her presence.

Hroarr let the roar of his voice carry. "My female is here to heal, but *no* one touches her." The crowd silenced for long moments, and he felt Sirena's irritation, but she was already moving to the cage where an unconscious male lay.

A middle-aged female with curly red hair was at Mist's side. "You can save my Erik?" the apparent mother begged Sirena, and he saw worry and only a hint of weariness there. They would be cautious of an outsider, but his command had informed them that she would be trusted.

That she was his.

His healer smiled softly and crouched outside the cage, her power sliding through to the injured male. Hroarr's jaw clenched when he saw the youth. The boy was barely into adulthood and could have been killed had his warriors not taken care.

*****

"My son was not himself, *þjóðann minn*," Sirena heard the tearful woman plead to Hroarr. The male was barely a man at all. His long hair was covering a face that couldn't even grow a proper beard. She frowned down, wondering if he was even twenty yet. Hroarr's reaction seemed just as appalled. He'd tensed at her back and his roiling emotion rocketed through her.

She listened as Mist assured the female, "Hroarr does not blame Erik or the others. It was poison that did this. Do not worry, Hildr."

A glance showed Mist pulling the female into a gentle hug as Sirena began her work through bars made of ice hard enough to be stone.

Remove the cage, she demanded of the God at her back. She felt him watching her and she knew he was using power to warm her skin. It was addicting and arousing all at once. She gritted her teeth, attempting to focus through it. The God might as well have peed on her or branded her ass as his property. She decided Alyssa deserved some sort of sainthood for dealing with Gregoire's possessive tendencies. This was absolute insanity.

His power melted away the bars, allowing her space to kneel at Erik's side. After demanding no one touch her, she was shocked that Erik's mother was brave enough to get near her, much less kneel at her side, but she did.

Sirena smiled softly. "Erik will be fine." She appreciated the fact that the Thulian language came easily.

Hildr relaxed at her side. "Thank you."

As she worked, she could feel the crowd growing. The females wore long wool dresses, likely to ward off the cold. The males, on the other hand, were in kilts. After Hroarr's announcement, the masses had silenced, yet now they were whispering as she sent her power to deal with the head wound first. It wasn't bleeding thanks to Mist, no doubt, but it had concussed the male and she eased the brain trauma.

The male's power was all over her now. She felt like he was claiming her body as his own right there in the middle of a damned crowd. She could feel him fighting himself, with guilt, jealousy, his duty to his people. At this point using their telepathic bond would only arouse them both further. All she could do was fight her way through the need and heal these people as quickly as possible.

She watched as Mist poured water through Erik's now parted lips and she felt when the priestess pulled power through the air and leaned down to whisper it just above the warrior's mouth, calming words spilled free with the thrall. The magic was beautiful.

Sirena stilled for only a second, knowing the power coming from the priestess was familiar. It was a softer version of what Pothos wielded with raw intensity. Sirena sought out the effects within Erik's body; the liquid and thrall Mist used worked together to eat away at the toxins Sirena had seen inside the boy. Sirena sent more healing warmth into the less dangerous knife wound along his side.

"What is that liquid?" she asked the priestess.

"It is the healing waters of Fólkvangr." Thule's version of Heaven Realm, and the place Gefn and Pothos had been trapped because it was a sacred place only priestesses of Thule could enter. Sirena found the fact that Pothos and Gefn had completed their mating bond there to be incredibly beautiful and romantic.

She shook off the fanciful musings and accepted Hildr's profuse thanks.

She needed to get to the next male quickly. "Who is next?" she asked Mist.

She was ushered to another male. This one was conscious and Laire was holding the male down as a green-haired priestess whispered the thrall into his lips. There was no time to talk. This one had a wide sword wound to the shoulder and another slice to his calf. She mended bone and muscle as Hroarr watched her from above.

She heard a female voice behind her speaking in the ancient language of the Creators. "We do not need her here, Hroarr."

Sirena turned her head to see the Goddess Kara at Hroarr's side.

Hroarr growled in the same language, "Your issues with Earth are your own, sister. Be useful or leave. My female stays."

The other Goddess bristled, snapping, "I will not leave my *þrír*."

Another God stepped up, and she quickly glanced back at the massive kilt-wearing male with long wavy brown hair, seeing him glare at the ice Goddess. "Kara, cease your vendetta against Earth. It will get you nowhere. You can see the healer is helping."

Sirena's lips twitched at the other God's words and annoyed tone. She knew of Hroarr's brother in theory, but she'd yet to meet him or Kara, and at the moment she didn't care to.

The second they'd arrived, Hroarr's power became more demanding on her skin, not only warming her, but caressing her.

She stood on shaky legs. Smiles were all she had time for as Mist stood with her.

Icy wind kicked up and Sirena realized it was Kara's exit. Sirena didn't bother to look. She honestly didn't give a damn what the Deity thought about her or Earth, but it seemed the icy-eyed Kara had irritated Mist. Sirena could feel the priestess' animosity toward Kara, it was just a low hum, but it was something she only now truly computed. It was the tie between a God of Thule and his priestesses, she'd felt it earlier and a glance into her mind's eye showed their threads leading to Hroarr.

She'd known about it, yet, suddenly, she wondered just how close they were to their God and a sharp surge of jealousy slammed through her so hard that she felt the rush of fire bursting through her body.

Hroarr had her in his arms within seconds, calling back the flames in an instant.

The silence in the space was near deafening as she looked down at the scorched grass beneath her feet.

Oh, God. Did I hurt anyone? She gazed up at him, panic flooding her.

No. Is this what happened when you were on Earth? he demanded while his emerald eyes searched hers.

She nodded.

I need to finish the healing, but I don't know if it's safe, she admitted. The need to heal was strong, but the fear of being out of control and harming an innocent was nearly paralyzing for her.

He stared down at her, his emotional battle there for her to feel. He wanted his people healed, but he wanted her away from there.

You are safe with me, völur. The words themselves could have been sweet, aside from the witch part, but his tone said it was a matter of fact—that he could control any surges of flames that came. That arrogant undertone was what she'd needed to ease her frayed nerves. The arousal was still horrible, but the panic had eased by the time he demanded, *Do what you must, but you will do it quickly.*

When he set her down before the next male and priestess, he commanded the silenced crowd, "No one speaks so my female can finish this quickly."

The utter silence was awkward, but no distractions made the work incredibly fast. Sirena did receive a lot of silent gratitude from those females being held at a distance after her power surge. She should have said... anything, but she only wanted to heal everyone and leave before something set her off again. All she managed was a series of forced smiles she hoped were comforting.

By the end she was exhausted, but not so exhausted that her body didn't hum for Hroarr. She needed him like she needed air, her nipples hurt, and her hands were actually shaking. Sweat beaded at her nape and chest, and the cold was not helping, because he never allowed it to touch her.

When Hroarr pulled power to open a portal to the palace, Sirena stifled a moan at the intensity of it. She was not walking into that watery air with him and his warriors. If it had the same effect as teleporting with a mate, she'd end up screwing him on the palace floor in front of all his people.

Before he could usher her through, she ported to his room.

Sirena, he growled. His displeasure at her disappearance was fierce.

Chapter 17

Hroarr's Palace, Thule

Sirena, Hroarr snarled as he watched his female disappear. He was in no mood to waste time hunting her when she belonged at his side. In his bed.

The watery air of the portal he'd called up hummed in front of him as he mentally stalked her location through their connection. The more he used it, the easier it became to understand and see.

His lips tilted when she stopped at his palace.

Ivarr, Laire and Ranulfr were waiting at his side. "Go through to the palace," he commanded to the three he was taking with him. His *þrír* and several guards were to stay with his brother and Kara until the toxins had been cleared from the clans.

He watched the males slip through the thick air and grinned before moving through to the palace steps. He lifted a hand and released the portal as he bounded up the stairs. The sun was still high as he made it through the marble pillars, with the males now at his back. Anticipation was licking at him. She was there, in his room, and he felt her drawing him in.

He barked commands at the warriors, "Laire and Ivarr, you will go rest. Ranulfr, ensure no one enters my chambers."

"Her belongings, *þjóðann minn*?" Laire questioned and Hroarr turned to the warrior, having forgotten that she'd asked for them to be retrieved from the inn.

"Give them to me." He seized the bag from the male before commanding, "Now go."

Laire slipped away silently and only Ranulfr remained until he approached his private chambers. Guards swept the doors wide and he left his elite warrior to ensure no interruptions

The second the door slammed shut, he slid her belongings to the ground and kicked off his boots. He turned through the open door of his bathing chamber, feeling her, hearing the water streaming. His shaft thickened as he remembered the last time they'd been in there: she'd been hidden in the shadows, naked and wet, watching as he thrust into his own fist.

She hadn't lit the torches, so she was partially hidden from him, the only light filtering in from the bedchamber.

Stalking forward, he sent flames to the stands beside the pool, illuminating her seductive form. Water ran down her small frame, sending tendrils of pale hair over her back. He could see her heavy breasts were already peaked and aching. They were perfect; every inch of her pleased him far too much. He growled when he felt her power gliding over his skin.

He tossed his shirt aside and then his breeches. With a burst of speed he was before her, gripping her hips and raising her into his arms. Her slick thighs wrapped around his hips and he felt her breath on his neck. Power rocked the entire palace as his need surged violently to mix with hers. He spun her back into the wall and slammed into her, harder than he should have allowed himself. Her snug channel accepted every inch, her slick walls pulling him in.

His shoulders tensed as he fought to control his strength while powering in and out of her, driven to near madness by her throaty moans and the sharp nails digging into his back.

He felt ensorcelled, like a wild beast.

His healer was taking every bit of his raw pounding. Her eyes were half lidded as she ripped the binding from his hair and tangled her hands in it. He could not take his eyes from her, watching as her head writhed against the stone.

"Harder," she breathed and he grunted his approval, flexing his hips, tunneling in harder and deeper until his shoulders tensed with the need to break down the walls around them.

He needed to be so deep that she would always feel him, would always remember who she belonged to.

The need to mark her flushed skin was relentless.

"You are mine, Sirena," he commanded. "Any time I wish it, you'll spread your thighs for me. You *belong* to me." His shaft pulsed inside her and he felt her anger and arousal at his words. She was nearly as lust driven as he, but she hadn't gone mad from it, as he had.

*****

Sirena was lost in the lust, but not so lost that his words of ownership didn't grate. Yet even though she didn't like it, a deep, long-dormant part of her reveled in every damned word. Her damned beast blood was clawing inside her now, wanting more of this from him.

But the beast was going to have to calm the hell down. This was the only kind of pleasure she could take at the moment.

Sirena was dizzy as his fingers dug possessively into her hips. He wasn't gentle, but she still felt him holding something back. A part of her wanted him to unleash it; another wasn't sure she was ready for the God at his most crazed. He lifted a hand to plump one of her breasts before pinching it; the bite of pleasure-pain made her dig her fingers into his hair and tug. It was too good and not enough.

His movements were furious, wild and demanding, as he moved a hand to tangle in her hair, pulling until her head was tilted to look at him. The Warlord God wanted her to see who owned her body and she could feel it all through the bond. Steam lifted up from their hot skin to join the water cascading down his massive back.

There was accusation and promise in his next words. "You created this need, *völur*, and you will ease it."

She gasped when he hit some magical spot inside her. It made her thighs tighten and her blood burn.

She could feel his lust and frustration when he decreed, "You will never leave my side."

She was too caught up to argue at that point, so she let him talk. She just needed to come, but when he thrust in hard, she was mesmerized by the straining tendons when his neck arched back. He slammed a palm into the wall, sending shards of stone down to the floor. When he snarled her name to the ceiling, she felt his cock pulse, filling her full of hot come. The second she felt that warmth she cried out in shocked pleasure, coming so hard her entire body tensed around him.

When his eyes came down to hers, she felt his tension and knew he was still hard inside her.

"Why is it never enough?" he demanded, his eyes flashing with frustration she could feel straight through their bond.

"I don't know," she bit out, but she did. Or she had a very good idea.

His eyes flashed. "Do not lie to me, Sirena."

Damn it, he'd felt her omission. She wasn't about to voice what she thought because she felt it had to do with beast blood needing more of a claiming. Needing more of his dominance, but she *felt* the need for him to take all of her in the ultimate dominance.

His eyes narrowed on hers as if trying to read all her secrets.

Arousal hummed inside her and she moaned when he started moving, rocking slowly in and out as he watched her. He was teasing her, tormenting her until her chest heaved with the need for more.

"What are you hiding, Sirena?" His voice was commanding and seductively arrogant all at once.

She let her head fall to the wall and closed her eyes, off balance and completely immersed in this slow agonizing pleasure.

"Tell me, *völur*. Tell me or I will stop this." Was it possible that the witch endearment was actually growing on her? Damn it, this bond was doing insane things to her mind.

Her eyes snapped open when she fully realized what he'd said. "You're making it impossible. Finish this; then we'll talk." She panted.

He stayed unmoving until she wiggled for more and then she squeezed around him. When he groaned, she sank her fingers into his shoulders for the leverage to grind against him and take what she wanted.

You will not go against my will, Healer. His lips met hers in a punishing kiss, his tongue demanding entrance, forcing her submission. She tried to teleport them to the bed, where she could take control and come.

They broke apart in pleasurable torture, but he ruthlessly stopped her from taking them anywhere. Instead he forced their bodies back to exactly the same position with him holding her against the wall.

Her nails dug into his skin and he nipped her lip before growling low. Without warning, her wrists were shackled above her head, held in one of his big hands. His other palm held her hips tight to his, forcing her to hold every inch of his cock inside her wet, aching channel. She could still feel his come inside her and it only made her more anxious for more. Something about it was addicting.

"You try my patience, Sirena. I am your *God*; your power is useless against me. You will learn that *I* rule your body and own your pleasure, *völur minn*."

She narrowed her eyes at him. He might be able to manipulate her skill to teleport, but could he resist her other abilities? She let healing power flow from her body to his, warm and seductive. Her lips tilted when it forced a groan from him, the pleasure making his cock throb inside her. "Yes, Hroarr, you are *my* God. *My* mate. That means *your* body and pleasure belong to me just as equally." She moved the power through his cock, not to harm, but to stroke and tease him to the same agony he was creating within her. In a way she was tormenting herself just as much.

They were in a battle and she wasn't losing without a fight.

His eyes flashed as he held her gaze.

"You will not win, little one," he challenged and then she felt what he intended. Her jaw clenched as he accessed her healing power and began manipulating it. Just as he'd done with her teleportation, he was easily using her other skill against her. It felt like his warmth was beneath the surface, underneath her skin, putting pressure on the spot deep inside her that made her wild. He didn't relent until she cried out, so close to coming she was panting, but he wouldn't move it, he only held the spot, torturing her.

I can feel the need clawing inside you, Sirena. Your blood heats for me. It knows you belong to me. So tell me what I want to know and I'll give you what you need. His full erotic assault combined to make her dizzy and stupid with lust. She wanted more, needed everything. He was right, there was clawing and it had become just as incessant as the arousal itself. The need was driving and relentless, and for a second she forgot she was trying to win their battle of wills. Suddenly losing seemed far more appealing.

She breathed, "I only have a guess and it requires a conversation."

"Tell me this guess and I will ease the ache." He was breathing hard, but would not relent in this. She had trouble finding any words that wouldn't actually unleash something Sirena wasn't ready for. Her beast might be all for a dominant God taking every last vestige of her body, but she wasn't.

Not yet.

His eyes bored into hers. "I have given you everything you have asked for, little one. Now, you will tell me what you're hiding."

His words jolted her enough for her to choke out, "All I've asked for?" Her mouth gaped as she hissed, "Are you serious?"

The seductive tone of his voice was back. "I vowed to fight for your world, Sirena. I also allowed you to go back to do your duty on Earth. And when you needed to heal, we stayed in the Northern Lands."

She tugged at her wrists and found his hold unbreakable, which made the clawing sound louder in her mind. He stilled for a second, seeming to hear it as well? His emerald eyes heated. "What is the clawing? I can feel your desire surge with my hold, but why is there a clawing?"

She swallowed. The asshole truly believed he had been nice and giving. "We *will* discuss your apparent generosity later." She gritted out, "I think the clawing is my beast wanting you to fuck me."

She took a shuddering breath and tried to focus. "I want to stop the relentlessness as much as you do."

"Beast? Like the dragon?" he demanded with narrowed eyes and she couldn't tell what he was thinking, because she was being held on the precipice of coming.

He groaned when she gripped him inside her. "I do not have another form. But there is some beast blood in me that wants you to do things." She lifted her chin. "Things I am not ready for."

He wasn't going to let it go no matter how much both of them needed to come. "What does it want? Is that why I can't get enough of you?"

"It wants everything."

"Everything?"

Her skin flushed, but she forced her eyes on his. "Everything." She gritted out, "It needs to be dominated."

His eyes flashed with wild heat.

Her breath stuttered out. "Doing this is still new for me. I'm not ready for your cock in my ass, Hroarr. Not yet."

He snarled in pure animalistic need and she swore he swelled thicker inside her as his power surged. Torches in the room flared to the ceiling as he tried to tamp it down. That alone made her eyes roll back. "Just let me get used to this, for now." She breathed and then met his eyes. "You vowed not to force me to do anything I wasn't willing to do."

He didn't speak; she wasn't sure he could. The muscles in his shoulders were vibrating when he leaned in and took her lips, devouring her mouth as he finally started to thrust. She clamped down on him in sheer relief and pleasure. She wasn't sure what emotion she was feeling from him, but it was raw and possessive as he drove into her harder and faster. He was still holding back, just giving her enough that her body was on fire, and the beast was clawing for more.

When he lifted his head, she could see all his animal need was spilling free as he powered into her body, hitting just the right spot over and over until she was crying out incoherently to the ceiling.

The second she tightened around him, he came hard and the entire room shook with his pleasured roar, "Mine."

Chapter 18

Hroarr's Palace, Thule

Hroarr did not wish to release her. The fact that she was now filled with his seed satisfied him far too much. Instead he stayed inside her as she fought for breath, her pale head resting against the dark stone of the wall. Warm water flowed down over his back and their connected bodies as sanity started to return to him in small degrees.

She was *his*. She groaned. "Let me down."

His grip on her only tightened until her eyes flashed with the annoyance he felt in their bond.

"I need to stand."

He was losing his mind where she was concerned. Even her sweet scent called to him beneath the surface of his earthy soap she'd obviously used on her hair and skin after disappearing from his side in the Northern Lands.

He clenched his teeth as he lifted her from his body with great effort, when everything in him wanted to stay inside her.

When she retreated from him to the spray of the water, he had to force himself to turn and wash her slickness from his softening shaft.

Now that he wasn't in need or touching her, he seemed to

finally be able to think again. Some primal part of him wanted to tie her to his side for all eternity, never allowing her to leave.

He rinsed off before commanding, "Get in the pool, Sirena." She would tell him everything he needed to know about this bond.

There was no mistaking the irritation in her voice when she snapped, "I'm not a pet, Hroarr."

"You are going to explain things to me," he growled as he turned to watch her.

"You think we'll *talk* when we're both naked?" she challenged.

He'd been rough with her and the healing waters were filled by his priestesses from the sacred rivers of Fólkvangr. She would go in them whether she wished it or not.

She'd already started to leave when he pushed his hair back and ran a hand down his beard, thankful that more sanity was returning.

But not enough.

With a burst of speed he was out of the falls, lifting her into his arms to descend the steps into the warm water. "Yes, Sirena. You will tell me everything about this bond and beast while you're naked because it pleases me to look at you."

He'd caught her off guard with his speed, and when she would have fought his hold, the water shifted over her skin, transfixing her until she groaned softly. "What is this?"

"Healing waters from Fólkvangr."

She let out a breath and let her head tilt back, the soothing liquid working its magic on her. He watched as her hair drifted beneath the surface, gliding over his arm. Her features relaxed as she sighed in pleasure.

He allowed it to ease her for long moments before speaking. "Now tell me about your beast blood, little one."

He'd already learned about those of her world having animal blood and he'd seen enough dead worlds to know that each had their own power structures and magic. Nothing could surprise him, but his lips curled in disgust as he remembered how he'd learned of Earth's differences. "Your God, Apollo, boasted of his skills with *enhancing* beings with the strength and senses of beasts."

Apollo had been caged in Thule at the time, and the unworthy Deity had attempted to use that information as a bargaining tool for his freedom.

He instantly felt disgust and sheer hatred through their bond and his eyes shot to hers. His body instantly tensed with fury as he growled, "This God harmed you?"

The water in the pool vibrated with his sudden rage. Had she been tortured and terrorized by the Deity like he guessed many other Immortals had? Apollo had been vivid in his descriptions of the armies he'd created and how long the Immortals had needed to adapt to the changes he'd wrought against their will. Apollo had been proud of the superior beings and his means of enslaving them for his purposes. He'd assumed Hroarr would find it all beneficial, yet Hroarr found the Deity to be far too like his own brother Tyr.

He'd traded Apollo to Hades for Kara's safe return to Thule; now he found he wanted the God back where he could make him bleed.

*****

Sirena slipped free of Hroarr's hold to stand in the chest-deep water away from him. The act hadn't improved his already irate mood, but she didn't care. She sucked in air, needing clarity away from his hold and the lulling waters he'd submerged her in.

Being battered by his emotion was distracting, she could feel his anger but couldn't decipher protectiveness from possessiveness, and there seemed to be a lot of both.

Ripples shuddered over the water as he growled, "What did he do, Sirena?"

Mentally shaking it off was all she could do. She and Hroarr weren't friends; they weren't even as intimate as she imagined real lovers would be. That meant he didn't need to know what her personal connection to Apollo was. Though she was surprised he hadn't already figured it out when he'd imprisoned the bastard. He had to have felt the similarity in her power.

She wasn't stupid enough to think he would accept no answer, so she shared what her world already knew. "Apollo was a monster. He harmed nearly every Immortal in my world. He captured them, bound them with slave cuffs, and experimented on them by infusing beasts into their bodies. If that wasn't enough, he forced them to breed like animals."

She'd felt his disgust for her father, but was that only because he'd assumed Apollo had harmed her specifically? After all, as Hroarr's pet, she was not to be harmed, or even touched, by anyone.

What unnerved her was that as the ruling God of Thule, he might see her father's actions as a justifiable battle strategy. She hoped not, but she didn't know him. Now that the thought was there, her blood ran cold at the possibility of being connected to another monster.

She teleported into his room, needing air and some space to think because she felt odd and irrational.

He snarled behind her, "I can feel your lie, Sirena. Your hatred was personal. And now you feel ill. What did he do to you?" When he spun her around and pinned her against the nearest wall, she glared at him and sent power to tighten his tendons, making him lose strength and drop her from his hold. She spun a few feet away, snapping, "Give me space."

Her traitorous body had already started melting for him and she just couldn't deal with that.

He growled low, "Tell me what you were thinking."

She shook her head. "I doubt you want the answer." She paused. "I don't know you, Hroarr. I'm feeling this way because I'm wondering if I'm tied to a God who would do the same things Apollo has done."

His fury slammed through their bond as he lifted her up to face him, snarling, "I am nothing like your Gods, *völur minn*."

"Then what are you like, Hroarr?" she shot back. "You demanded I be your sex slave as payment for helping my world. You summon me like a pet. You tell me I belong to only you and you're the only one allowed to put his hands on me. What does that tell me?" She felt a wave of his anger and offense at her words, and that was fine. He'd offended her by demanding her as a damned payment for services rendered.

He snarled, and she found herself back on her feet in a flash. His speed was so incredible she'd barely seen him move, but she could feel him battling with himself, silently seething with anger as he stood naked before the now open balcony doors. His back was to her, and in between his shoulder blades was a tattoo, the design comprised of three triangles pointing down, making a Y in the middle. With a frown she knew she'd seen the symbol in Earth mythology. It was known in her world as the eye of the dragon, who knew what it meant here. She forced her eyes from his body art and the muscular back and ass that were far more beautiful than the icy seas beyond. His body was far too captivating to her and she needed to look away just to focus. The second she felt the cold wind starting to waft over her skin, his heated power came in to replace it and it felt too damned good.

She wasn't an idiot; she realized that a lot of this was likely their unfinished bond turning him into a bigger ass than he might truly be. Fate had done this to both of them, not just her, but she'd only been dealing with it for a day and she felt like a crazy person.

"Would you enslave races and force power on them to fight for Thule if it meant more strength in battle?" she finally asked because she needed to know what kind of male he was and didn't want to play games right now.

His muscled back and shoulders tensed impossibly further. "I do not need to force my people to fight for Thule." He growled with a sense of arrogance and offence she'd seen often enough with Hades. "There are no slaves here, nor have there ever been, Sirena."

She begged to differ. He had at least one.

He shot her a hard look over his shoulder and she felt him waging some internal war.

Good. She was waging one of her own. Her emotions were all over the place, the beast driving her one way and their combined need and confusion turning everything into insanity.

He wasn't letting the rest go. "You were innocent before me," he growled. "The God did not touch you or use you to breed, which would have earned him a fate far worse than death." She felt the truth in his words before he slowly turned to her. "He is your father,

Sirena?"

Bingo. He'd finally figured it out and she wasn't exactly happy or upset. She just was.

"That's none of your business," she pointed out.

She felt a blast of possessiveness and he stalked back to her. Her eyes slid to his cock on their own, as if drawn there. She closed her eyes, frustrated because she could already feel the arousal threatening to come back.

"Everything about you is my... *business*, Sirena." He'd mastered her language as well as she had the Thulian tongue.

She didn't need to open her eyes to know he was in front of her. His warmth was seeping into her already.

They were getting nowhere fast. She ground out bitterly, "You seem to expect me to trust you with all my secrets while giving me none of yours."

She felt too exposed for any real conversation. A glance told her the bed had been made at some point, and with a thought she called the sheet to her. Before he could reach for her, she headed for the seating area by the fireplace, wrapping her body in the soft material.

A fire blazed to life in the hearth as she turned to look at the shelves housing some of his things. Answers to who he was.

She noted the old books mixed with some metal objects. They looked like ancient works of art, because they weren't weapons or technology that she could tell.

"What are these?" Wasn't it her turn to learn something about him?

The exhaustion she'd felt before porting away from the village was sliding back in. It wasn't physical as much as it was a feeling of being mentally drained. She frowned to herself because, by all rights, she should probably be comatose or at the very least her energies should be depleted.

But they weren't. Her strength was fine.

He moved to her side and shocked her by actually answering the question. "They are artifacts and books from long-dead worlds."

"Why take them?" she said, pointing at the books and artifacts. "Can you even read the languages?"

"No," he admitted.

Before she could process the fact that he'd shared something semi-personal, he ruined it by stating, "Apollo is your father, yet you will not admit it."

He was so damned relentless. She shook her head as she moved away to curl into the edge of a supple leather couch. He wasn't going to let it go, he was like a beast with a bone. "Would you? Apollo is a vile being and my one half-brother by him was just as bad, if not worse. I've never met the God, but his tainted blood flows in my veins," she said in utter disgust. Let him judge her for it. "I'm surprised you couldn't feel his power in me."

He was watching her closely and surprised her by speaking again. "Your power does not feel the same as his."

She had to admit she liked the sound of that.

He added a moment later, "My sister Kara likely sensed your God blood, but she did not say and I do not share that particular skill."

She raised a brow. "So you're not so all-powerful after all?"

He tilted his head. "You mock me, *völur minn*?"

"Yes," she answered honestly.

He leaned a naked hip against the shelves directly in front of her. He seemed to look into nothingness for long moments, his thick arms crossed casually over his chest. She noted rivulets of water were still sliding from his wet hair down all the dips of his muscle.

Her eyes only slid back to his when he spoke. "I thought you shared mental bonds within families. I see several threads in your mind, but I do not sense one that feels like his."

He was adapting terrifyingly well to her powers and she wasn't sure she liked that. Now he could see her links to the Guardians, and next he'd be teleporting.

She shook off those thoughts and focused on what he'd said. When he wasn't acting like a caveman, he was asking uncomfortably shrewd questions.

She needed to pick her battles, and this was not the field she wanted to die on, so why fight him for answers? It had to be her beast causing the constant need to challenge him, to rile him for little reason like she was doing now. She shook it off because this mating was permanent and they needed to find a way to get along, and that meant getting to know each other the old-fashioned way.

Would it be more prudent to just suggest they blood bond? She wasn't sure that was something she wanted to do. She finally understood her brethren's reticence when it came to that portion of the mating bond, and she had far fewer horrors in her past than any of them.

After a deep breath she finally answered him slowly, "My connection to Apollo was severed when I was a baby. He did not want to be tethered to any being and I'm more than grateful for that fact."

"How is it that you have never set eyes on him?"

She hesitated for only a moment. "I'm sure I did after I was born, I just don't remember it. My mother was able to free me from Apollo's island when I was an infant. I was hidden away and given a new identity so he wouldn't know I survived the escape that apparently killed her." She took a breath before continuing, "I was raised with Drake in his mother's palace, and *only* my Guardian brethren know that I am that bastard's daughter." At that she gave him a hard, warning look. "It's not something we speak of." The only Immortals Hroarr would likely see were her brethren, but it wasn't a subject she liked to discuss even with them.

She could feel him processing that information.

Frustration was tensing her muscles as she leaned her head back on the couch. They were both millennia old and neither trusted the other, yet they would have to learn to do exactly that eventually. "If we would have bonded the *right* way, you'd know all this. You'd understand me and I'd know why you think the way you do." Though in all honesty, their unfinished bond didn't seem to be bringing out the best in either of them.

He narrowed his eyes. "Explain what the *right* way is."

Chapter 19

Hroarr's Palace, Thule

Hroarr's female was driving him mad, and not only with lust, it was with her constant challenges and upset over his claim on her. She was his, and at the moment he wanted nothing more than to turn her over his knee and remind her just how much she belonged to him. She made him *feel* for the first time in millennia and he didn't know what to do with it. Nothing about it was rational or logical, yet he craved her. He was obsessed with owning her after having lost real interest in anything but duty long ago.

Logic demanded he get answers about this bond between them, but logic was getting harder to see.

"What is the difference between our soul bond and my sister's? Gefn said she has Pothos' memories." Hades had connected his essence to Sirena's within moments.

She eyed him before speaking. "Yes, Gefn has Pothos memories and he has hers. We skipped that particular part of our bonding."

"Is that all we skipped?" he demanded, knowing there had to be more if her *guess* was correct about the beast creating the constant need between them.

He could feel her irritation as the need started building between them again.

He would grant her patience in his claiming her in the way of beasts, but only for as long as it took him to prepare her body to insure he did not hurt her more than necessary. If her beast needed dominance to stop the relentless desire, he would provide it.

He would task his *brír* with finding the items it would take to prepare her for his full possession in the morning.

After moments lost in thought, she answered him. "It starts with what we call a frenzy, which is what we're pretty much going through now. It's the constant need to have sex, but in normal cases our souls would be pushing us as well. After we'd had enough of the constant need, we would have spoken vows and been branded with mating marks." She paused as he processed all these odd steps and then added more, "After that we would have exchanged blood, which is how memories are shared. After learning all about one another, we would have consummated the union." She was shaking her head as she continued, "It's a way of easing two complete strangers into the deeper connection souls generally need to bind together completely."

There were too many parts to this.

He growled, "Start with these vows and the purpose of a brand?"

She shook her head. "The vows and markings are more of a tradition, like that of any marriage or joining." Her eyes were on him as she continued, "The blood bond is the part that would have helped us know one another almost completely before we sexed our way into the soul connection."

"What about your beast?"

"It would generally have connected at the same time our souls did. It wants to manifest a match inside you. My beast has no separate form, so the only change you'd know was a more primal urge toward me. Unless you've always been possessive like this with females?"

That thought sent a surge of jealousy through her and it pleased that odd animalistic part of him that she'd spoken of. He doubted any beast could truly manifest inside him as she'd said; he held far too much power.

"What is your beast?"

"I have a finite amount of dragon blood."

That made him still for a moment. Had there been a more in-depth reason for his parents having given him the symbol of the dragon? Had the Great Beings known he would be linked to a female with the blood of such a beast?

*****

Sirena was already feeling the effects of the bond. She wanted him all over again and their conversation hadn't been able to distract her from constantly stealing glances at his cock. Her body hummed with need when it started hardening for her. How could he suddenly be lost in thought when he was definitely aroused?

This need was insanity, but she wasn't going to fight it and she had no intention of waiting for him to lead this time. She wanted to feel what it was like to have the God at her mercy instead of being the one completely taken over.

His intent gaze was on her the second she slipped from her seat, and she was entranced by the way he stilled as she unwrapped the sheet. Tendrils of his power slid over her skin as she prowled toward him.

Hroarr was tensing, ready to pounce, when she infused her voice with compulsion. "Let me touch."

He groaned deep and she could see the barbarian inside him trying to slip its leash. He wanted to grab her, she could feel it.

When she set her palms to his chest, her body slicked at the thought of what she could do, emboldened by the twitching of heavy muscle beneath her fingers. She was mesmerized by the dusting of dark chest hair as she let her nails trail through it before scratching lightly against his nipples. His body jerked and one hand came to cover hers, not to stop, but to lead it down to his hard cock, growling, "This is where I want your touch, Sirena."

She stifled a moan at how hard and hot he was in her hand, and she stroked him once while leaning in to kiss his chest. *What if I don't want to touch? What if I want to taste?*

His neck tilted back as he fought her powerful voice in his head. She licked her way lower while he throbbed in her grip, a grip he forced tighter with his hand around hers. She moaned when he thrust into her palm.

She smiled against his hot skin. "Will you tell me how to suck it, Hroarr?" She knew the reminder of her inexperience would bring out his more primal instincts. It didn't make sense to play with fire, but she felt compelled and couldn't seem to stop. He felt too damned good and her beast wanted to play as it clawed for more.

Empowered, she scraped the nails of her other hand down his stomach as she lowered to her knees. His cock was too high with the height difference, but she was able to tilt her neck and lick his sac while keeping her eyes on his, reveling in the tormented raw need surging from him.

He growled and she felt him losing control. "Do not tease me, *völur minn*." At some point she'd started to enjoy his calling her a witch and it made no sense.

She sent telekinetic power out for the couch cushion. She knelt on it without letting go of her grip; his hand over hers wouldn't allow it anyway. She sighed when finding it the perfect height. Without conscious thought, she slid her cheek over him. It felt incredibly silky even though he was so hard beneath the hot flesh. His power whipped around them as he snarled, and she felt almost possessed by it when she looked up. His hands moved to her hair, pulling it from her face, and she felt the tug as he wrapped the wet strands in one fist.

His eyes were dark with raw passion and she taunted the God by licking slowly from root to tip. *Like this?* she teased into his mind.

He'd gone down on her and it had been mind-blowing every single time, but she'd never had control over him.

When her tongue slid into the pre-come at the tip, she closed her eyes and moaned. He tasted so damned good. She'd been told Aletheia semen could be addicting to humans, but this... *You taste incredible.*

He groaned a command, "Take me in your mouth, Sirena." He seemed to be fighting the need to fuck her. She smiled before sliding her lips over him and sucking just the thick head. She couldn't help flicking her tongue over the slit. *Give me more to taste.*

When she moaned around him, his cock jerked and then his fingers were gripping her head. "Take more of me, *völur minn*."

There was no way she'd get him all in her mouth even if he pushed past her gag reflex, which she was sure would happen. He flexed his hips until he was all the way in and she squirmed with need of her own as he commanded, "Swallow around it. You will take more of me."

How could his demands make her want more? At that moment all she wanted was to come she was so wet. When he pushed, she breathed through her nose and swallowed as he forced more of himself inside her throat.

"Again," he growled, after pulling from her and pushing back in. He was holding back, barely containing himself. The scent of sex filled the air as she sucked, released and repeated until he was pumping between her lips, his hand moving hers to stroke the remainder of him at the same time she sucked.

When she gripped his ass in her other hand, he moved it to his sac. "Touch," he commanded.

And then his hands were back in her hair, gliding her mouth up and down his shaft. "Get me wetter," he demanded when he pulled from her.

She spit on him and let her lips glide over his cock and was rewarded with more come to lap up.

"Suck me harder. Finish what you started, Sirena," he demanded as he shafted in and out of her mouth until her jaw ached and her thighs were slick for him.

She mewled around him and he took her harder, furiously thrusting to the back of her throat until she felt the first jets of hot come filling her. "Drink it all."

She did, moaning the whole time, until finally he slipped from her lips so she could tongue the last bit from his throbbing flesh.

She was panting by the end.

That had been incredible.

"Sucking me made you wet, Sirena," he growled, and she could see his skin had flushed and his massive chest was rising and falling with his harsh breathing.

"Yes." She wouldn't deny it, she was in too much need for that.

He had her in his bed in record time. She tensed when he flipped her to her stomach, pillows miraculously slipped under her hips, and protested, "Hroarr, no!"

He smacked her ass. "I will not take you here. Yet. But you will get used to my touch," he growled as he pressed her back until her breasts were on the bed, his thumb against her ass. He wasn't pushing in, but he was there, letting her feel him there.

She wasn't sure she believed he would contain himself, but she was too flushed with need to talk. Her body was tense, waiting for him to break his vow, but he didn't. Instead he caressed her hips and slid through her wet folds. She stayed down, gripping the bedding as her body betrayed her with each seductive touch. He hadn't moved that damned thumb.

"Do you want to come, Sirena?" He was showing her he was in control and the clawing raw need was relentless enough that she almost begged him for more, knowing he could feel her rampant desire.

"Yes," she gritted out.

"Then you will not move."

He pushed her thighs wider, and she felt her knees up against the edge of the bed. Her hips were tilted so that she was completely open to him. She waited for him to slam inside her, but he didn't.

That one digit on her ass was driving her beast insane. When she felt his tongue on her clit, she nearly shot off the bed. Another sharp slap landed and she snapped, "What the hell, Hroarr?" That had stung, but her damned animal thought it was incredible.

"Do. Not. Move."

When the sting morphed into pleasure, she bit her lip to stop from moaning.

*****

Hroarr's cock was rock hard again. He loved the taste of her. It was unlike anything else and he was quickly learning he could feast on her for hours and never get enough.

Every new discovery his innocent female made only served to please him more, binding him tighter to her.

He lashed his tongue through all those sweet juices once again. Every jolt of her pleasure slipping into his mind belonged to him. His little *völur* had teased him while taking him in her mouth and he would tease her now.

He would also push her.

She was open and wet as he slid his tongue over the nub that made her ache for him.

He nipped at the inside of her thigh as she made catlike noises into his bed.

"It is your turn to give me more, Sirena," he taunted as he added a little more pressure, circling his thumb lightly against the tiny hole that made her jump and twitch. The clawing grew louder as he licked and sucked her pussy.

Your animal needs me here, Sirena, he taunted, *but it will take time to prepare you for such a possession.*

She bucked and he smacked her bottom again before gripping and caressing the perfect flesh. He spread her open so he could look his fill. She made a sound, half moan, half snarl. She'd liked the firm hand, though she did not want to.

Her beast loved it.

He smiled against her before pushing two fingers into her pulsing channel. "Yes," she groaned until he moved his thumb and replaced it with his tongue. He thrust inside her, loving how she sucked him in and tightened around anything he gave her: his tongue, his fingers, his shaft.

Come for me now, he commanded.

He pushed his fingers deep, using his thumb on her hard nub as he tongued her ass until she begged for more.

He smiled when her entire body tensed, pushing back against him, slicking his fingers.

He slipped them free and buried his shaft inside her still-throbbing passage. He groaned when she tightened around him. He put his thumb back on her tiny hole as his hips powered against her. She got up on her forearms and pushed back to meet each punishing thrust and he allowed the movement.

His healer had gone wild for him. Her fingers were digging in the bedding as she arched and slammed back for more.

The curve of her spine and the perfect flare of her hips made a near perfect picture. He fisted her hair, loving having her neck arched back for him.

Grunting, he slammed into her until she cried out.

When he shouted his own release, she came again, whimpering as she caressed him with her body.

His chest was still heaving when he realized she'd fallen asleep with him still inside her. As he slid free, he felt a certain animalistic pleasure knowing his seed was still inside her.

He stayed there looking down at her for long moments.

He felt more clear and alive than he had in centuries and he didn't want to leave her, but he had duty to attend to.

Chapter 20

Hroarr's Palace, Thule

Gefn reformed into the empty room of her guard, Laire, her body was still shaking from hearing of the battle and her friend's injuries. The navy comforter hadn't been disturbed, so he hadn't been there recently. She'd already checked the healing pools favored by Hroarr's *þrír* and found them to be empty.

I'll be right there, Pothos assured her as he sent soothing energies. Spa and Velspar appeared at her side and she could feel their concern for her and maybe Laire, as well.

I'm fine. Stay in your meeting. The clan members said Laire walked through the portal with Hroarr. That Sirena healed him. I only need to see him for myself. She'd already told her *maðr*, her consort, what she'd heard upon teleporting into the Northern Lands moments ago and she knew she was being irrational, but it couldn't be helped. He'd been in the Northern Lands because she'd suggested he watch over Hroarr's priestesses while she and Pothos took time to themselves. A fact that was causing guilt and worry to eat at her from the inside out.

Gefn reformed in the great room that was her brother Dagur's work space, her beasts appearing at her side on their own. Her instant presence earned a curse from her brother before he growled, "Do not enter that way, sister." Gefn was fully aware of her obnoxious brother's displeasure with her intrusion, but she didn't care.

She noticed the eight-foot-high bronze God prison he and Hroarr had fashioned long ago had been moved into the middle of the space. The cylinder shape of the otherworldly metal encasement had been etched with magical runes that glowed into the space.

Dagur settled his hands on his kilted hips, his golden eyes flashing with annoyance. "Since you are here, you can deliver the chamber to Earth yourself. Hroarr said it was yours."

"Good." She nodded before quickly asking, "Have you cast the spell I asked for?"

He threw his hands in the air. "When was I to do that, sister? In the half hour since my return to the palace?"

Spa chuffed her annoyance at his tone and it drew Dagur's attention.

Gefn firmed her lips because she'd asked him to do this last night. He could have done it before she and Pothos had come to the palace to have him and Kara relieve them in the Northern Lands. What he'd likely done instead was frequent the chambers of Kara's *þrír* to slake his constant lust for the priestesses.

They needed an update about when the Destroyer of Worlds would come for Earth. If the Tria were calling it there, she wanted to ensure its speed hadn't increased since the last time Dagur checked. She was on edge as the Guardian's prepared to contain the evil beacon. She gritted out, "Will you please do it now, brother?"

Spa and Velspar paced around, glaring at her brother.

Dagur eyed them wearily before admitting, "That was my intention."

It took all her strength of will not to berate him. "Thank you,

Dagur. I cannot find Laire. Was he sent to some task?"

"I have not seen him since the Northern Lands. Your warrior returned to the palace with Hroarr in the last hour. Kara and I did not return with all the *þrír* and the remaining warriors until a half hour ago."

She nodded. "I will return to take the chamber away."

She teleported to the hallway without another word and asked the first guard she found, "Where is Laire?"

"He was in the kitchens moments ago. Should I fetch him for you?"

Some of her tension eased at that information. After a quick, "No," she teleported away, again with her entourage, as Pothos called the cats. They'd been so busy sitting outside the baby's room she'd actually missed having them at her side.

If she'd been thinking clearly, she would have considered that Laire might have become hungry after his ordeal. She was relieved to know he was well enough to eat.

When she reformed to see her guard with a leg of cooked meat in his hand, relief surged through her. There was a clanking of pans hitting the floor and soft curses when she appeared out of nowhere.

"Why are you not abed?" she chastised before starting forward. His long blond hair was tied back and he wore only a leather kilt and boots, as did all the guards. His weapons harness and staff were lying on the long wooden table that held his plate full of food.

Guards and cooks moved quickly out of the massive room the second she arrived. A fire was in the hearth and it smelled warmly of stew and baked breads. Laire was smiling at her as he set his meal down to stand before her. He was a large warrior, nearly seven feet tall, yet she bent to see his bare stomach, forcing him to move side to side so she could see where the injury had been and whether Sirena had had time to completely heal him. The cats were there at his side as well, bumping him as he chuckled. She found no blood or evidence of an injury, so he must have cleaned and changed in the time since coming back to the palace.

"I am fine, my Goddess. I swear it. Hroarr's priestesses were here only moments ago, fussing. They too said I am whole and were confident enough to leave me to my food," Laire informed her, grinning at her in the same charming boyish way that enamored the priestesses. Her guard had a way with any and all the females, young and old.

Her body finally released some tension as Spa slid her silky head under Gefn's hand. Laire had been her friend and guard for over a century, but he was mortal. She might only have a few centuries left of his mortal life, and many of those would be as he grew older, and it was going to devastate her to watch it.

She narrowed her eyes. "You are certain you feel completely well?"

"Yes, my Goddess. Only hungry."

"Very well, when you are finished with your meal, gather your things." He would be going with her to Earth.

"I am back to my duties, then?" he said as he eyed her closely. Laire was a male and a warrior and his pride would sting if she fussed too much, but she was having difficulty not doing it. He would not have been harmed if he had been at her side, where he had been for over a century.

"Yes. There is much to do on Earth and I will need my guard with me."

Laire watched her with knowing eyes and after a glance around the room asked, "You no longer need time with your *maðr*?"

Only Laire would question her.

"Laire, I know I am acting a little mad, but you will have to indulge me. I need you at my side."

His voice got soft. "I was only injured because we were attempting *not* to harm the clan members and a young one almost cut his own father's arm off. I assure you that Mist largely healed me before Sirena arrived. My wound was not so terrible." She had a feeling he was lying.

Pothos appeared in that instant and nodded a greeting. "Laire."

Gefn relaxed as soon as he curled her into his side, his warmth soothing all her raw nerves.

After gazing down at her, Pothos returned his attention to Laire. "Has your Goddess explained that we need you back on guard duty?"

"Yes, my Goddess' *maðr*," Laire said formally.

"P works just fine," her male informed her friend.

Laire bowed his head respectfully.

"When you are finished eating, gather your things and meet me in the great room," she said to Laire.

With another bow, he grabbed the piece of meat and was out the door.

Gefn looked up, noticing her male was staring into nothing for a moment before she realized what he was about. A glance into her own mind's eye found Hroarr's connection had moved.

"I need to have a word with Hroarr before we leave."

She nodded before checking for Hroarr's location. He seemed to be moving in Dagur's direction. "I told Dagur I would be back for the first God prison for Earth."

P looked down at her and grunted. She knew he was thinking about his sister, who was the reason Hroarr was releasing the weapon to Earth. Pothos was worried for Sirena, so she didn't say anything. He would have his word with Hroarr and hopefully feel better. She understood the need to protect those you cared about. Before they left, she turned into his arms fully and lifted to give him a fleeting kiss. "Thank you."

He kissed her on her head. "For what?"

"For understanding my need to keep Laire safe." Until Pothos, she'd had very few people she cared for, and there had been so many she'd lost through the years. The loss never became easier.

"It was purely self-serving, love. I'm hoping he can babysit your damned fur-covered menaces." He grinned wide when Velspar knocked into his side as the beasts huffed and disappeared. "You see?" he pointed out. "Who the hell knows where they're going. Drake's losing his damned mind about it."

She laughed. "Laire can't teleport."

"We'll figure something out. Maybe we can come up with some magical leash for him to hold onto."

She shook her head, smiling. "Okay, let's go so you may lecture my brother." She wasn't worried. Even if Hroarr lost his mind and attempted to battle her *maðr*, he would find the error in his ways.

Pothos' priestess mother had gifted him her power with the protection runes down his back. Even the all-powerful Hroarr could not harm her male.

No God of Thule could.

Chapter 21

Hroarr's Palace, Thule

Hroarr slipped out of his chambers and away from his sleeping female to stalk down the hallway.

When Ranulfr stepped from the shadows to follow, Hroarr demanded, "Has Dagur returned?"

"Yes, *þjóðann minn*."

"Where is he?"

"I believe he is in the Great Room." The room his brother had long since made his work space.

Hroarr bounded down the steps in that direction. The massive spelled doors were swept wide when he neared and he felt the magic his brother wielded. Dagur was in a leather kilt with his long brown hair tied back in a knot as the air swirled around the room. He noted a swirling black sphere filled one side of the massive space. Dagur stood still before it, speaking ancient words that echoed through the room.

The second the doors clamped shut behind him, he crossed his arms over his chest and waited.

After long moments the spell was finally cast and magic whipped through the room and sucked back into nothing with a whoosh that vibrated in the walls. His brother might be foolhardy more often than not, but there had never been another God with Dagur's ability to cast such immense spells.

Hroarr finally spoke. "Were the clans cleared of the toxins before you left?"

"Yes, brother." Dagur sighed. "I assure you we did not leave until the *þrír* completed their tasks."

"Good. I am leaving to retrieve more materials for the prisons you will create."

Dagur put his hands on his hips as he nodded. "Gefn is here somewhere looking for Laire. I told her to take the one prison we have, per your instruction." Sarcasm laced the male's tone and Hroarr raised an eyebrow. He had good reason for the need to oversee Dagur's tasks, the other God had been patently reckless his entire existence.

The doors burst open and he turned to see Gefn and her male striding down the steps.

"Brother." Gefn acknowledged him with a nod. "I am taking Laire with me when we leave. When will the other prisons be made?"

"I am leaving to retrieve materials for them now. If they have all twelve Gods, then they will need seven more."

The tension coming from his sister's male was heavy as he spoke. "We'll need eight."

"You will need four Gods to work the spell. One for each element," Hroarr advised.

"Drake and I will handle the fourth position."

Hroarr tilted his head. The power wielded by the two Guardians was strong. "We will have them done within the week."

Dagur sputtered, "A week!"

Hroarr pinned him with a glare. "A week." They had long since created molds and Hroarr would be the one to melt the metal while Dagur etched the ancient runes with magic. After that it would be up to the Earth Gods to get their Deities inside and seal them using the elements and a portion of their life forces to lock them in.

"Good," Gefn said. "They will be containing the Tria in about the same time."

"If they are calling out to the *ófǫlr*, you need to contain them now," he commanded.

"We will handle it," Pothos challenged.

Gefn stepped between him and her *maðr*. "Hroarr, they are handling it. They have a much bigger world and there is a chance these beings will die and cause mass destruction. They are doing this as quickly as they can while working to minimize loss of life." At that Gefn turned to Dagur. "That is why I need updates on the Destroyer's progress toward Earth."

"I have sent the spell. It will take days to get it back," Dagur informed her.

When Hroarr moved to leave, Pothos stepped up. "We need to talk, Thulian."

Hroarr eyed the male. "You have five minutes. In my study."

"Please, no fighting," Gefn snapped as Hroarr took the steps with the Earth male at his side.

Dagur groused something about wanting to know what was

going on and then the door was shut behind them.

Once they were alone in his study, Hroarr turned and waited, crossing his arms over his chest.

"You've put me in a fucked-up position, Hroarr."

Hroarr merely raised a brow.

"You are my mate's favorite brother, who she believes is honorable. Yet you're also the dick who disrespected my sister."

"Your sister?" Sirena and the male were cousins by blood.

"Sirena has been a sister to me nearly my entire life," the male said as he tilted his head, studying Hroarr before adding, "You are at a disadvantage, Hroarr. I know all about you and Thule through Gefn's memories, but you don't know a damned thing about me or the female you were fated for. I hope for your sake that you are treating Sirena like a fucking Goddess, because I don't believe you're worthy of her."

Possessiveness swelled inside him until he narrowed his eyes and stated with harsh finality, "She is mine."

Pothos eyed him for a long moment as Hroarr's power swirled around the room.

When the male finally spoke, he was shaking his head. "My sister has spent her entire life putting everyone else first. Everyone. She's worked night and day doing things no one else in our world could. She was chosen as a Guardian by our Creators because she is special and her heart is fucking pure. She deserves a male who will put her first and care for her. Your sister is fucking cherished as the center of my world. That is the very least of what my sister deserves and you had better be doing the same for her."

And at that the male was gone.

Chapter 22

Guardian Manor, Tetartos Realm

Sirena's hand snaked out to feel cold sheets at her side and she lifted up. She was alone in Hroarr's bed and that rankled. She felt for his connection and her shoulders tensed sensing he was worlds away and that distance agitated her and the animal beneath the surface.

Waking alone should have made her happy, not only had she spent millennia waking up that way, but it had the added bonus of not having to fight about leaving for Earth.

She shook it off and teleported home with a frown.

Drake had obviously been watching for her return to the manor because the second she'd ported into her room at the manor, he summoned her to his office.

After a quick shower and throwing on some clothes, here she was, staring into the dragon's worried face. His green tee shirt stretched over his chest as he crossed his arms, assessing her too closely. He rarely used the desk he leaned a hip against.

"Is Hroarr being a dick to you?" Drake growled after two seconds in his presence.

"Listen to me closely, Draken." Sirena glared, using his full name like his mother would because if he wanted to treat her like a child, she could return the favor. After taking a breath she continued, "Hroarr and I are in a mating frenzy he knows nothing about while trying to get to know each other at the same time. I'd say he's no more a dick than any other male in his position." She was being generous, but the point was to get her brother to stop worrying, not piss him off more. "Considering that, I won't be here long today. I just wanted to find out what's happened."

Smoke filtered from her brother's lips.

She raised her hands in the air. "I'm here, right? I'm not a prisoner and he hasn't harmed me in any way. The only reason the bond isn't complete is because I needed some time to get to know him first. I'm allowed to take a day for myself, so stop reading into things and being difficult."

He grunted in annoyance.

"We have far more important things to talk about than my mating," she said, raising a brow while cocking a hip. Her black pencil skirt didn't allow for a lot of movement, but that didn't deter her from trying.

The staring contest with Drake finally ended when she asked, "Has Era been checking in on Lucy?" Sirena had been the only Guardian healer for millennia and it had never been just a job to her, which made accepting help from anyone incredibly difficult, but necessary. At the moment she was grateful as hell that Era was there now.

"Yes. Both baby and mother are fine."

"And Gregoire?"

Drake grunted. "As well as he can be with a new child and the end of the world knocking at our fucking door."

She nodded. "I'll check in on them tomorrow after I have more control over the new powers."

"They know you're dealing with your mate," Drake bit out.

She nodded. "Good. What else have I missed?"

Arousal was already humming beneath the surface, so she needed this to be a quick trip to grab some more of her things and get information before getting back and summoning the God to take care of this.

They would be finishing their bond today. Waiting hadn't been smart and she'd never planned to drag it out for long. A day or two to mentally deal with being intimate with a male she didn't know was what she'd given herself. Though she had no doubt it was still going to be a challenge to allow herself to be so physically vulnerable to him. Her beast was all for it, so she guessed she'd let the animal's instincts run free when the time came.

Drake blew out a frustrated breath. "P and Gefn brought over the first prison from Thule last night per Hroarr's instruction."

She stilled and stared at him. "I didn't realize P and Gefn were there." Hroarr had left her after she'd fallen asleep and she hadn't even known it?

Hroarr had woken her throughout the night like a male possessed, demanding her body over and over again until she was writhing and begging for more, but talking had been the last thing on his mind.

Sometime in between his wild bursts of lust he'd actually been keeping to his part of the bargain; that made her happy. Drake also told her about Dagur checking on the distance of the Darkness and the fact that Hroarr would build eight more prison slash weapons for

Earth by the end of the week. She wondered if that was what he was doing now. She knew the metal used in the weapons was from a dead world.

Drake leaned back against the desk, still staring at her.

She nodded. "How are the plans for the Tria?"

The dragon's eyes hardened as he spoke. "The world's too fucking big to manage all the damage we could be looking at. When Gods died in Thule, the entire world was affected—earthquakes, tsunami's, volcanic eruptions. I've wanted the Tria dead for their entire existence and now I'm hoping the bastards live through the purge of the stasis units so we don't have that mess." She felt Drake's frustration. The Tria were the most evil beings ever created, fed dark energies of death and suffering even from Artemis' womb. There was absolutely nothing good in them.

After a pause he continued, "We can't predict what areas will be hit. The populations of Earth are too damned high everywhere, but Conn devised a plan. He, Vane and the wolves are preparing to hack computer systems in the mortal Realm to get warning alerts out worldwide for the areas that are most susceptible. If that works, humans will get more advance notice to evacuate. It's a heavy task even with the help he enlisted, so we can't do anything with the Tria yet."

"It can't be helped." She nodded. "We have to do all we can." They were Guardians; they couldn't just allow massive amounts of casualties if they could do something to prevent them. The Creators said that humanity needed to evolve without the interference of more powerful beings. They didn't say the Guardians should turn a blind eye to mass destruction if they knew it could be coming.

"Did Conn say how long he needs?"

"He thinks it could be up to two weeks to do whatever tech shit they need to do."

Sirena didn't like it either. "What about Tetartos?"

Smoke lifted into the air. "We meet with the heads of the cities tomorrow."

Sirena was processing everything. "Is Apollo going into the prison we got from Thule?"

Her father was currently in an actual prison cell since his stasis unit had been ruined when he'd been freed. A part of her wondered if there was something wrong with her that she had absolutely zero empathy for the Deity whose blood ran in her veins.

Drake was watching her. "Yes. As soon as we do the modifications, we're testing the locking mechanism on Apollo's."

"What are you doing to it?"

"Hroarr and his siblings locked their brothers in the weapons using a portion of their life forces and the elements of Thule. Athena is making changes to the locking system since we've already used too much of our life forces to imprison the Tria." She knew that Drake, P, Hades, Athena and Aphrodite, plus the Goddesses' mates had to use extreme power to lock the powerful fiends in the bowels of Hell Realm.

"What is Athena doing?"

"She's siphoning some of the Creators' power from Hades' stasis unit to use some of it as a seal around the prison's opening. I hold the key to the stasis power, but Athena is actually skilled at manipulating it. If all goes well, it should be a solid lock without impeding the weapon's purpose in both imprisoning a God and being able to free the Deity's power as a weapon when we need it."

She felt her head was spinning at how complicated that all sounded.

She looked off, thinking that her father's power was finally going to the protection of their world instead of being a horrible self-serving prick of a God.

Hroarr's comments about Apollo made her lips curl.

"What is it?" Drake demanded, more smoke filtering in the air.

She shook her head before admitting, "Apollo bragged to Hroarr about everything he'd done to the Immortals." The God might have been purged of dark energies, but he obviously hadn't been good to begin with.

Drake nodded. "I figured as much. The second Apollo saw Hades waiting at Hroarr's trade for Kara, the bastard did his best to get Hroarr to keep him in Thule."

She contemplated for a moment. "I wonder if Apollo's horrible traits will turn into the same kind of toxins Hroarr deals with in Thule?"

"P told me about them. If it happens, we'll burn it away like Hroarr does," he said thoughtfully, "but the alternative is to allow him and the other eight asshole Gods out of their confinement to fight at our side when the Darkness comes. I'd rather drain the bulk of their power as a weapon than fight beside any fucking one of them. Apollo is a prime example that none of them were good to start with."

"I agree."

Their world was about to change in big ways. Once the Tria were contained, the Guardians wouldn't be in constant battle for the first time in millennia.

"Is there anything else I need to know?" She needed to grab what she came for and get the God to finish what they'd started.

He shook his head and groaned when they both felt the power.

Aphrodite.

Damn it.

Sirena tensed the second the Goddess entered the room in a sea of white silk. The blonde beauty was at least six feet tall and built with curves that men craved. She was in the same Grecian style that she'd always favored, so it was as if she and Ladon were going to a costume party. Drake's father looked almost identical to his son, other than his longer hair and lack of beard. The dragon was currently wearing white silk tied over his hips, showing a lot of skin.

Even with high heels Sirena was several inches shorter as the Goddess beamed at her. "Sirena!"

With a respectful bow Sirena greeted her, "My Goddess," thankful as hell that she was with Drake when seeing Aphrodite for the first time in millennia. That meant her power was under wraps.

Hades came in with Sacha at his side a moment later. One look at her sister Guardian and Sirena's lips twitched. For the calmest of Guardians, it had to be a nightmare watching over Aphrodite. Hades seemed more than happy with his sister's presence. The God grinned wide as he tucked Sacha into his side. His ebony wings curled around her sister Guardian until Sacha relaxed into him.

"You look well, child," Aphrodite said, her brilliant blue eyes assessing Sirena as Ladon grinned down at her before her aunt chastised, "Where have you been? Why have you not come to see me?"

Sirena wouldn't go so far as to say Aphrodite actually raised her, because this was, after all, Aphrodite. Child rearing wasn't the Goddess' forte, but the Deity had provided Sirena sanctuary.

"Please accept my sincerest apologies. I have been kept busy a world away or I would not have missed greeting you. We are excited to have you home." What the hell else could she say? "Unfortunately, I must get back to Thule now."

She was out the door before anyone could protest.

She smiled when she heard Sacha's voice in her mind as she rushed through the halls back to her room with a speed that she'd never possessed. *Are you doing okay with Hroarr?*

I am. But I still have a bond to complete, and being anywhere near Aphrodite is trying even when I'm at my best. How has she been? Sirena shot back.

Interesting. As long as Drake is near, she behaves. When he's not, I want to murder her, Sacha gritted out.

Issues?

You have no idea. At least Hades insisted both she and Athena stay in the Immortal Realm for the time being. He thinks the Creators' confinement spell around Tetartos can block the Goddesses' presence from the Tria's radar. They send possessed to Hades every time we're in Earth Realm, but nothing ever happens like that here. We'll see. I'm just glad that they seem to be playing by those rules. After that Sacha sighed. *I need wine.*

Sirena smiled. *Maybe we can find time tomorrow.*

Yes. Her sister's tone was emphatic enough to make Sirena grin.

Sirena entered her room as she answered sympathetically, *I'm sorry.*

Wine tomorrow. I want to hear how things are going with Hroarr. Brianne and I haven't wanted to interrupt your time together.

Tomorrow, she promised.

For now she planned to gather some of her things and get back to Thule.

She had a bond to complete.

Chapter 23

Hroarr's Palace, Thule

Sirena reformed with her clothes and shoes, setting them on the wood drawers in the middle of Hroarr's massive closet. Two dark wood walls were lined with glowing green blades of different sizes and shapes. Only one side held any clothing, and what was there consisted of a line of the exact same outfit in brown or black leather with boots to match. The heavy wood unit in the center held drawers of daggers or what she assumed were throwing blades spaced with precision.

The small bag from the day before had only held a few items, but she decided if the God wanted her, he was going to need to share closet space.

A flash of awareness told her someone was in the other room and she tensed as she assessed the situation. When she realized who was there, she slipped through the doorway, her high red heels clicking against stone until she was on a thick rug.

Mist, Hroarr's priestess, was setting things on the bed and she had to tamp down the jealousy at seeing the female in front of the bed she shared with Hroarr.

Mist turned; the nearly transparent blue dress she wore flitted around her legs and her snow white hair lifted as she moved. The priestess looked ethereal as she smiled in Sirena's direction, and there was no mistaking the warmth in her pale blue eyes. "Hello,

Sirena. Hroarr asked me to bring some things for you both. He is with Dagur right now."

After a deep breath, Sirena moved closer and saw the items in question. Her cheeks flamed when she took in the sight of what the oaf had tasked the priestess with bringing into their room. It was an array of creams and what looked like several anal plugs of varying sizes.

A glance back in Mist's direction showed the female's eyes were sparkling with amusement. "Do not be embarrassed, Sirena. There is no shame in pleasure. We priestesses have extensive needs, which have resulted in the design of plenty of such devices to make such things very pleasurable. I will be happy to explain all of them."

Oddly enough, Sirena's embarrassment wasn't nearly as strong as the jealousy that reared up at the topic of the priestesses' needs. Hadn't Gefn shared that particular fact when she'd mentioned Pothos' mother? She gritted her teeth and forced images of Hroarr with a naked Mist away with a strength of will that was flimsy at best. The female hadn't acted jealous of Sirena, nor had she made it seem that she and Hroarr were lovers, but Sirena needed to know.

In a tone as calm as she could muster, Sirena asked, "Mist, what exactly is your relationship with Hroarr?" She knew the God was linked to his priestesses with a basic emotional connection, a thread that Sirena shared with them as well. She sucked in a deep breath in an attempt to think logically. If Hroarr had been sleeping with his *brír* before his mating with her, she would deal with it, but it would never happen again or she'd end up killing the God, painfully.

The male infuriated the hell out of her, but that didn't mean she would share him.

Ever. He was her mate.

Mist's ice blue eyes took her in as she thoughtfully tilted her head. "It is not the relationship I believe you are imagining, Sirena. We have never shared pleasure with Hroarr. Our emotional connection to him would make it *odd* even if we had not raised him from childhood."

There was unmistakable truth in the priestess' words and that eased the jealousy she felt. She was truly happy she'd asked the question because the images she'd conjured had her beast clawing for blood and she'd barely been able to hold back the flare of power at her fingertips.

She took a deep breath and nodded, suddenly wondering who exactly Hroarr had been sleeping with all this time and wondering if there would be problems from that end.

That was a question for the God, not Mist.

Sirena did have another question for the priestess. Since she was now linked to them through Hroarr, would the females feel things from her? She didn't think they had while she'd been in the Northern Lands, but she needed to know if it was happening now. "Can you feel my emotion, Mist?"

Mist frowned for a moment before shaking her head slowly. "No, we cannot feel your emotions." After another second where the priestess seemed to be making a decision, Mist asked, "Would you care to sit and talk with me while Hroarr is busy with Dagur?" Something oddly comforting came from the female and it helped Sirena ignore the humming of desire as she moved to the couch by the fireplace.

"We owe you more than you know, Sirena. Not only for what you did yesterday, but for saving Spa and Velspar. And also for what we hope you will do for Hroarr," Mist said as they angled their seats to face each other. "We can feel the link you share with Hroarr and have heard that what you share with him is the same as what Gefn shares with Pothos. But we were told that Pothos and Gefn shared memories? If you had Hroarr's memories, you would know that we were not his lovers, so are we misinformed at how the bond works, or is the bond different for you and Hroarr?"

Sirena wondered how much to share. It wasn't really any of the female's business, but Mist was a big part of Sirena's new world now, so she found herself answering, "We did not share memories as Pothos and Gefn have, but our souls *are* bound."

"Why did you not share memories? Is it because of Hroarr's power?"

She explained that Hades had bonded their souls without the usual steps of a mating. After answering a great deal of questions, she ended up sharing everything that had happened in her lab.

Mist shook her head, obviously shocked. "You came into contact with his sjá?"

"Yes." It had rushed out as if eager to engulf her, so "coming into contact" didn't seem a strong enough description. As terrifying as the isolation had felt, she'd never felt any danger from the power, and if she hadn't seen Pothos' memories of her body seizing, she would never have known it had happened.

It took long moments for Mist's shock to abate, but once it did, she shot more questions at Sirena in rapid fire until she'd eventually explained every detail in an Immortal mating, including blood bonds and everything in between. The priestess grew more excited as she devoured the information while filling in the blanks of her current knowledge of Gefn's mating to Pothos. She also knew about the beast forms certain races of Immortals could take, but her information had been limited until Sirena explained them all.

She ignored the building need, enjoying her conversation with the priestess. Sirena hoped to find more mates for Immortals from Tetartos in Thule.

"You believe more of those in your world are compatible with those of Thule?"

"From the few blood samples I took from Kara's warriors, I would say yes. I would need to test more to be sure."

Mist's excitement only added to Sirena's.

A huge part of Sirena's duty had been finding mates for the Immortals of her world, usually in Mageia, mortals with elemental abilities, but even that was rare. Thule had actually opened up more chances for her to help her people, and theirs, because both worlds suffered low birthrates.

Mist was shaking her head. "This would be truly incredible."

Yes, now they just needed Earth to survive the final battle, which was a rather sobering thought.

Mist's silently processed it all and after a moment looked at Sirena. "So you and Hroarr will not share memories?"

Sirena shook her head. "No." It wouldn't happen unless she asked him to, and even then she wasn't sure he would do it.

Mist seemed to contemplate something for a while before she spoke almost reverently. "What Gefn and Pothos have is truly beautiful. Regin, Geiravor and I desperately want that for Hroarr, Sirena. He has always been the most powerful of our Gods, but with his strength came immense duty. It has been a burden that only he can bear and it has taken a toll. All he is driven by is duty to our world."

Sirena felt love coming through the bond from Mist; it was almost maternal. She had a moment of stillness as the warmth of that soft caring emotion from Mist was influencing her feelings toward the God just the tiniest of fractions. If nothing else, Sirena understood what it was like to be driven by duty, and having some kind of common ground with him was a start.

That meant she and the God had two things going for them. Sex and a mutual drive to protect their worlds. It could be worse.

Mist took a long indrawn breath before making some kind of decision. When the priestess continued, Sirena had a feeling Hroarr wouldn't appreciate her sharing personal information about him. "Hroarr's emotions are closed off from us, but even so, we *know* that pleasure and amusement are things he lost interest in centuries ago."

Sirena let that sink in. "Are you saying that he doesn't have lovers?"

Mist shook her head. "No. Not for centuries." Sirena felt altogether too much pleasure at the knowledge.

"Why are you telling me this?" Sirena asked.

There was no mistaking the hesitation. "Hroarr deserves to see beauty and passion in life, in the world he protects. He also deserves to feel true companionship and happiness, but I'm not sure he will know how." Icy blue eyes bored into Sirena. "You will need to show him how to *feel* again."

Chapter 24

Hroarr's Palace, Thule

The second Sirena closed the door after Mist's exit, she took a deep breath and went in search of her bag from the day before. After setting it down on the bed, she gazed at all the things Mist had left and shook her head. She wouldn't need any of the plugs or creams, so she sent them into the closet with a thought. She dug into the bag and found the jar she was looking for at the bottom.

She turned and sat for a moment, spinning the jar in her hand, thinking about everything Mist had shared about Hroarr.

Standing up, she released the black belt over her snug champagne-colored sweater. With shaky hands she unfastened the tiny buttons that ran down the front as she breathed into Hroarr's mind, *Come to me.* Her body was on fire for him, which meant it was time to finish this.

There was something gratifying about the way he appeared so quickly in front of her. His power licked over her skin as she took him in. He was sexy as hell with the leather clothing and boots. Even when he narrowed those emerald eyes at her, she wanted to climb his body. His heat was sliding over her skin as he demanded, "What is it, Sirena?"

His gaze had zeroed in on her fingers as they released the last delicate button. When it slipped free and she eased the snug material from her shoulders, his eyes stayed on her breasts. Her body responded to the possessive growl as she slid down the zipper from her high-waisted skirt and shimmied it down to step free of it. Gooseflesh rose over her oversensitive skin as his eyes devoured her, and raw heat pulsed through their bond.

"I'm ready to finish this," she breathed.

He kicked off his boots, his gaze nearly singeing off her high-waisted black garter belt and matching lacy panties.

"These items please me, but I want them off," he commanded and she unclasped her bra before reaching for the delicate straps and shrugging to let it fall at her feet.

She slowly unhooked the garters from her silk stockings and slipped the panties down first. She reveled in his harsh hiss as he watched her. He'd already tossed his shirt aside when she slipped from her high heels and lifted a leg to roll the soft material from her skin.

He was naked in seconds, lifting her up before she got to the garter belt, which was torn from her in a flash. Her legs wrapped around his waist as his lips claimed hers, demanding she part for him as he invaded her mouth. He ravaged the warm recess with fierce animalistic need and she mewled, dizzy with desire and the taste of her male. She pulled the tie from his hair and dug her fingers in as she matched each crazed thrust of his tongue, grinding her wet pussy against the stiff cock trapped between them. When he gripped her ass to slide her clit up and down, she broke the kiss, panting, "More."

Her nails dug into his shoulders, his muscles bunching for her as he held back from her. She groaned. "You don't need to be careful with me, Hroarr. I can take it."

Careful was the last thing her beast wanted; the clawing animal needed him as wild as she was for him.

"Where are the items Mist brought?" he demanded as the fingers of one big hand dug into the soft cheek of her ass while the other pulled her hair back. His head lowered and his tongue and teeth licked and bit at the vulnerable slope of her throat.

He ignited every nerve ending in her body and riled the beast to epic proportions. Before she knew it, his cock was at the entrance of her pussy, slamming her down hard, making her cry out at the raw pleasure of being filled. When his fingers moved down the crease of her ass to gather wetness from their joined bodies, she moaned. The second those thick digits slid back and pushed inside her, she was far too ready for what he would do. Her beast was going wild at being trapped and full of his cock with just the tip of his finger invading her ass, her throat exposed to his lips.

He snarled, "Where are they, Sirena? I will have you here." He pushed another finger inside her back entrance and she cried out at the bite of pleasure-pain.

She panted. "You won't need them."

He growled against her skin. "You enjoy pain, then, little one?"

How could she think, her eyes had rolled back in her head with his possession. "No."

"Then do not play games, Sirena."

"The jar." She was having a hard time breathing. He wasn't moving and she was desperate to come. *Use the cream inside me. And on you.* With the words she sent him a mental image of the jar on the bed.

He released her hair and she was suddenly looking into his eyes. "Good." And she felt his pleasure that they wouldn't have to wait to stretch her with toys.

In a flash he brought them down to the bed, covering her with his weight as he thrust hard and fast, his finger still inside her as she cried out, bucking and coming. He roared his pleasure to the ceiling and she couldn't look away from the sexy tendons of his neck as his warmth spilled inside her, pulling another climax from her pulsing body.

Why did she come every single time he did?

He moved his finger, but not his cock, and when his intense gaze met hers again, she was captured by the wildness there. She felt him fighting the need to stay inside her and her body responded by clenching, and there was no mistaking the sheer male satisfaction tearing through their bond.

They didn't speak or move as their breathing evened out, but after a moment she couldn't resist the desire to touch him, to feel his warmth against her palms.

When her fingers hesitantly moved over his back, the heavy muscle twitched and she swore their connection was getting stronger. She felt his pleasure at her touch as if it were her own and that sent a wave of desire running back through her body. One of her thighs slid over his hip until he throbbed inside her.

When he leaned down to capture her lips again, she fell into the magic of his kiss. He had talented lips and that thought brought up images of his head between her thighs. He'd spent a great deal of time devouring her and she loved every second of it.

He growled into her mouth as he rocked into her body. *You are mine to feast on, Sirena.*

Her legs gripped him and then she groaned in the bond, *I need you to finish this.* If he kept fucking her, she'd pass out before they ever ended this, and her body and beast needed them to complete what they'd started.

When he lifted away, she had to stifle the need to protest, but when he flipped her onto her stomach, she felt her heart slam against her chest. She was on fire for him and was definitely ready now. Pillows were pushed beneath her hips and she groaned as he sent her images of how she looked facedown in the bed with her ass up, inviting his invasion. She couldn't help but spread her thighs wider and he was definitely happy about that. His massive palm kneaded her ass before smacking it.

He showed her exactly how it looked as his come slid to her thighs. "I like my seed on you, Sirena. But I am more pleased when you hold it inside." Possessiveness hit her hard, and she closed her eyes as she listened to him twist the lid of the jar. When she felt him coat the cream over her back hole, she instinctively pushed back for more.

She wanted this. Her body needed it and she wouldn't deny it anymore.

She wasn't sure if Mist had eased her thoughts about the God or if the beast blood inside her was taking over, but it didn't matter.

"Let me in, *völur minn*," he commanded as one finger circled and pushed into the tight muscle there. He growled, "Relax and give me what I own."

His words made the beast blood hum and she swallowed. "Yes. More."

With a growl of approval, she felt him push two fingers inside of her. The cream was relaxing her muscles and taking away any pain, replacing it with supreme pleasure.

Her hips jerked back to take more of him. "I can take more."

Her fingers were digging into the bedding when his fingers left her. Her hips were undulating against the pillows as she panted, waiting for what seemed like a lifetime before she felt the head of his massive cock at her ass.

He slowly tunneled into her and it felt like too much and not enough all at once. When she turned her head to see the harsh look on his face, she groaned. His eyes were on his cock in her ass and every single muscle in his body looked tense. So much that she could feel his pain as he held himself at bay.

Her beast was losing its mind. “You will not hurt me. Hroarr, please,” she begged as she squeezed around him. He snarled when she pushed back, taking more than he was giving her. She sent him images of what she needed, of him holding her down and ramming his cock inside her until she bucked for more.

With a fierce snarl his body came down over hers, nearly covering her as he braced his hands at the sides of her head and slammed inside her.

“Yes.” She felt so full like that and she thought she’d die of need.

“Put your arms above your head,” he commanded and she obeyed because she needed this.

“You are mine, Sirena,” he growled and the words caused more clawing inside her. “Your pleasure belongs to me,” he snarled as he slammed into her. “You will accept *only* my cock.” He was ruling her beast, giving her everything she wanted as her body flowed with a blinding pleasure unlike anything before. “You exist to please me, Sirena.” She bucked against each violent thrust of his cock, loving the sound of his harsh grunts and the slapping of flesh against flesh.

The room smelled of sex and she was drunk with it.

When he moved back and pushed her thighs tight together, she felt her body gripping his cock tighter. She loved his hiss of pleasure so much she couldn't help but push back for more, and then he settled his bulk over her back until she shuddered with excitement and need. His massive thighs caged her legs while trapping his cock inside her, and she thought she'd come from that alone. Then he rocked his hips, pushing her into the pillows. One hand slid under her to circle her aching clit and the other collared her neck, lifting it back until she was caged and forced to accept anything he would give, and she lost her mind. She was completely dazed as he powered in and out, his hips tunneling hard and fast, with his beard against her cheek as every inch of his big body commanded hers.

She came so hard her vision dotted with black and her entire body tensed and pulsed around him until her hand reached back to grip the side of his neck, needing to touch, to feel those strong tendons as they tightened with his pleasure. He slammed down against her ass and snarled her name, but the second she felt the warm jets of come, a whirlwind of power flared from them both until she was wildly ensnared by his sjá.

Its brilliant light was both beautiful and terrifying while isolating and encompassing her in warmth.

Suddenly flashes came flying at her at the speed of light, yet she could see and understand it all.

She was shown Hroarr as a baby and felt the moment the blinding purity of his Creator father hovered above him. There was no mistaking the love as the being gifted Hroarr with a piece of himself. A sacrifice. Instant knowledge flooded his small body. Duty surged inside him with clarity that no baby should know. The tattoo she'd seen on his back was from his father. It was the mark of his power, his sjá, and the emotion coming from the Great Being as he gifted it was full of such pure encompassing love that she nearly fell to her knees from the sheer beauty of it.

Later she saw him as a child God with his *þrír*; Mist, Regin and Geiravor were all doting on him.

She felt his affection for them as if it were her own.

Another flash showed his sister Gefn and her *þrír*. The small girl was playing and rolling around with the mystical cats who held a piece of Hroarr's mother. Both Great Beings had given of themselves to champion Thule. To give their world a chance to survive the Destroyer that would come for them. His sister smiled up at him with such trust and joy.

Love.

Then she watched him spend decades traveling from world to world, seeing birth and death so many times it wore on his mind and soul. Knowledge of those worlds filled him and now her. The dangers of technology. Of Gods and mortals bloated with power. Destruction ravaging worlds before the Darkness ever even came for them. She felt his constant fury at the arrogance and ignorance of those who ruled through pain and fear. Over and over it was the same until it turned to numbness. He would return to Thule and let the elements replenish him every time, taking days to recover from the drain of his special ability.

She was there when Hroarr came home to Thule to see the death and destruction wrought by his brothers. He was enraged to learn that his brother Tyr had decided to harness the power of the Gods and priestesses for his own purposes.

She saw him setting protections for his siblings before traveling the worlds with renewed force, seeking a way to fix the damage Tyr had caused in Thule.

Each time he used his sjá, more numbness seeped into his soul. It felt as if his power had been trying to protect him, yet it slowly stole his ability to feel more than echoes of true emotion.

Her heart was racing with the bombardment of knowledge. His power was a living thing, just like her beast or the beasts of her brethren.

It wanted her to understand. To help him.

The cats somehow directed his attention to a world that held a special metal that could be used to imprison his siblings while being the perfect weapon against the Darkness. Anything held within the material could not be touched by the Destroyer, a fact he learned when opening a box from that world and finding a bit of magic held inside. She felt a faint echo of pleasure at his find.

Then he returned to have the prisons built.

Later he was drawn to his sister's palace. She felt Hroarr's rage when he found Gefn's dead *þrír* and his sister at the mercy of their evil brothers.

She watched him capture and imprison each of his siblings, caging them into the weapons with Kara, Gefn and Dagur's help.

More dead worlds.

Flames against the toxins that seeped from his siblings into Thule. More decades passed with only numbness and duty residing inside him.

She felt that void and it actually hurt a part of her soul.

She suddenly knew that he used the emotion filtering from his *þrír* to remind him of what he *should* feel. Just as the old tomes and artifacts were a warning of what could happen if his sense of duty was lost.

She felt the way his mind worked; it was so logical and cunning. Only flickers of emotion leeched in. Like the hint of disgust he'd experienced when he'd met Apollo, her father reminded him of his brother Tyr.

And then he felt her healing power when she'd come to help the cats.

Suddenly he started feeling flickers of *need* for the first time in centuries.

When he saw her in his bathroom, he was slammed with a possessiveness so strong it jarred him, until he craved her with a certainty, a primal knowledge that overloaded all logic. He'd needed to have her no matter the cost.

She'd made him *feel* after thousands of years.

She felt the pleasure of when he was inside her or tasting her. It had been so strong for him it was nearly painful at first and he became more addicted each time they touched.

Mist was right; all he knew was that he wanted her and craved her power and body and would never let her go. But he didn't understand any of the feelings, so he allowed instinct to rule where she was concerned.

A lot of that had to do with her beast pushing to connect with him, it had to be. Her animal craved his dominance and now it seemed Sirena was addicted to it as well. What he did to her was beyond pleasure, it was pure euphoria that she'd never known existed.

Whether he knew it or not, they truly belonged to one another.

He was hers.

Chapter 25

Hroarr's Palace, Thule

The second Hroarr felt his hot seed spill into his female, power rippled through the room. Her warm healing power streamed through his body, nearly making him come again, but it was his sjá surging free in a wild rush that nearly stopped his heart. Battle rage slammed into him as worry for Sirena had him fighting the power back. It would not relent, it sucked him under as it always did, but this time he wouldn't be shown the birth of a world.

This time it was his female's life flying before him.

A beautiful blonde female cried as she held her baby tight. Sirena's mother holding her as a newborn.

Later the same female was whispering words of love to the tiny bundle as she secreted down a dark tunnel. A blast rocked the entire space and it began to collapse around her. Fire surged wildly through to them until all he heard were screams as she held the child and filtered all her healing ability into the infant to keep her safe, kissing her until the flames had gone and the mother lay half crushed and burned, barely breathing.

Sirena was crying when rock and dirt filtered down and finally a male came into view. A mortal. The female looked up as if expecting him. She weakly lifted her baby up and begged, "Take her to Aphrodite. *Please*." The mother's tears slipped to the dirt-covered floor until everything stopped and the female was dead. The male lifted the child up and carried her away, hearing the final collapse of the tunnel as he carried the baby to a boat. The sea took them to an island housing a palace of gold. Guards met him at the banks and he knelt with the child.

A blonde Goddess, Aphrodite, appeared dressed in white with a golden crown. She lifted the child into her arms before casting a spell on the mortal and sending him away confused. She did the same with her own guards as the Goddess' bright blue eyes assessed the infant and then cast a spell to mask the baby's power before carrying her away.

He watched as his female grew older in the palace of gold, alongside a young Drake and Pothos. The bond between the three was as close as siblings. He watched her worry over Pothos' struggle to maintain his power to enthrall. Something no one of Earth would have truly understood, as the power was that of Pothos' Thulian mother, which was something Hroarr could feel even through these memories.

He saw her love for her brothers and felt her loneliness and isolation.

When she was fifteen summers, the Goddess finally told her about her mother's death and that she was Apollo's daughter.

He felt the weight of her father's blood settle on her slim shoulders. Apollo was hated on Earth; he abducted any Immortal he could find in their world. It was only safe for her to stay within the confines of Aphrodite's palace.

He watched her enter secret meetings with Drake, Pothos and some other males he had never seen. They were planning to call their Creators back, against the wishes of Hades and Aphrodite.

Sirena honed her healing skills and worked spells as best she could to help those they rescued from Apollo's island.

He saw so much, the Creators of their world coming and deeming her a Guardian of their world; he watched her constant battle to atone for the horrors of her father and half-brother. Drake and Pothos futilely badgering her to rest. She lived for her constant work, day and night, until exhaustion forced her to renew her energies in a lonely cavern.

He saw her bond with the Guardians and felt her shame when they learned she was Apollo's daughter. He vibrated with protectiveness until they embraced and accepted her wholeheartedly.

Work and duty was her life. He saw her meeting and convincing mortals with magical power to come to the Immortal Realm of their world. He understood it all. Everything about the confinement spell by their Creators, the sleeping Gods, and how the mating spell came to prevent Immortals from birthing children with anyone but their soul mate.

He felt his female's worry.

Centuries of her healing Immortals or her brethren.

He even saw her battling at their sides; her power to stop organs had saved hundreds of mortals. She was a healer but would kill, if needed, to protect the world or those she cared for.

He saw births of babies. Mating ceremonies with her brethren, where she funneled her power through the pairs in order to mark them. He watched over and over as she helped them with their mates and felt genuine joy for her family. Yet all the while his female accepted that she would never have the same. Both his female and her beast blood would only accept a more powerful male.

This pleased him immensely because she had been waiting for him. As his power released him from the visions of her life, it was to find that he was still inside her body. Only moments had passed.

He slid from her to lay at her side as she sucked in a deep breath. When she turned to her back, she was breathing hard and so was he.

"How long was I out?" she asked, shaking her head.

"Not long. You woke right after I did."

His first real look at her sent a growl from his lips. He quickly lifted her into his arms and tilted her neck to see the small marking on the side of her throat; it glowed gold in the shape of his dragon insignia, the eye of the beast.

His sjá.

Yet inside the triple triangles that were marked by a Y in the center was the mark he'd seen her use with mated couples of her world. Three sets of twin dragons in the shape of an eight and held together by their tails filled in the space of each triangle. This was a branding of his power that said for all the worlds that she belonged to him and him alone, which satisfied him deeply.

"What is it?" she asked when he examined his symbol on her smooth skin.

"My power has marked you, little one."

Her eyes shot to his, her mouth open as her gaze moved to his neck, her finger lifting to trace something warm on his skin as she frowned. "What does mine look like, Hroarr?"

He sent her the image of what he was seeing.

She sucked in a breath before confirming, "You have the same mark. It's a mix of the symbol on your back and the mating mark of my world."

He commanded, "It is the mark given to me by my parents. Show me."

When he saw it, he was shocked, but not displeased.

She took a deep breath and nodded. "These aren't from my power, Hroarr."

He smiled down at her. "I believe they are from our combined power, *völur minn*."

After long moments she asked him, "Why were you unconscious?"

"My power was showing me your life, little one."

She looked into his eyes. "It showed me yours as well."

He wondered what exactly his sjá had shown her as he stared down at her through new eyes. The bond between them had tightened, he could feel it. He felt different emotions running through him now, possessive and protective, but also a sense of pride after *seeing* her. His power had marked her, claimed her. It was a power too intense, too immense, for anyone but him, yet it had reached for her twice and now had branded her as its own.

He silently lifted her into his arms and carried her into the bathing room. Her hand moved from his neck to hers, and even as he washed her skin, she didn't speak. He quickly rinsed his own body before lifting her back up and carrying her into the pool. When the soothing waters slid over her skin, she moaned and relaxed further into his hold. She seemed to be lost in thought as he felt the immense need to care for her.

He sat with her in his lap.

Everything had changed. He suddenly felt clearer than he had ever felt. His possessive instincts hadn't abated, but he could think again.

He closed his eyes, still holding her.

He felt… at peace.

Chapter 26

Hroarr's Palace, Thule

What Sirena had shared with Hroarr the day before had changed things for them, and now they were both trying to figure it out. She could feel his struggle with understanding all the emotions rolling through him in new blinding clarity.

Instead of talking about it after his power had marked them, she decided to give him time to get adjusted to it. He'd carried her from the healing water and made slow love to her for the first time and then he'd left to work on the prisons with Dagur. All the while she felt him struggling and couldn't do anything but let him figure it out. He'd been numb for centuries and he deserved some time to deal with it in his own way.

Instead of lying there alone last night, she'd gone to see the baby and made time for a glass of wine with Brianne and Sacha, sharing her new mark with them. She liked it and felt oddly proud of it. When she'd returned to Thule last night, he'd blown her mind in bed, but she'd woken up in bed alone again, which wasn't starting her day well.

They both had duties and he was determined as hell to get the prisons done as quickly as possible. She could respect that. She should be grateful, but a part of her craved his warmth.

She got up and dressed, dreading the day to come.

Quickly tracking Drake and the others, she knew exactly what had them gathering in one place. Sacha and Brianne had told her what they'd all planned to do today.

This was the day they would put her father away for all eternity.

She steeled her nerves and ported to the cavern system.

The dim stone walls shook with power as Sirena heard voices coming from the cavern at the end.

"You cannot do this." The autocratic voice was filled with power and she instinctually knew it was her father, and that alone made her stomach twist. She stilled for only a second to catch her breath before moving closer to the cavern holding her brethren.

What is it? Hroarr demanded, obviously feeling her upset.

Nothing. I'm fine, she assured him.

The clicking of her high heels against the stone sounded almost deafening to her ears as she fought the hatred and odd hollowness she felt for the male she would finally see.

I can feel it is not fine, he growled and his voice in her mind actually made her less nervous about what she was about to face in the cavern ahead.

She assured him, *It will be fine.* A part of her wished she'd stayed in their bed.

Forcing back her nerves, she stepped into the cavern and felt all eyes on her. Brianne smiled and moved toward her. Vane was at her sister's back with a wink for Sirena as Brianne sent, *Are you sure you want to be here? You've never wanted to see the asshole and there's no reason for you to be here now.* The reminder that her brother and sister Guardians had never held her blood against her quickly relaxed her.

It's time I face what I've been fighting against.

Brianne nodded slowly, her wild red hair shifting as she leaned in and grabbed Sirena's hand and squeezed it in support.

A quick glance showed all the Gods up front with Drake and P and their mates. Hades' wings were unfurled and flexing as he informed Apollo of his fate. There was no missing his blatant pleasure at sending Apollo away for good. She noticed Sacha turn to her and Sirena felt her sister's warm greeting through their telepathic link.

Sirena felt Aphrodite's stare, and when she looked up, the Goddess nodded and winked.

At Aphrodite's left was the Goddess Athena and her male, Niall. Though Sirena'd never seen them, they were unmistakable both in power and the female's striking resemblance to Alex. The Goddess was far taller than her daughter, over six foot, but the seriousness and power coming from both her and her warrior male were immense and incredible.

Without looking, she knew all the Guardians, mates, Alex's brother Erik, and his female, Sam, were all there. It seemed the only ones missing were Gefn's cats, Alyssa, little Lucy, and Conn's wolf in-laws, who were likely busy working on hacking Earth's emergency systems.

Her eyes met Gregoire's. His massive bulk was tense as he nodded at her. She was surprised to see him there, but knew so many of her brethren had suffered at her father's hand and would likely *need* to see him put away forever. Finally. Her heart ached for the male as she smiled reassuringly at him.

The top of the eight-foot-high prison was visible beyond the taller warriors and she was struck by the familiarity of the power built into the Thulian runes etched all over it. The cylinder was split in two, showing the hollow opening, and the edges glowed with blue Creator power siphoned from one of the stasis units. That bit of power would be used to make a permanent seal. If this worked.

She moved on shaky legs to stand between Brianne and Bastian, listening to Apollo argue and taunt Hades as she got the first look at her father.

Apollo was kneeling beneath the weight of a golden net infused with Thulian power, and just seeing him made bile rise in her throat. This was the male who had ruled her life even though she'd never set her eyes on him. Her life and duty had been formed in order to somehow atone for his sins.

Suddenly she felt wild furious power and warmth as Hroarr appeared behind her, pulling her into his side as he assessed the situation through narrow rage-filled eyes. His crackling waves of power rocked the cavern beneath their feet. Thankfully there had to be a spell holding the walls in place or the mountain would have come down around him.

Everything happened in a split second.

Pothos' power lashed out and enthralled the instantly battle-ready Goddesses, who had never met Hroarr, and she was grateful for P's speed. The Goddesses and their mates likely saw Hroarr's presence as a threat.

Especially as furious and protective as the God was right now. Her brethren gave them a wide berth while watching her closely. Many had never met Hroarr, but they did know of him. All talk stopped and she instantly sank into Hroarr's touch and put her hand on his chest to calm him.

What are you doing here? She wasn't angry as much as surprised and grateful for his warmth, she'd needed it.

You were upset. It displeased me, he growled after his eyes had taken in everything and landed on her father with barely leashed power.

"Release your power now, Pothos," Athena commanded. "And tell us who this is?" Both sets of Goddesses and their mates were beyond furious that Pothos had trapped them in his thrall.

Hades' voice commanded the room. "This is Hroarr, ruling God of Thule and Sirena's mate." A second passed before Hades growled, "Calm down, sisters. The God is our ally." The Gods were obviously aware of Hroarr, considering the fact that they were standing in front of a prison weapon he'd created.

"Why choose now to meet our *ally*?" Niall growled.

Hades' eyes were on her and Hroarr, and he smirked before turning to address his sister's mate. "Don't flatter yourself, brother. He's here for Sirena, not you. In fact, I believe he couldn't care less about anyone else in here."

Apollo looked up at Hroarr and she heard him hissing in recognition. Then he attempted to barter with her powerful mate for his freedom and it not only disgusted and angered her, it embarrassed her, when it shouldn't.

She didn't even know the male, but when his eyes landed on her, he seemed to jolt under the metal net covering him. His eyes were assessing, the violet color a match to her own, his hair was dark to her light, but she could see his moment of recognition. "You are my daughter," he accused before a spark of glee entered the God's gaze. "You cannot put me in this weapon. I am your father. Would you put your own blood away for all eternity?"

"You do not address her, ever!" Hroarr growled and the entire room rocked with her male's fury, and flames suddenly trailed over Apollo's entire body. The God screeched until she siphoned the power back. Her male hadn't intended to kill Apollo, but there was deadly threat in Hroarr's next words. "Do I make myself clear, Apollo?"

She sent her male calming emotion as she watched Apollo twitch while his flesh knitted back into place.

She swore she heard a female, Nastia, excitedly cheering for more.

Suddenly she saw her father for what he truly was. Pathetic. After centuries of trying to make up for his horrors, she found a God who needed to pay for his own crimes. Her father only had power over her because she'd allowed it, and she refused to do that anymore. She was a Guardian because she had a sense of honor and decency he would never know or understand.

Ignoring everything else, she lifted her eyes to her male's. When Hroarr's gaze came down to meet hers, she felt so much protectiveness toward her that she smiled and sent something far sweeter to him: appreciation and affection so strong it jolted his body, and then he was holding her tighter. After sighing, she sank into his hold and explained what she needed, *Just stand with me while I do what I need to. No more fire.*

After a moment he nodded.

She turned her eyes to Drake. "Are you done with Apollo?"

The dragon growled, "Yes."

When she looked down into the cold, furious eyes of Apollo, she said, "I have spent my life atoning for the fact that your blood runs in my veins. You're a monster, Apollo, and it's time you pay for your crimes against this world and those in it."

The God's mouth opened, but he looked at Hroarr and he shut it again, wisely. She sent a breath of telekinetic ability with a flick of her wrist and slammed Apollo into the prison. The God's angry roars echoed in the room as Hroarr infused her strength, and Apollo's body shot upright against the back of the cylinder before the net was ripped and all of her brethren used their own abilities to slam the heavy metal shut, silencing Apollo in the powerful casing.

The magical runes etched into it glowed brilliant gold against the dark rock.

The beautiful glowing blue seam ran around it and she felt the Gods and Goddess along with her brethren infuse the runes with elemental magic from Earth. Her hair rose with the electric charge in the room as finally Drake released the spell that sealed the power with the touch of the glowing key imbedded in his palm.

Magic rocked the entire room as Apollo was trapped forever.

When it all settled, Hades stood with his hands on his hips. "Now to see if it works."

She felt Hroarr's confidence in that fact as he held her to his side, and she smiled. This test was needed, after the modifications they'd made to the seal, to ensure they could still access an imprisoned God's power.

Athena, Hades and Aphrodite all stepped forward using the ancient language and the entire room charged with power until, with a loud roar, brilliant white energy surged up through the rock and dirt. It felt incredibly pure and contained.

It worked and the sense of relief in the room was palpable.

Just as quickly as it was unleashed, the Gods said more ancient words and the light was sucked back into the casing with a wild rush.

Hades was smiling brilliantly at the end. "It will do." And his smug smirk made its way to her male, but Hroarr ignored her arrogant uncle.

When she turned to talk to Hroarr, everything seemed to still and then Gregoire snarled, "Mother fuck." The massive male staggered to a knee before disappearing right before their eyes.

The room erupted in noise and 'what the fucks' as they all mentally tuned to the Guardian's location in their links.

It stopped at the manor and Gregoire's voice growled through the Guardian link, *Lucy pulled me to her and Alyssa. Something isn't right.*

Sirena's heart stilled as she ported away.

Chapter 27

Guardian Manor, Tetartos Realm

Everyone appeared in a large living room in the manor. Chairs were overturned and there was a singed hole in the wall letting in cool mountain air. That wasn't what had them all entranced, it was the wild bubble of intense swirling power holding not only Alyssa, Gregoire and Lucy on the couch but also Spa and Velspar at Alyssa's feet. The beasts seemed oddly serene lying there as both parents ran their hands over their daughter's head and stomach. "It's okay, princess. Papa is here," Gregoire rumbled. "Nothing will hurt you or your mama."

Sirena felt Hroarr's warmth at her back and his presence soothed her more than she'd like to admit. She was worried about what this meant and started forward slowly.

Before she could take that first step, she and Hroarr were gripped in the power and forcibly pulled into the bubble directly in front of the baby.

Hroarr gritted out, "What is this?"

Gregoire looked up and Sirena knew her brother Guardian was one second from losing his damned mind at having Hroarr anywhere this close to the baby. No one touched her, at least not when Gregoire was near. She and Hroarr stared down into Lucy's frowning face and were entranced when her tiny frown turned into a beautiful smile as she reached chubby hands up to them. The bubble released with a pop of power that rocked through the room and calmed Sirena's heart rate.

She felt sorry for Gregoire as he glared at Hroarr, his power mounting. *Do not touch the baby, Hroarr. Gregoire is incredibly possessive of his female and his young.*

As he should be, Hroarr returned, his eyes still on the sweet face smiling up at him until he tilted his head, his eyes warming. He didn't smile, but she felt her male's approval and... amusement at the baby's actions. After a moment he stepped back and nodded respectfully to Gregoire and calmly stated with blatant approval, "She is a very special child."

Sirena stood there in shock as she watched, feeling the lightness in her male. He liked the baby, Lucy's magic having had the same effect on all of them. Special might have been an understatement.

Uri's urgent voice suddenly filled the severe silence of the room. "I'm getting telepathic reports of mass hell beast attacks in all Tetartos cities."

"Conn?!" Drake snarled.

"On it," the wolf said as he looked off, obviously sending a telepathic call to his in-laws that were in his office. The Lykos was the one who dealt with Mageia reports of demon possessed on Earth. The wolf nodded after a second. "Hagen and the other wolves are fielding messages now. We have demon possessed in five major cities on Earth so far."

"We need those prisons, Hroarr," the dragon gritted out.

Hroarr nodded before turning to her.

She looked up at him. *I need to stay close and ease Gregoire and*

Alyssa.

He was waging an emotional war about leaving her there, but finally growled, knowing he was going to let her stay. The information on attacks had not pleased him, but he also knew he needed to get the prisons done. He lifted her up and kissed her, demanding entrance into her mouth and making her insane for him before setting her down on wobbly heels. His intention was clear, he was marking her as his own in front of her family while fighting the desire to carry her home with him. She was still dizzy with pleasure when he disappeared.

Sirena's cheeks flushed bright as she looked around the room. Thankfully, Drake was already barking commands to the others. She was only called out when forces were thin, but she didn't want to be a world away if that happened.

"I guess this means the Tria know about Aphrodite and Athena's presence, or maybe they were just in the mood to fuck shit up," Jax growled.

Gregoire snarled, "Language, cat!"

Jax just shook his head.

Sirena smiled a little, but she didn't feel good about any of it.

Chapter 28

Heaven, Earth

After days of constant battles and getting Gods in prisons, Sirena stood looking down at the serene blue lake glistening in a valley nestled beneath green mountains. The Realm of Pure Souls had a beautiful soothing magic. Flickering blue and white lights flitted beneath the blue spelled dome covering the entire lake that prevented souls from getting out and hell beasts from getting in.

Would they one day be able to take the dome down, or would the coming Darkness prevail and consume them all? She didn't like thinking about that, it didn't serve any purpose.

The last few days since Apollo's final imprisonment had been a rush of constant work and battles.

Hroarr and Dagur had managed to create four more prisons, of which Drake and the Gods had gotten Ares, Artemis, Poseidon and Hermes safely locked away. They were scattered into the highest spelled mountain caverns of Earth Realm. Each imprisonment had perpetuated a mass of beast and possessed attacks, but so far they'd had few injuries and no casualties.

Sirena took a deep breath before porting down to the banks of the lake. Looking down, she saw the female lying beneath the waves, her iridescent Nereid tail barely flitting in the waves. Her blonde hair flowed around her as Charybdis stared into the blue skies above.

Sirena had long ago tasked Uri and Alex with trying to help heal the female, but her catatonic state wasn't only because her mind had fractured, but that a huge portion of her soul was missing. The stream of pure souls that moved through the waters had seemed to ease the female for all the millennia she'd rested here.

This was Apollo's doing. This was her father's legacy. He'd taken an Immortal who'd already been abused and tormented by Poseidon, at one point left chained to the bottom of the sea, and instead of caring for her, Apollo had experimented on her. He had tormented and bred her until she couldn't bear to lose another child to his warrior camps. She'd used a portion of her own soul to create the mating spell, preventing any more Immortals from breeding for his army. Now, only those with the bond could produce young.

She kneeled at the water's edge, leaning over to put a hand in the female's. "Apollo can never harm anyone again, Charybdis. His power is finally going to be used to protect this world." Whether he wanted it to or not.

She continued speaking, adding power into her voice in hopes it would do something for the Nereid who'd sacrificed so much for the Immortal races. She told her more, about the prisons and how they would be used to save their world.

The female blankly stared up into the sky, but Sirena swore she felt the female's hand tighten a fraction, though it was likely her imagination. Sirena had spent millennia trying to find a way to help her, but nothing worked. Even Hades' power over souls wasn't capable of regenerating one.

After sitting there for long moments, Sirena finally stood.

Hroarr was suddenly there with her. Anytime she was upset or angry, he would come. Many times he would merely assess the situation and leave before she'd even spoken.

She smiled, because her God was learning to feel, just as Mist had hoped.

*****

Hroarr felt his Sirena's sadness and was drawn to her. The last few days had been a war with duty and his growing *need* not just to possess, but to ease this female who'd changed his world.

Seeing her past, her life, had changed things. He respected her, yet she still challenged him. He allowed her to do what he felt she needed, but refused to allow her to work to exhaustion. He allowed her only the same amount of hours that he worked, though he found himself forcing the tasks to completion because the prisons needed to be finished quickly. Any time he could demand they break free, even for an hour, he did, spending the time sharing his favorite places in Thule. Showing her the new world she now belonged to.

The Darkness would come far too soon. The spell his brother had cast to detect its distance had failed, and Dagur had sent another one out the day before.

Hroarr didn't like it.

He came to Sirena's side, looking down at the female floating in the water. He'd seen the female in Sirena's memories.

Sirena looked up at him. "Aren't you supposed to be working on more prisons?"

The urge to touch her was always so strong and he pulled her into him as he spoke. "I just delivered two more. Dagur is finishing the runes on the last now." His own tasks were nearly complete. He would deliver the units once his brother was finished.

Her eyes widened as she gazed up at him. "That was fast."

"It needed to be," he pointed out.

She nodded in agreement.

"Why are you here, Sirena?" Though he thought he knew the answer, he wanted it from her lips.

"Did you see Charybdis in my memories?" she asked him.

"Yes."

"I wanted her to know Apollo would never be free again." The Guardians had been keeping the female's life a secret from the Immortals of their world. Sirena had always felt driven to save the female who had given up everything to save all of the Immortal races from eternal torment at Apollo's hands.

"You believe she knows what you say?"

She nodded and he could feel her sadness again. "I hope so. Why are you here?"

He looked down at the female for long moments. Instead of killing Charybdis to see if the mating spell would die with her, Sirena had found a way to help those of her world while caring for this broken Immortal. His caring healer had made it her life's work to end her father's horrible legacy without destroying whenever possible.

He had hours before Dagur would be done and he wished to spend time with her. "Show me your world, Sirena."

She looked up at him with a hint of pleasure that turned to uncertainty. "There will be attacks again the second Drake puts another God in a prison."

"Then do it quickly."

She was struggling as much as he had been to find balance between duty and desire. She breathed out before making her decision. "Just for a moment." Her small hands came to his, their fingers twining together until she was taking him somewhere.

When they reformed, she was smiling up at him and the look on her face made his cock twitch.

It was hard to tear his eyes from hers.

She smiled up at him. "This is my home. We're in the city of Paris in the mortal Realm."

He narrowed his eyes and growled at that. Her home was with him.

"Let me rephrase, this is a home I own. Does that please you?" She was mocking him as she grinned. His healer had not only taken over his bed, choosing to sleep with her face in his neck, but she'd burrowed into his mind and made him *feel* again. This one small female had healed his soul and even his power had marked her as its own. She was becoming the center of his world.

He set a thumb on her red lip, pleased at the way she sucked in a breath. He found he craved her smiles. Her control over him should be infuriating, yet he found she only pleased him.

Her eyes heated when he pulled her closer into his chest. "Show me, Sirena."

Her eyes sparkled for him as she pulled away, showing him framed pictures of half-dressed females in shining black frames. Her furniture was small with soft fabrics and a lot of the color red. The noises of her city slipped from the now open balcony doors. When she led him out to the cool night air, she spoke of her favorite things: shoes, movies, wine.

All the technology he prevented in Thule was here to see in the masses. These were the things that destroyed many worlds. They usually led to mass destruction before the Darkness ever came.

"You don't like it?" she said without any upset. It was merely a statement made with curiosity.

He stared down at her. It was different seeing a city this way, but he preferred the magic that filled Thule. "What pleases you about this place?"

She smiled. "Nice evasion."

She turned, still twining his hand in hers. When they were inside, she moved through different rooms until they were in her bedchamber. Pale blankets covered her bed, with one red one and a mass of deep crimson curtains bunched on either side of another balcony. She grabbed a small black box and pushed buttons until the curtains closed and a thin white material lowered from the ceiling.

"This is what I like best," she admitted before crawling up into her bed and patting a hand on the area beside her. His eyes moved to her still-clothed body and he felt his cock respond.

She warned, "No, Hroarr, do not burn my clothes off. We don't have time for sex. I could be called to work at any moment."

His eyes shot to hers and he was pleased by the way her breathing had changed; even her eyes had dilated in the dark. Curiosity moved him to lay beside her as the screen lit with images. A villain with bloody blades and a scarred face was terrifying the humans he chased and taunted.

She laid her head on his chest to watch the scene while sharing, "When you saw my office and frowned at the busts I had in the cases, this was what I was trying to explain. This is a movie. A very bad one." Her laughter vibrated against his chest. Something about what they were doing made her happy in a way he hadn't felt. It wasn't the pleasure of his touch, it was different. He'd found her monster infatuation odd, yet he would not deny her this.

He rubbed his hand over her hip as they lay silently watching the screen.

All too soon he growled at Drake's voice through her Guardian link: *Be ready. Zeus is going into his box.* Hroarr had long been intercepting her mental communications with other Guardians. The access to their information satisfied him, but he did not enjoy that others were touching her mind as he could. His more primal instincts obviously were still there, only now he was better able to control them.

When she sighed and moved to get up, he pulled her down for a deep kiss that made her body melt against his chest. One of her hands slid to his hard cock and he growled at his teasing female.

Another Guardian signaled, *We've got hell beasts in every fucking city.*

She snuggled into him for several moments, both delaying their duties for just a little longer.

Chapter 29

Hroarr's Palace, Thule

Sirena reformed in their bedroom, stretching her arms above her head.

It had been a tense few days since showing Hroarr her Paris home. She and her mate had been connecting at an entirely new level that made her happy, but the stress of duty had weighed on them both. They'd barely had any time to truly enjoy each other and the new bond between them due to her commitments on Earth. His tasks with the prisons had been done days ago, so he'd insisted on helping her world and stealing hours together whenever possible. After Paris, he'd demanded to see all of Earth and its Realms and he'd shown her the beautiful magic of Thule in short trips. She smiled at his relentless determination to convince her to love his world.

He'd succeeded in that task, she did love her new home, but that didn't mean she loved Earth less.

She shook off her amusement, looking forward to whatever he planned today now that she finally had more than just a few hours. The last of the nine Gods was now encased in her new prison and the Guardians had just finished dealing with the ensuing aggression from the Tria. They were all hoping for a reprieve of a day or two before Drake took steps to contain the evil three.

Now all she wanted was to see her male and re-energize.

Sirena rolled her neck.

She knew for a fact that Hroarr had gone out with Hades several times to kill hell beasts and deal with possessed while she'd been healing injuries or watching over Lucy. Her male was a force of nature and she appreciated how he'd been helping. Only once had he had to take care of toxins in Thule.

Taking a deep breath, she relaxed as the magic of Thule infused her depleted energy stores until her strength was quickly renewed. There was something about this world that made it a seamless experience. That meant either come to Thule or go sit in a cavern in Earth and meditate until she felt energized.

It wasn't a difficult choice.

When she turned to their bed, she smiled a little to herself. Over the days she'd come home to a great deal of changes to their space. First the pin-up art from her home in Paris had mysteriously found their way to the wall beside his bed.

The next day blankets that looked very much like the ones from her room found their way in. She knew they couldn't be hers because his massive God-sized bed was larger than the one she used to sleep in.

When she saw the newest change, her smile widened. She honestly thought he couldn't outdo himself after the gift he'd given her yesterday. A glance at the shelves by his fireplace made her lips twitch, the heinous monster face staring back at her through red eyes had been yesterday's perfect gem. It wasn't real, but a replica like those of her B movie busts. She laughed as the creature glared at her, looking very much like the werewolf of London. It held a special place next to his artifacts and a few busts from her office.

Now it seemed her God had actually found time to go and bring her something else she loved. Sirena's eyes were at the foot of the bed and she felt her stomach flutter in excitement. His new gesture had to have taken time and magic because electricity was not the same in Thule. But if you were a determined God with a brother skilled in spell casting, you could apparently make anything happen. The sight of her projector and screen meant he would be forced to watch her terrible movies with her every night before bed. She actually laughed out loud because she knew he would deeply regret this decision in the years to come.

He'd definitely made this a home she felt comfortable in.

He might never say the words, but she felt the depth of his affection for her in their bond. The sweet gestures only strengthened her feelings for him. He more than cared for her, and if she were being honest, she'd admit that she more than cared for him as well.

Feeling lighter and more relaxed than she had when she'd arrived, she tracked his location and teleported from the room, needing to see him, to be in his arms.

When she reformed, it was in his office. A glance said that he was alone behind the desk. Shelves of old tomes and artifacts rose up the two stories of the wall behind him. Her male was looking at her, papers in front of him forgotten. His eyes trailed over her face at first warm with affection and then heating to an inferno as she stalked toward him.

She trailed her fingers over his desk as she sauntered around it. He pushed the chair back as she stopped to slowly shimmy the tight pencil skirt up over her ass in order to climb over his thighs to straddle his lap.

She leaned in and took his lips. *Thank you for my gift.*

He instantly took command of her lips, fisting her hair, moving her head where he wanted her. *Show me how much it pleased you, völur minn.*

She circled her hips against his leather-covered cock.

Her fingers moved to his fly, and she trailed the back of her knuckles over the hard bulge before releasing him. She didn't tease for long, she was already too eager for him, which seemed to be their norm.

She slid her panties to the side and gripped him in her fist to guide him in. He groaned into her mouth as she slid down, moaning into their link. Rough hands pushed her sweater and bra above her breasts until his palms found her swollen flesh, plumping them before pinching her hard nipples. She moved on him, becoming wild as he ruled her body.

He broke the kiss and ordered, "You will come all over me, Sirena."

His hand went back to her hair and pulled it back to expose her throat and her mating mark to his lips. He sucked and licked the sensitive symbol until she cried out her release, bucking on him until he came inside her.

After the tremors subsided, her forehead met his in relaxed bliss.

His hands caressed her back, keeping her in place. She breathed through the dizzying pleasure in knowing what he was feeling at that moment. Smiling, she lifted her head away to look into his eyes, "Do you understand what it is you're feeling right now?"

One cocky brow rose as he rumbled, "I do."

His hands moved to her ass and squeezed as he watched her

closely.

"Would it make it easier for my big Thulian God if I told him I loved him first?" She asked knowing her eyes were twinkling with amusement.

The deep satisfaction he felt from her words made her laugh.

"I am pleased you finally admit it, *völur minn*." There was enough arrogance mixed with pleasure that she playfully nipped his lower lip.

"And." She prompted.

He grunted, "You can feel what I do, Sirena."

She smiled wide, "And yet I'd like to hear it."

With a growl he pulled her down for a devastating kiss while sharing, *Yes,* völur minn, *I love you*.

She smiled against his lips, happy to finally hear the words. When the kiss broke he snuggled her against his chest, both completely content to stay like that forever.

They were so caught up in the moment that Dagur's urgent voice jolted them as the door tore open.

Hroarr roared, "Out," before sending a rush of power to send the heavy wood crashing shut, likely right in his brother's face.

She was already standing and righting her clothing as Hroarr's fury and power lashed into the room.

She sighed. "Well, next time I'll remember to lock the door."

He growled, but couldn't speak yet, he was still too angry.

"I'll meet you in our bedroom," she said, before teleporting away.

Before she could undress and get in the shower, she felt a blast of anger and something else. Urgency made her quickly clean between her thighs with a towel before porting back to his office.

"What is it?" she asked as she watched Hroarr pace. Dagur was tense and looked just as agitated.

Her heart was pounding in her chest when Dagur gritted out, "The latest spell came back and the Darkness is getting closer." The last spell hadn't worked for some reason, so this was the second one to go out in the week, to Dagur's great ire.

Her next words were calmer than she felt. "How close?"

"Months."

"How many months?" she demanded. They'd had a year just weeks before.

"Two."

"I need to use my sjá to see what these Tria are doing. This stops now," Hroarr growled.

It felt like her world was crashing around her as she stared off, sending the information to Drake. He was right, they needed to know what the Tria were doing immediately. A year was bad, but now it had escalated to two months?

She was in his mind, telling him about the new time frame and Hroarr's intent to use his power to see what had been happening in the Realm, to which Drake growled, *Do it.*

Her brothers were set to meet them in Hell Realm. They would fend off the hell beasts while they were there, using his sjá to see all the Tria had been doing in the Realm.

She only wished they'd done this sooner, but they'd thought they had things covered with a plan to contain the Tria. Athena herself said that the Creators had instructed her to put the evil beings in the stasis units.

If not for Dagur's spell casting, they'd have had no idea their time had been cut in a third after mere weeks.

Her heart was thudding out of her chest when they ported away.

*****

Sirena's worry was like a blade slamming into Hroarr, and he clenched his teeth against the need to *ease* her immediately. The only way to do that was to find out what the evil Gods were doing.

Pothos, Hades and Drake were already in Hell Realm of Earth with their females when he and Sirena arrived. The stench of death and dark power permeated this plane, most coming from the creatures charging up the mountain where they stood. Their red eyes glinted in the sunlight. His lip curled at the scent and evil wafting from the slick black beasts, like those he'd destroyed at Hades' side the day before.

Dark clouds were moving in as Drake snarled, "How long will this take?"

He glanced at the dragon before deigning to answer, "Moments."

His eyes narrowed at the pitch-black beasts with red eyes charging up the mountain toward them. Accessing the flames that rested inside him, he waved a hand, calling them to disintegrate the first wave easily.

Death and smoke filtered into the air around them as Drake commanded, "You worry about what the fuck is going on. We've got the beasts."

Before he could respond, Drake morphed into a massive green dragon, shooting into the air to clash violently into two smaller black versions soaring in their direction. The green creature tore the smaller dragons from the skies, severing scaled necks and sending them crashing to the valley below. Hroarr felt Sirena's power burst free in a raw wave until more charging creatures dropped to the ground as she tore into organs and then used her flames to set them ablaze.

Hroarr sent more flames, watching Hades and Pothos fly into the hordes, their blades slashing and tearing flesh as the beasts screeched in fury. Their females cut down even more while keeping an eye on him and Sirena. More Guardians appeared all around them with blades, destroying the fire-breathing creatures.

Satisfied they had the situation under control, Hroarr found his sjá and knelt. With a wave of pure power, he slammed a fist into the rock and dirt, shaking the mountain with the force of his magic releasing into the core of this Realm, his neck arched back as flashes of images sped behind his eyes.

He felt Sirena's presence in the power and the sensation was pleasing if odd.

The sjá sped through flashes with a will of its own, forwarding beyond the birth of the beasts and the Realm until he saw the prison and the Tria, three dark-haired Gods covered in the blood of their victims, roaring in rage-filled fury as they violently tried to break free of their cavernous cage. Their eyes turned black with wild demented wrath and soon the beasts of the Realm were compelled to enter their underground lair and forced to take the evil beings' dark blood. His sjá flashed with greater speed through the torture and enslavement of the beasts, so much that the rock walls and ground seemed as if they were bleeding on their own. Decades flew by before the Gods found a way to direct the dark souls to be released into the Realm. They captured and tortured the dark souls with terrifying laughter. It was sick, and the stench of terror and the horrors enacted drove Hroarr to try to force Sirena from his power.

His female would not see this.

Her voice was hard when she spoke. *Finish this. I am not leaving you here, so stop fighting me or I will do this myself.*

She took control and sped the images faster until they saw light souls pummeling into the dark cavern of death and defilement. He felt Sirena's gasp of horror as the bright lights were devoured in the vilest of ways. He gritted his teeth and sped the disgusting images faster, seeing the beings growing paler until their skin was gray and the fiends' blood-soaked hair ran to their waists. Images of their twisted glee at breeding more beasts, making the creatures' poisons deadlier with spells before sending them from the Realm to see through the eyes of their beast servants.

Demon souls were infused with tainted magic and forced out to possess the mortals in the primary Realm of Earth. With each year they became more bloated with tainted power and sickness unlike anything Hroarr had ever seen. Eventually their entire prison became shrouded in dark magic until even his sjá could not detect the acts within the pitch black.

Years passed where nothing was revealed in that space until his sjá narrowed to a vaporous stench that filtered out from the mountain into the air, invisible but unmistakably magical, seeping purposefully out into the ether.

This was their call.

And it had started less than a year ago.

Chapter 30

Hell Realm, Earth

Sirena held it together long enough that she didn't retch all over her shoes when she and Hroarr came out of his sjá and the images of the Tria's horrors. The nightmares she'd seen would haunt her for decades.

Hroarr's anger at her refusal to leave was making him insane. *You should have obeyed me, Sirena.*

I wasn't leaving you there, she gritted out, still too out of sorts to take umbrage at his choice of words. She could feel his furious need to protect her, but it was too late. She couldn't unsee any of that, but neither could he.

Her shaking body only started to relax after Hroarr pulled her into his chest, but her stomach was taking longer to calm and she was aware that the stench of dead hell beast and sulphur wasn't helping in any way.

After turning in Hroarr's tight hold, she gave a fast explanation to Drake and the others. Smoke filtered in the air, and below them the nightmarish landscape was littered with dead beasts as far as the eye could see. Both Goddesses and their mates were there in a rush of air, dressed for battle with blood-soaked blades like all her Guardian brethren, who now circled them. Everyone was there sans Gregoire, who'd been instructed to stay with Lucy.

Hroarr snarled at Hades, "Pull them free and I will place them in the stasis units."

"We have this, Thulian," Ladon snapped. "You are here as backup."

Tension and grappling for control ensued between Ladon and Niall and their Goddesses, sending power tearing through the hills and valley below, making Sirena want to snarl at all the powerful beings to shut up.

Drake ignored them all as he turned to Conn and snarled for him to get the hack of Earth Realm's warning system on line now. Even an extra hour could help if the world's elements were upset when they contained the fiends. Uri was getting the word out through the Aletheia throughout the cities of Tetartos, and Drake ordered Bastian, Tasha, Sander and Nastia to bring three of the stasis units to Hell. Only four still existed.

"There was nothing more? No hint at what they've been up to in the last decade?" Hades bit out.

"No. It went black, but they are far more powerful than when they were first confined." She hated it, but the visions she'd seen meant they'd royally screwed up in their role as Guardians. They'd had no clue what was truly going on here.

"More powerful how?"

"They've been doing spells and using the beasts and possessed to see everything happening in the Realms. They bred the animals to provide a never-ending fountain of pain to feed from and they devoured souls sent into Hell Realm. They're bloated with more dark power than I ever imagined possible." She was frustrated with her lack of knowledge of exact details.

"I will bring Dagur to handle their spell casting," Hroarr stated while still holding her tight.

The three stasis units appeared with her brethren a second later.

"Should we do this in a Realm of their beasts?" Era asked.

Hades growled, "We will have to. I won't take the chance of not being able to gain a solid grip on the tags in their souls from another Realm."

"We will only have one to deal with." Niall scoffed with the arrogance of a God, or a Goddess' mate in his case. He was right. They had Guardians, Gods and even Gods of Thule and the magic confinement web that should incapacitate them the second the vile beings were loose. They could take one at a time and still deal with any hell beasts that were still alive after those that had died in the week of constant attacks. Not to mention those that died while she and Hroarr were in his power.

The beast populations would have been thinned by now.

Then why did she still feel a sense of foreboding?

"All three have the ability to sense your worst fears and terrors and use them against you," Hades informed the crowd. "I will pull Phobos first, since Deimos seems to be the one in charge, judging from their interactions with me through possessed. I want to see their tricks from the weakest of the three first. We'll take Deimos second."

Drake snarled, "They will likely target those of us who put them away first, but we will be vigilant." That meant all three Gods, Niall, Ladon and P would be primary targets.

"Then all of you should be in another Realm while Hades pulls

Phobos free. I will stay and get him into the unit," Hroarr commanded.

Sirena was tense, waiting for more uproar as everyone argued over who was doing what.

Suddenly a heavy power permeated the space and all eyes fell to Alex. Her dark hair was rising as if charged and her stance changed and her blue eyes glowed.

What is this? Hroarr demanded in Sirena's mind.

Even Alex's voice was stronger and her mate, Uri's eyes glowed silver as she spoke. "Hroarr and Sirena need to go protect Lucy, with the cats." The female's blue eyes landed on Hroarr. "Have Dagur and Kara there with you and take some of your sacred waters."

Hroarr stiffened at her side, not one to obey commands from others. Sirena sent him calming energies. *Heed her. She truly knows things. I know it's odd, but you had to have seen her abilities in my memories.*

Alex went on as if in a thrall, directing people to different positions, adding, "Only one stasis unit stays here. The others go to the manor."

Alex's voice boomed with more commands. "No God or Goddess is to step foot on this mountain."

Suddenly Alex turned to Gefn and P, commanding, "Gather waters directly from the sacred place in Thule, as many bubbles of it as you can hold, and bring them to Hell." It was becoming eerie just listening to her.

How? Hroarr demanded before growling, *I do not trust this power.*

How do you see the birth and destruction of a hundred worlds? she responded.

When he didn't seem to be moving, she snapped, *If she thinks the baby needs protecting by the Gods of Thule and their powerful beasts, we need to get moving, Hroarr.*

He only grunted.

Smoke was filling the air around Drake as he watched Alex move with purpose. The dragon was fighting the same battle Hroarr was with handing over control in something as important as this. Aphrodite and Ladon argued as Athena and Niall looked down at their daughter with pride when Drake finally commanded everyone to do as Alex said.

We need to get Dagur and Kara and go to the manor, she said when he hadn't moved.

I will collect them. Go to the manor now, he growled and was gone.

Finally it was Era who snarled, "Enough." Her feral power flooded the area in her ire and it stopped all the arguing from the Deities.

She disappeared with a sick feeling in her stomach. It was time to dust off her fighting leathers and blades.

*****

Gefn and P reformed in Hell after making the trip to Fólkvangr, where the healing waters were the most potent.

She was tensely standing in the position she'd been directed to by Alex, still shocked at the speed this was happening and wondering at the real accuracy of the female's skill with *knowing* things.

Pothos was seething at her side, wanting to send her away yet knowing that would not happen. He could argue all he liked; she would not leave his side. She sent him soothing energies in hopes of calming him some.

The stench of death in the air was thick as she gripped the spelled Thulian confinement net in one hand and her blue spelled blade in the other. If all else failed, she could throw energy balls, which was her sister's preferred weapon.

She felt waves of tension coming from Pothos as they waited.

I am a Goddess and more than capable of battling at your side. Do not forget that. And your father is only releasing one for all of us to deal with. Everything will be fine, my love, she tried to assure him, but in all honesty she didn't have a good feeling. It had gone far too silent in the Realm.

I don't like it and I hate the idea of having you anywhere near these assholes. They are the worst evil ever created, thea mou.

I understand. I do not like you being here either, but would you allow me to send you away? He growled and pulled her into his arms as she continued softly, *Your cousin Alex thinks I am needed. You told me to trust her knowledge; now you must do the same. I love you, Pothos.*

He kissed her hard, both keeping their weapons at their sides while he devoured her lips until she was dizzy. *And I love you. Now promise you will not get anywhere near the fucker,* he commanded.

She was spared the need to respond when Hades' voice boomed, "Be ready." The God seemed just as furious and protective as he looked at his mate, yet Sacha stood tall at his side, not budging an inch.

All those present took defensive battle stances as Hades summoned a blast of pure power that sucked the air from her lungs. Suddenly before them was the evil visage of Phobos. The vile God looked as though he had bathed in blood, and the small amount of skin that showed was sickly gray. Obsidian eyes gazed at them and suddenly his laughter echoed with the clawing sound of terror-filled nightmares. His long black hair was tied back to show a vicious maw, and as his eyes met hers, she'd never felt such terror permeate her body. Everything about his dark presence and horrifying magic made her entire body feel covered in filth.

The demon's body seized and he cried out as Gefn called a rush of wind to project her net. It covered the creature, whose screeches rang like claws on glass. Terror and soul-shaking images of Pothos lying in a pool of blood at her feet filled her mind as she fought Phobos' evil power, breaking free of the illusion that made her heart pound in dread.

She saw others suffering the same effects as they charged the evil God.

In an instant the top of the mountain erupted into the sky as a dragon three times the size of Drake's and several serpents just as large burst free to hurtle down toward them.

"Mother fuck," Pothos snarled. "Don't let the venom of these beasts touch you," he shouted as a tsunami of black fog rushed through the valley. Gefn felt Pothos fall at her side. Agony tore from his lips and she could feel an insidious spell tearing at his organs. He somehow summoned the strength to push her free of another swarm of wild beasts that appeared through the open holes forming in the mountain. She guarded his body, sending energy fire from her blade and slicing through thick beast flesh, spattering acid blood all over them both.

Drake and his father, Ladon, were a mass of green and gold as their dragon forms roared and screamed, falling from the sky when the spell overtook them as well.

Gefn watched, horrified, as those who had imprisoned the Tria fell to whatever heinous spell was cast. Hades, Drake, the Goddesses and their mates, and her Pothos were all down, writhing and screaming in agony.

Tasha and Bastian quickly advanced on a dragon that had formed in the pit of the mountain. The winged creature's eyes glowed such a deep red it was nearly black and as hot as the center of the sun. Just as suddenly the two warriors were gone as the beast screamed its fury, belching sulphur while its severed halves crashed to the ground. Not far away, Nastia and Sander furiously took on a massive serpent while Erik, Alex and Uri desperately fought to guard their fallen parents.

Several Guardians were holding their ground above the bodies of Aphrodite and Ladon, while more joined Sacha, killing beasts coming for Hades.

Gefn ruthlessly powered the winds, creating a maelstrom that whipped the smoke into a tunnel and carried it away. As she poured healing water into Pothos' throat, she relied upon her spelled blades to destroy any beast that neared.

Sending the healing water out in her wind she ordered, *Put the water into the fallen's mouths,* while crouching above her male. The terror caused by the illusions was relentless and nearly stole her sanity as she battled against them. Her concentration was such that she didn't even see the real threat until it was upon her.

One of the vicious dragons, the putrid color of decaying flesh, soared down, its talons ripping into her shoulders, snatching her from the ground until she ported free.

Gefn violently wielded her blade, shooting power from the tip to destroy the dragon above and any other beast who dared near her mate as she stood above his agonized body. The healing waters from Fólkvangr were easing his spelled torment, but not fast enough. All the warriors were fanned out protecting those they could as Phobos laughed with pure terrorizing elation. Her eyes narrowed when he sneered in her direction before snatching the net from his body and caused it to disintegrate in his hands. When he spoke, it was with the echo of gleeful pain and death, which nearly stopped her heart.

"Soon your body will feel the rending of ours. Pothos' toy will be our plaything."

P snarled, "Get him in the fucking box." Gefn's mate was attempting to rise, but was still too weak, his power affected by whatever the creature had done. Conn tried wielding his incredibly powerful telekinetic ability, but it didn't budge the evil God.

Before she knew what was happening, Phobos disappeared and reappeared in flashes all over the area, laughing maniacally with delighted triumph, taking blades from one warrior to slash into others as if he were playing with them. This was a game for the twisted creature and they were not powerful enough to withstand it.

A feral Era laid waste to hordes of beasts flooding the area as Brianne's battle cry rang out. Phobos had set his sights on Hades, and Sacha was decisively protecting the writhing God, seemingly anticipating the creature's every move and teleporting to defend him against it time and again. The laughter suddenly stopped and the malicious being roared its fury at being denied its prize.

P and the others were starting to stand, which only infuriated the creature more.

Finally the beast stilled enough that Tasha and Nastia were able to attack it with their deadly blade-filled mist, but just as the head started to sever, it reattached. He gripped a hand into the air and forced Nastia into form as Sander hit it with blast after blast of fire until Phobos threw her.

Bastian's voice was in the link. *We can't force a teleport. He's too fucking strong.*

With a thought Gefn tried forcing some Fólkvangr water into his open maw, which jolted and infuriated the creature, but didn't stop it.

She turned to fire more power at the massive serpents surrounding them, their fangs dripping venom, and they sent waves of flames everywhere until her blade's power finally penetrated through their eyes straight to the brain.

Phobos was all over the place until Alex landed on his back, powering her blade deep into his neck.

Alex screamed a telepathic order to Gefn, *Force all the water into him.*

As the beast roared, she slammed the water into his open mouth. He snarled and shrieked and threw Alex off him and batted Uri with his fist.

He'd found new prey in the form of Alex, who'd attacked him. Uri's blade struck true, slicing into Phobos' stomach, and the shrill howl nearly destroyed Gefn's eardrums. It was actually feeling the pain. When the fiend lashed out at Alex, the roar of a furious massive lion rent the air; her father had risen again and charged with a surge of speed and power. Athena was at his side with her blade arcing and rending Phobos from neck to crotch.

The evil God roared and flew with wild power into the Goddess, taking advantage of her spell-weakened state, and impaled her on a venomous fang of a massive serpent on the mountain. Vane and Erik ripped off the creature's jaw bellowing in a fit of fury for their mother.

Alex and Uri ported to Athena's side, but Phobos was too fast. His blade shot straight through her mother's neck before they'd gotten there. Niall's furious and anguished roar rocked the ground as the male attacked in lion form, tearing at Phobos' throat with sharp teeth before crashing to the ground and reforming to a man.

The creature laughed in maniacal glee as he lifted Niall's bloody heart in his fist, crushing it with relish. Even as the evil God's wounds bled out all over the ground he fought the Guardians who finally wrestled him into the stasis unit. Drake got there in time to set his hand over the chamber and the Realm rocked with the force of the power of its closure.

Just as suddenly the ground erupted across the valley as a sea of black blasted into the skies. Two demon Gods flew high and then one came down to the fight. The remaining Tria were free.

"We will devour your pretty, pretty world. All it took was one death. One death and now you all die, because we are freeeeeee." The evil God's voice was of pure venomous delight until it saw the stasis unit and its brother.

Its shriek severed Gefn's eardrums until all she could hear was a humming. It pounded its fists on the casement and the stasis unit only burned its hands.

With a wild and furious hiss it advanced and then suddenly it sniffed the air like an animal and its eyes lit up with new horrendous purpose and it was gone. She could only hear faint screeching from the remaining creatures she fought as her eardrums started to heal. The elements were growing wilder all around them. With a sudden pop her hearing returned only to take in Alex's anguished cries of fury mixed with her brothers' rage filled roars. They were kneeling at their parents' side. Era had tried everything but nothing could be done, Athena was still, her gallant mate lay at her side. In a final heartbreaking act of love they died holding hands.

*****

Sirena was losing her mind with worry as she followed the hectic battle as best she could through her Guardian link.

She was jittery and on edge. Changing into fighting leathers before Hroarr had even returned, she grabbed a blade she hadn't used in centuries to stand beside the baby. Lucy had already encased her mother, father and the cats in some form of protective bubble while the wolves as well as Dacia, Rain, Sam, Havoc and Laire crowded into the room. Sirena could tell Sam and Rain were seconds from losing their minds with both their males out battling in Hell Realm.

As everyone circled the baby, Sirena felt something sickening, a hideous kind of wrongness, and when the cats stood and hissed, releasing a wave of immense power, she knew it wasn't good. Abruptly Than appeared, and Hroarr, a force of wild power, stepped in front of her. Dagur and Kara flanked their brother, weapons at the ready.

As the wolves and Laire closed in behind her, a snarling Havoc charged and tore at the evil monster, who proceeded to slap the pup away, crashing him through two walls, bringing a harsh yelp of pain.

The God was so much bigger than she'd ever imagined, his massive frame nearly hitting the ceiling. The cats held the snarling

God paralyzed in power for moments, but the fiend finally stutter stepped as if in a horror movie. Sirena was already summoning her power to stop his organs as she lulled with her powerful voice to still it and disorient it.

Hroarr sent his flames to the creature's body as he cut the God's head, severing it, but it reattached, laughing.

Pure terror shot through her when she saw Hroarr and all those she loved in a pile of death at her feet. *It's not real*, she sent through the room with magic in her voice as she heard the others cry out at the horrible illusions the creature was capable of.

"Yummy, yummy, yummy baby," the vile being crooned. Gregoire's roar of fury was bloodcurdling as he positioned himself before his female and their child within Lucy's shield.

Dagur cast a wild spell into the air against the terrors as Kara sent wave after wave of energy power with no results.

Gefn sent a telepathic call, *The healing waters weaken it.*

The room was too small to contain all the Guardians teleporting from Hell to help.

Kara sent a wave of healing water into the creature's mouth as Sirena used power to sever organs and set them ablaze, and this time they weren't regenerating as quickly.

Hroarr's flames were finally burning the evil creature. Its neck arched as if enjoying the flickering heat until Hroarr snarled and used his blade to sever the beast's head again and kicked the evil God into the open stasis unit the wolves had telekinetically moved closer.

The entire world shimmered and then violently shook.

Sirena felt as if everything was crashing around them, and

Than's voice bellowed with pleasure, "You're too late." His voice echoed in horrifically childish glee and made her skin crawl as Drake locked the unit and ended the God's delight as the body shook and convulsed inside.

The Realms were collapsing, toppling into one another; she remembered the feeling from Hroarr's sjá. The air was thick around them, making it hard to breathe. The lights of souls from Heaven flitted frantically beyond the windows and she swore she heard the eerie howls of hellhounds outside the walls.

Deimos had successfully called the Darkness. She felt dizzy as she looked up at Hroarr in abject terror.

"We have to stop Deimos," Sirena snarled.

The baby remained oddly quiet, as if waiting for something, when Alex's somber voice filled the Guardian link, *Do not leave Lucy alone, but the Gods need to activate the weapons now.*

The end of the world was here.

Chapter 31

London, Earth Realm

Deimos' laughter echoed down to the masses below. He had always loved the debased cities of the world and now they would all be *his*. He stood atop a massive building of glass and metal, relishing the way the clouds and Darkness began converging and blacking out the sun.

The Realms converged the second the obsidian Destroyer soared into the atmosphere, rocking the ground, sending cars plummeting from the bridges below. The building he stood on groaned and glass shattered as he watched through the eyes of his beasts as the creatures tore into flesh and bone, feasting on human flesh and life forces as the screams of terror filtered up to his perch.

He swayed as he enjoyed the new thickness in the air, likely suffocating the feeble mortals below.

All it had taken was sweet beautiful death to free him, the destruction of two life forces to create a crack in his prison. That it was the demise of Athena and her mangy mate was but a sweet added bonus for him.

He was only furious Phobos had played with the fools so long instead of instantly killing one of their captors to gain Deimos' freedom.

Both brothers deserved their deaths for not obeying him in all things.

Though, he had to admit Than had found the perfect shining morsel for Deimos to feast upon after he was finished devouring the Darkness flooding the skies to finally funnel down to its master.

He roared with insane laughter as it poured into his open mouth. It was a turbulent storm of pure death as it tunneled from the sky, its power rocking him as it violently descended.

Come to me, he hissed, his cock hardening as all that succulent destruction fed his insatiable hunger for power. He opened his mouth further, greedily sucking in the Darkness. His body seemed to expand with the evil energy filling him.

This would be his plaything for all eternity, giving him the ability to travel the worlds and hoard all magic for himself.

The second his hard body, mind and strength connected to the flood of Darkness, he felt glorious pain as the entity fought for control. Control it would never have over him. The Darkness captivated him, filling him with immense power, his body expanding as he invited yet more in. It wanted to consume him and instead he was devouring it inch by lush inch.

It could suck the life from a world, but he was dominating it, siphoning the mass of pure wondrous destruction as it raged, hoping to turn the tide against him. He roared his pleasure with each and every thrash as it battled uselessly, and he opened his arms to the skies, forcing more to come to him. It would never break free no matter how it struggled. His laughter grew as he easily snuffed its will.

He relished the carnage wrought by his beasts as they tore through the cities of the world, ripping and shredding the mortals. Their horrified shrieks were lullabies for his soul. Immortals were fighting against his venomous beauties even as gunshots of mortals rang in the air. The humans were fighting those attempting to save them and he roared with pure laughter at their weak minds. Their fear and panic infused him with more power to suck in the scourge in the skies.

It was sheer rapture to him.

Abruptly, bright streams of pure light and power flooded the skies from all around the world. His body tensed as he fisted his hands, watching through all his creatures as this magic was destroying his meal before he'd consumed it all. He bellowed in fury, fighting to absorb more, but was denied. The power of the Gods was taking what was rightfully his.

He demanded more! He was owed it for the thousands of years he'd spent caged in that squalid place, forced to sup on pathetic, weak souls for his very survival.

He whirled in the air, his power ripping through metal and glass, before teleporting toward the bright Guardian light. The baby his brother had coveted would be his. They would all suffer after he devoured the light of the infant while they watched, helpless and weak against him.

He reformed in a room, in the presence of puny Gods and Guardians easily swept away with a wave of his hand as he stalked, intent on his prize. The baby was indeed powerful and it would be the best of desserts. Sweet. Succulent. Juicy.

He felt the pull on his body as powerful cats hissed and tried to stop him.

Flames licked over him; blades entered his body. He barely noticed. None of their pitiful powers could touch him.

He sneered, "I am your God now. You have no hope to win against me, feeble creatures."

Then the infant's light suddenly lashed out and encased him, capturing him in her light. Deimos roared, furious, as he fought and writhed for freedom from the very power he'd come to ravage.

How!

It was suffocating him, stealing his Darkness with the light, snuffing out the Darkness until panic and fear infused him, his slamming fists and lashing of power only constricted with his every struggle.

*****

Sirena was horrified at the sight of the God. The very moment Deimos appeared in the room, they all threw everything they had at the malevolent being. Uri was reporting that Immortals were fighting hell beasts in the Earth cities they'd landed in. The weapons were all powered and they'd been waiting for information on where Deimos was. Hades hadn't been able to pull his soul to him after the God had been weakened by the Tria's deadly spell.

Uri snarled, *New reports say he devoured the Darkness before the weapons started working.*

She could feel it in him. The creature stank of dark energies, and nothing they did touched the massive evil God.

How had he been devouring it!

It didn't matter. He was the Darkness now, only worse. He was pure terrifying death.

And he was fixated on Lucy as they all fought him, including the cats, who were draining all their power just to slow the evil God's movements. Even the waters of Fólkvangr were not touching him. The stasis unit was slammed into his leg and it didn't faze him as his neck angled as he moved to the baby with soulless black eyes.

"I am your God now. You have no hope to win against me, feeble creatures." His laughter chilled her very blood.

The baby seemed far too calm, not uttering a single cry while Deimos' evil words rang out. Gregoire bellowed as the unthinkable happened, Lucy's pure light lashed out, wrapping Deimos in her power as if she'd only been waiting for him to get close enough. The God lifted from the ground. His shocked, rage-filled roars were deafening as he writhed and fought the power holding him.

Spa and Velspar finally fell, panting for air, having used all of their power to hold the evil creature for the moments they'd had him.

Drake commanded through the telepathic link, *Infuse every bit of power into the telepathic link to Gregoire, Alyssa and Lucy.*

The air charged as everyone sent power through the Guardian and his mate and into the baby. Lucy moved the trapped God above the stasis unit and she forced Deimos inside. Drake placed his hand to it and locked it with a resounding rush of power that shook the entire room.

The room silenced in shock until suddenly Lucy freed her family from the shield around them, and Sirena rushed to her, sending healing tendrils out and through the infant as her parents choked out tears and held her close.

Her tiny body was perfectly whole as tiny hands reached up to her parents.

Mother and father were an emotional wreck, but a quick check showed they too were unharmed.

They were in better shape than she was at the moment.

Sirena was exhausted and drained when Hroarr came to hold her in his arms, infusing her with love and warmth.

They all watched as Deimos' body seized and seemed to feed upon itself until it was nothing more than gray flesh over bone inside the blue containment unit.

When the baby reached for the cats, Gregoire growled but let her touch them, and the beasts started to purr lightly. Suddenly Havoc limped to lie beside Spa with his head on her back. The pup had broken bones that Sirena quickly mended. Lucy made an impatient noise and tried to get free to be down by all three beasts. Sirena was already checking the cats and found them as depleted as they'd been when she'd healed them in Thule. Their organs were shutting down on her, yet whatever Lucy was doing seemed to be healing them.

"Is anyone else wounded?" she asked. She hadn't seen anyone in need, but that didn't mean they weren't.

Drake said, "Era patched up everyone that was in Hell." After saying it, the dragon leaned down to kiss his mate, who was tucked into his side.

"Were the weapon God prisons turned off before the Deities died?" Sirena asked, because the elements would be in turmoil all over the world if they weren't.

Drake nodded. "They were set to only expend so much power before stopping."

Of course the dragon would have thought about that.

"We need to see to the damage," Sirena said.

"Dagur and Kara will help wherever needed," Hroarr said with a hard look at his siblings.

"We would be happy to," Kara said, which seemed to surprise everyone. The Goddess was looking down at Lucy with such reverence that it brought a smile to Sirena's face.

Uri spoke with a tearful Alex snuggled into his side. "The healers in the cities need help."

She nodded. It was going to be a long day, or more likely decade. Hroarr hugged her to him before saying, "Thule first so you have enough energy."

She was anxious to get to it, but he was right, even a few minutes in Thule would reenergize her so that she'd be of more use.

She looked up at him and nodded, feeling him sending her energies as he ported her away.

Chapter 32

Guardian Manor, Tetartos Realm

Sirena cuddled into Hroarr's side in the crowded war room of the manor. Guardians and the Gods of both worlds had spent the past two exhausting days healing and helping fix the damage in the Realms, and it wasn't over yet. Luckily they'd had the more elementally skilled Thulians helping them or who knew what destruction they'd still be looking at. The deaths of the Tria, Athena and her mate had hit Earth hard.

"The Darkness has been destroyed," Dagur informed them after having cast his spell into the ether days ago. "There is no trace of it left."

Thank the Creators for that.

They'd lost Athena and Niall, but the rest of their family had thankfully survived. Sirena knew that Alex was racked with guilt that her power hadn't been able to save her parents and the female likely still saw them dead on the mountain she'd warned no God set foot on.

It was a sober meeting where everyone shared their progress. Mass destruction had occurred all over Earth, though they'd minimized as much as they could. Even with Conn's warning system going out early, earthquakes and tsunamis had hit before humans could evacuate certain areas and islands. There was less destruction in Tetartos only because there was less *to* damage.

"We have settled the elements." Hroarr confirmed. At least now the humans could start to rebuild, but it would still take decades.

"The Internet and television stations are all over the mythical creatures running rampant in the cities. They even have images of the Gods. This is huge. They will never get over it." Conn groaned.

"Eventually we'll have to do major diplomatic work, because with the Creators' confinement spell down around Tetartos and Immortals being able to get to the mortal Realm, there's no going back," Bastian pointed out. "They are all helping to fix the damages and rescue survivors, but Earth officials have no idea what to think."

"My sister and I will handle the humans." Hades scoffed.

Drake grunted at the God. The press was already all over Hades and Aphrodite. After a minute the dragon ordered, "For now we fix the damages we can, but there will need to be new rules for everyone. Including you, Hades. And you, Mother. We are still the Guardians of this world."

Hades snorted.

Jax growled an interruption of that argument, "I'm just fucking happy that when the Realms reconnected, the beings and beasts all landed back where they came from. Fuck, humans were shooting the Immortals who'd been trying to help save them from the beasts. It sounded like utter chaos."

Dorian added, "Yeah, for ten motherfucking minutes of convergence." The entire thing felt like it lasted hours, but in reality, Dorian was right about that. The Darkness hadn't even touched the ground. Actually Deimos made it far easier than if the Destroyer of Worlds had encased Earth and done what it normally did; they'd have far bigger problems.

"What now?" Sirena asked as she enjoyed the warmth of her male holding her.

Drake snarled, "We go back to work, fix this, and start a new beginning."

The world would rebuild.

The Darkness would never come for Thule or any other world again.

Hroarr kissed her and she felt truly optimistic and free for the first time in her life as she looked around at Guardians and mates and felt the pureness of love they all felt for each other.

Epilogue

Paradeisos Island, Tetartos Realm – Ten Years Later

Sirena sat on a lounge in her fifties-style white one-piece with her red heels at her side. The sun and sea breeze felt amazing as she listened to the clear aqua waves crashing over the white sands of Paradeisos Island. They'd all meant to take a girl spa day at Paradeisos, renting the entire pleasure island for themselves, but it had turned into a family day with mates showing up and crashing their trip of indulgence.

She put a hand up to shade her view as she watched sea creatures converging all around Dorian, Rain and their little two-year-old boy, whose delighted giggles could be heard all the way up to the beach.

She smiled at Gefn, saying, "They are adorable."

The Thulian Goddess was too busy grinning into the blue skies as her own four-year-old boy soared using his sleek black wings. Pothos and Hades were up there with him, laughing and spinning as they taught him how to fly. Hades' bellowing laughter echoed into the winds as his three-year-old daughter rode his winged back as if he were a pony instead of using her own tiny wings.

She saw Laire off talking to Conn's male in-laws, drinking what looked to be beer.

Sacha came to curl into the lounge next to her with a glass of wine in her hand.

Decades ago, Sirena would never have even considered taking an entire day off to sit basking in the sun or getting her nails done. She'd always done her primping on her own and quickly.

She also would never have imagined seeing any of this. There was so much peace and sheer happiness in the air.

The Realms were still working to find a way to blend lives, with mortals and Immortals living together. Hades and Aphrodite were helping to heal their world the way Deities were always meant to, but it was all a very big change, no matter how much of celebrities the two Gods had become to the humans. There were great struggles, but at least it was becoming better.

It would never be the simple life of Thule, but it was becoming the best version of Earth.

She smiled thinking of her own Thulian God. She couldn't wait to get back to him because she had something very important to share. At the moment he was with his brother, so she planned to indulge in a little more time with her family.

She laughed when she saw Lucy, the oldest of the children, playing with her younger brother. Havoc and the cats were lying in the sand at her side. Alyssa and Gregoire's boy was only three and his sister loved him like no other. Lucy's chestnut ponytail whipped in the breeze as she lifted her brother's tiny horse form into the air with one of her bubbles. The toddler spun and reformed inside it, giggling at her. His bright green eyes and shock of red hair looked wild and thrilled as he set his hands to the bubble's edge, wanting his big sister. When she let the power dissipate, he fell into her arms, laughing hysterically as he cuddled into her before his father swooped him into the air to ride on his shoulders while hugging his daughter and mate into his sides.

Dacia and her wolf sisters came down the steps from the spa, laughing, until Conn came in and lifted his pregnant mate away from them. The sisters were unfettered, choosing to change form and bound into the sand to wrestle while Sirena and the others laughed at their antics.

Ileana, Era and Brianne were talking closer to the water's edge. They were the only ones not pregnant or with children running around. Suddenly their mates appeared, tucking them into their arms as they all spoke. Seeing Drake relaxed was a miracle of its own and Sirena's heart felt huge because of it.

Sam and Erik were further down the beach on a couples lounge covered by a huge blue umbrella, their tiny baby in their arms as they spoke intimately. Erik leaned down to kiss the child.

Alex and Uri were up on the steps, talking to Tynan, the Aletheia who owned the island. The dark-haired male was grinning with enviable charm as the bundle in Alex's arms reached for him repeatedly.

When the twins Nastia and Tasha moved around Alex and Uri, Sirena noticed the redheaded Mageia Brigitte with them. She was an old friend and the once manager of an erotic club the twins used to own in Earth Realm. Brigitte now managed Paradeisos Island, as Tynan was spending far more time on his Caribbean island in Earth Realm, creating the ultimate erotic resort catering mostly to humans with vampire fantasies. The Aletheia were the Immortal race whose existence created the myth in the first place, and it seemed this would be a lucrative decision for him.

Sirena raised her eyebrows as she drank some cucumber water

and watched a pissed Nastia stalk toward them with her sister at her side.

Brigitte was saved from the display when Astrid, a Kairos they all knew and loved, intercepted her.

Both twins were pregnant, but Nastia's white tank top said it all: "Touch my stomach and" was written in a small scrawl across the female's boobs, but the "I WILL CUT YOU" was in bold block letters over her massive belly.

"You knew!" Nastia snarled at her twin.

Tasha sighed. "Sander didn't take them all."

Nastia turned to her twin with deadly intent. "He took my fucking Bugatti and *hid every other* damned car and motorcycle that had any guts in them!" The female liked speed and so did her mate, but he'd obviously put his foot down on using anything while she was pregnant with his baby. The Phoenix was not to be crossed in this and everyone knew it.

Tasha groaned as she took a drink of what Sirena guessed was juice. "Don't be so dramatic. He left you something to drive if you want to, and I agree you need to be careful with my niece in there."

"I'm fucking Immortal! And so is the baby!" Nastia roared before ranting in a more despairing tone, "He bought me a minivan, Tasha! A motherfucking minivan! He obviously hates me *and* baby Anarchy!"

Everyone there tried with great power not to laugh, but it was impossible.

Nastia spun on them, narrowing her eyes.

Come to me, love, Hroarr sent.

Sirena thrilled with excitement and sent quick goodbyes as she tossed on her cover-up and shoes before porting away.

She reformed with a jump into Hroarr's massive arms. He laughed as he held her to him, and when she looked around, she realized they were in the great hall, and her heart skipped a beat when she saw what he'd done. There was a huge two-story movie screen on one wall, and smiling warriors, priestesses and staff all sat in dozens of big leather chairs. She smelled the scent of popcorn, and on the screen was a chainsaw-wielding madman.

She gazed up at her male with incredulous joy.

He'd made her a movie theater in their home, and even though he still mostly eschewed technology in Thule, he'd been breaking some of his rules.

For her.

He kissed her nose. "Do you like it, love?"

She nodded, a little choked up before saying, "I have something for you too."

She smiled when his eyes crinkled at the sides the way she loved.

"I already have my prize, little one," he said as he cuddled her in his arms, leaning in and kissing her deeply.

As their mouths parted, she breathed, "How do you feel about having two prizes?"

It took him a second to understand, and when he did, his eyes flashed with love and feral possessiveness. He growled in blinding satisfaction as he leaned her back to gaze at her currently flat stomach.

His voice was gravelly when he spoke. “You please me too much, *völur minn*.” And then he teleported them to their bed, where he made soft sweet love to her before moving down her body to kiss her stomach reverently.

Sirena felt all the happiness in the world at being encompassed in his love.

In all her millennia she’d never dared to dream that she’d be gifted with a happily ever after that spanned two worlds and all of eternity.

The End

Glossary of Terms and Characters - For Reference Only:

Agnarr – God of the world Thule, long ago ally of Hades

Ailouros – Immortal race of half felines, known as the warrior class, strong and fast

Aletheia – Immortal race with enhanced mental abilities and power within their fluids, can take blood memories, strong telepathy, the race that spawned the vampire myth

Alex – AKA Alexandra, Demi-Goddess daughter of Athena, sister to Vane and Erik, mate to Uri

Alyssa – Hippeus (half warhorse), daughter of Adras and Ava, mate to Gregoire

Aphrodite – Sleeping Goddess, one of the three good Deities, mother to Drake

Apollo – God who experimented with the Immortal races, adding animal DNA to create the perfect army against his siblings

Ares – Sleeping God and father of the evil Tria who are imprisoned in Hell Realm

Artemis – Sleeping Goddess and mother of the evil Tria who are imprisoned in Hell Realm

Athena – Sleeping Goddess – One of only three Gods that were good and didn't feed off dark energies and become mad, mother of Alex, Vane and Erik, mate to Niall

Bastian – AKA Sebastian, Kairos (teleporter), Guardian of the Realms, diplomat for the Guardians within Tetartos Realm, mated to Natasha (Tasha)

Þjóðann – Thulian word for ruler

Brianne – Geraki (half ancient bird of prey), Guardian of the Realms, hybrid, mated to Vane

Charybdis – Immortal abused by Poseidon and then sold and experimented on in Apollo's labs, she gave a portion of her life force to create the mating spell, aka mating curse, so that no Immortal could breed with any other than their destined mate.

Conn – Lykos (half wolf), Guardian of the Realms, mated to Dacia

Creators – Almighty beings that travel worlds sowing the seeds of an ancient race, creating Immortals and giving birth to Gods

Cyril – Demi-God son of Apollo, Siren/healer, dead bad guy

Dacia – Lykos, mated to Conn

Dagur – God of Thule

Demeter – Sleeping Goddess

Demi-Gods or Goddesses – Those born to a God or Goddess

Dorian – Nereid, Guardian of the Realms, mated to Rain

Drake – AKA Draken, Demi-God dragon, leader of the Guardians of the Realms, son of Aphrodite and her Immortal dragon mate Ladon

Efcharistisi – City in Tetartos Realm

Eir – Long dead priestess of Thule, P's mother

Elizabeth – Aletheia – evil female who found a way to free Apollo

Emfanisi – Yearly, week-long event where Immortals and Mageia of age go to find mates

Era – AKA Delia, powerful female experimented on by Cyril, mated to Drake

Erik – Demi-God son of Athena, Ailouros (half-lion), Vane's twin, Alex's younger brother, mated to Sam

Fólkvangr – Sacred Realm of Thule that is much like Earth's Heaven

Gefn – Goddess of Thule

Geiravor – Priestess of Thule, bonded to Hroarr

Geraki – Immortal race of half bird of prey, power with air

Gregoire – Hippeus (half warhorse), Guardian of the Realms, mate to Alyssa

Guardians – Twelve warriors of different Immortal races chosen by the Creators to watch over the four Realms of Earth.

Hades – One of the three good Gods, father to P (Pothos)

Havoc – Uri and Alex's pet hellhound that was rescued as a pup and bonded to Uri

Healers – AKA Sirens, Immortal race, power over the body, ability with their voices

Hellhounds – Massive black hounds blood bonded to the Tria in Hell Realm

Hephaistos – Sleeping God

Hera – Sleeping Goddess

Hermes – Sleeping God and Apollo's partner in the experimentation and breeding of Immortals for their army

Hippeus – Immortal race of half warhorses, power over earth

Hroarr – Ruling God of the world Thule

Ileana – Ailouros (liger), Jax's mate

Jax – AKA Ajax, Ailouros (half tiger), Guardian of the Realms

Kairos – Immortal race whose primary power is teleportation

Kara – Goddess of Thule, imprisoned by the Guardians after her attempt to take Hades

Ladon – Immortal dragon, mate to Aphrodite, father of Drake, friend of Jax

Laire – Guard of the Goddess Gefn of Thule

Limni – City in Tetartos Realm

Lofodes – City in Tetartos Realm

Lykos – Immortal half wolf with the power of telekinesis

Maðr – Thulian word for husband or consort

Mageia – Evolved humans, mortals compatible to be an Immortal's mate, have abilities with one of the four elements; air, fire, water, or earth.

Mates – Each Immortal has a rare and destined mate, their powers meld and they become stronger pairs that are able to procreate, usually after a decade.

Mating Curse – A spell cast in Apollo's Immortal breeding labs that ensured the God wouldn't be able to use them to continue creating his army. Charybdis cast the spell using a portion of her life force and now Immortals can only procreate with their destined mates.

Mating Frenzy – Starts when an Immortal comes into contact with their destined mate, a sexual frenzy that continues through to the bonding/mating ceremonies.

Minn – Thulian word meaning my

Mist – Immortal priestess of Thule, bonded to the God Hroarr

Nastia – AKA Chaos, Immortal created by Apollo, twin to Natasha

Natasha – AKA Tasha and Nemesis, Immortal created by Apollo, Nastia's twin

Nereid – Immortal race of mercreatures, power over water

Ófǫlr – Thulian word for the Darkness or Destroyer of Worlds

Ouranos – City in Tetartos Realm

P – AKA Pothos, Guardian of the Realms, Son of Hades, second to Drake

Phoenix – Immortal race with ability over fire

Poseidon – Sleeping God

Þrír – Thulian priestesses or Immortal three who are bonded to a God or Goddess of Thule

Rain – Mageia, destined mate to Dorian, best friend of Alyssa

Realms – Four Realms of Earth; Earth - where humanity exists, Heaven - where good and neutral souls go to be reincarnated, Hell -

where the Tria were banished and evil souls are sent, Tetartos – Realm of beasts – where the Immortals were exiled by the Creators

Reginleif – Immortal priestess of Thule, bonded to the God Hroarr

Sacha – Kairos (teleporter), Guardian of the Realms, diplomat for the Guardians within Tetartos Realm, Bastian's mother

Sam – AKA Samantha Palmer, mated to Erik, power over metal, Mageia/Ailouros

Sander – Phoenix, Guardian of the Realms

Sirena – Siren (healer), Guardian of the Realms, primarily works to find mates for Immortals in Tetartos

Spa – Massive black lynx looking cat gifted to the Goddess Gefn at her birth, one of the two Guardians of Thule

Tetartos Realm – The Immortal exile Realm, once known as the Realm of Beasts

Thalassa – City in Tetartos Realm, where the Lykos clans live

Thea mou – Endearment meaning my Goddess

Thule – Once thought a mythical land to the north, it is a world where Hades long ago found allies in God's birthed by different Creators

Tria – Evil Triplets spawned from incestuous coupling of Ares and Artemis; Deimos, Phobos and Than

Tyr – Evil God of Thule

Uri – AKA Urian, Aletheia, interrogator, Guardian of the Realms, mate to Alex

Vane – Demi-God son of Athena, Ailouros (half-lion), Erik's twin, Alex's younger brother, Brianne's mate

Velspar – Massive black lynx looking cat gifted to the Goddess Gefn at her birth, one of the two Guardians of Thule

Völur – Thulian word for witch

Zeus – Sleeping God

Thank you

I truly can't thank you enough for taking this incredible journey with me. I hope I did justice to each and every one of my Guardians and that you love them as much as I do.

COMING SOON!

New Releases

Subscribe to Setta Jay's newsletter for:

book release dates

exclusive excerpts

giveaways

http://www.settajay.com/

About The Author:

Setta Jay is the author of the popular Guardians of the Realms Series. She's garnered attention and rave reviews in the paranormal romance world for writing smart, slightly innocent heroines and intense alpha males. She loves creating stories that incorporate a strong plot accompanied by a heavy dose of heat.

An avid reader her entire life, her love of romance started at a far too early age with the bodice rippers she stole from her older sister. Along with reading, she loves animals, brunch dates, coffee that is really more French vanilla creamer, questionable reality television, English murder mysteries, and has dreams of traveling the world.

Born a California girl, she currently resides in Idaho with her incredibly supportive husband.

She loves to hear from readers so feel free to ask her questions on social media or send her an email, she will happily reply.

Where you can find her:

http://www.settajay.com/

https://www.facebook.com/settajayauthor

https://twitter.com/SETTAJAY_

https://www.goodreads.com/author/show/7778856.Setta_Jay

A information can be obtained
w.ICGtesting.com
in the USA
Bn1305300818